Knightfall

ANN DENTON

Le Rue
Publishing

Le Rue Publishing
320 South Boston Avenue, Suite 1030
Tulsa, OK 74103
www.LeRuePublishing.com

ISBN: 978-1-7335960-1-5

To Cindy. Hope you enjoy.

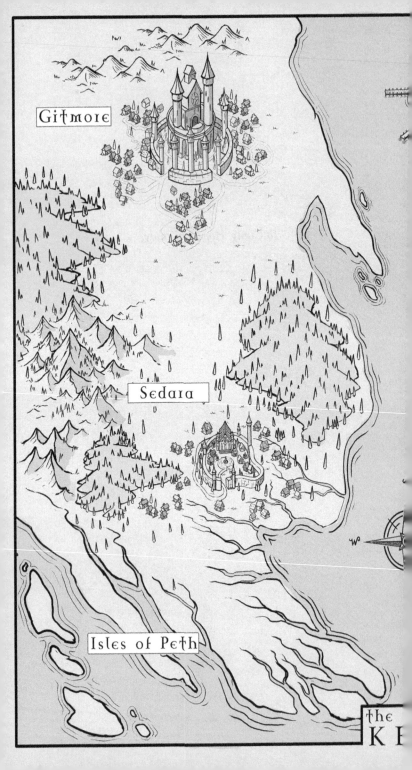

Gitmore

Sedara

Isles of Peth

the
K E

CHAPTER ONE

*T*hat dirty, liver-eating shitehole threw ale all over me!

"This tripe's disgusting!" he snarled. "Cost a whole half-penny and tastes worse than my boot!"

I was soaked and freezing. My eyes glazed over with rage. I swiped a hand over my sopping face and focused on the jerk holding the empty cup. I ignored the table I was serving.

There was a reason this asshole's food tasted awful. It was three-day-old fish I'd saved specifically for him. I bit down on my smile.

The inn was crowded with miners on payday. Here to play until their pockets were empty. Entitled as shite because they had two coins to rub together.

Case in point, Tripe-man picked up his plate, ready to toss that at me, too.

Asswipe. He thought he could steal from Kylee, and then waltz back in here? That tripe would have him heaving in no time. But I had to pretend I didn't know that. That I was outraged by his attempt to attack me with it.

I held up an arm to block him. "I didn't cook it, you piss-pot! If you don't like the food, leave."

"I want my money back, you soulless witch!"

My power flared. Oh, if he only knew. I shoved my power down and grabbed Tripey by the collar. "You want roasted duck? Go to the palace and try your luck there! Of course, I hear they like suckling pig. You might end up *on* the table."

"How about you suckle my pig!" a nearby miner shouted.

"You mean piglet!" I yelled at the heckler as I dragged Tripe-face toward the door. I'm not that strong, but he wasn't that big, and rage was a big motivator. I tossed him into the dirt. "Don't come back."

"Sard you!"

"In your dreams, Tiny!"

I turned to go back inside and nearly ran into a wall of a man. Green vest, gold pocket watch, pressed shirt. All covering a body that used to be pure muscle. But, running an inn and gambling hall made Kylee soft. It was the only explanation for why the brute hired me. He was soft in the head. It was how jerks were able to steal from him.

I bit my lip and looked up. "Sorry, sir."

"Bea, you can't keep throwing out patrons."

I sighed. "I know."

"Gonna have to—"

"Dock my pay. I know."

Damn it all. I needed that money.

But I didn't argue. Kylee didn't know what I was doing. And I wouldn't embarrass him by saying I knew he'd been swindled. No man liked to feel a fool.

"Learn to control that temper, Little Dragon. Then I can toss you in the back with the fat cats. They'd love you." He nodded left toward the double doors that opened onto the gambling hall, where the nobles and merchants sat, laughing and playing as much with the prostitutes on their laps as they did with the cards in their hands.

I shook my head. "No thanks."

Kylee ruffled my hair. "Well, if you don't want that, get your pretty butt upstairs and change before those tits start a riot down here."

I glanced down. Sure enough, my wet shirt was see-through. My nipples had pebbled and were straining the transparent cotton.

"Don't tell Abel or Marcus," I wagged a warning finger at Kylee as I tromped over to the servant's stairwell.

"They're probably already up in your room, panting," he barked out a laugh and shuffled back toward the poker table.

I rolled my eyes and hiked up my skirts to climb the stairs, hoping Kylee was wrong.

He wasn't.

Two handsome stable hands stood in my doorway gawking, eyes glued to my shirt.

"No. I'm working. Get out if you want a repeat of the other night." I jabbed a finger at the hallway and went to my trunk to rummage around for a decent shirt. I swore under my breath. My poor drunken decision-making had led me to make out with the pair of very horny halfling grooms and they'd been heckling me for a repeat performance ever since.

I rustled through the trunk, careful not to jostle the false bottom. I couldn't find a clean shirt. I'd have to put on my black dress. The one that had become far too tight recently. Damn spelled disguise was reaching its expiration date. I'd have to get another soon.

I grabbed the dress, tossed it on the bed, and turned to pull up my top only to find two very naughty stable hands still staring at me.

"I said no!" I felt my power flicker again, in response to my annoyance. I shoved it away.

"Please, Bea, just let us watch," Marcus whined.

I took a step toward him. "So help me Marcus, I will use that horsewhip on your hip."

Marcus grabbed Abel and sprinted out of the room.

I laughed and tossed my sopping shirt on the floor. I got rid of my green skirt and pulled on the black dress. A few weeks ago, my bust expanded because of this stupid spell. Spelled disguises tended to go wonky as they reached expiration. The spell had made my bust grow a cup size. I'd tried to hide it. But men have an annoying sort of perception when it comes to breasts. Never hair. Never my clean face, though I supposed I should be thankful my nose hadn't grown instead. That might have caused awkward questions. But the curves had started causing chaos.

It didn't help the fact that I caused enough chaos on my own before then. Kylee called me a dragon because he said I spit fire. I couldn't help it. My tongue had been reined in for so long growing up. Now it just unleashed. Even four years on my own hadn't been long enough to tame it.

I went to the looking glass to fix up my hair. I finger combed my brown locks, pinched my cheeks, added some extra kohl around my spelled brown eyes. That stupid miner. He'd cost me two pence, which would delay my next disguise. I might have to head out to the Cerulean Forest. Abandon Kylee's place and just run. Sard it all.

I turned to leave just in time to see Jenna come up the stairs, her gown ripped at the shoulder. I started to ask what happened to her, but it was pretty obvious. Jenna worked the gambling hall.

"Bea, can you cover for me?" Jenna turned her little nymph face on me. "I just need to change. I'll be done in a jiff. But there's a drink order and a stew order up and—"

I rolled my eyes. "Yeah, but hurry back. You know I hate that place."

Jenna nodded seriously. "Absolutely! You're the best!"

I tromped into the kitchen, grabbed Jenna's orders, and headed toward the gambling hall. I even pasted a fake smile on my face.

"Here you are m'lord," I pushed my accent a bit more low-class as I handed our very own Duke Aiden his stew.

My rump got an approving smack. I gritted my teeth to keep the smile on my face as I turned to serve another jerk at his table.

I set the drink down. The man made eye contact with me. He smirked.

I nearly dropped my jaw. Not because I knew the man. I knew his crest.

He was the palace spy master. And by the look in his eyes, he'd found what he was looking for.

Me.

*I*t took all of my self-control not to run, right then and there. But he would have caught me. I was sure he'd have posted guards around the inn. I had to be stealthy.

So, instead I widened my eyes like a sodding fool, gave him a deferential nod, and pushed my arms together so the girls would pop just a smidge more out of the black dress.

He didn't even look, though his mouth curled up a bit more at the corner. As if I amused him.

It was a fine mouth, thick and sensuous. I tried not to think about it as I turned and headed for the kitchen.

I tried not to think about how fine a specimen he was at all. I tossed his grey eyes, pointed elf ears, and clipped black beard out of my head. Because I had no use for handsome spies. The only good thing about seeing him was that now I had a face to go with the name of my enemy. Quinn Byrne. The queen's spy master.

Once I reached the kitchen, I doubled my speed. I nearly bowled Jenna over.

"Whoa now!"

"Delivered your orders. Tell Kylee thanks for me."

Jenna raised a brow, but I simply darted up the servant's stairs. I raced to my room, threw open my trunk, and fished around to unlatch the false bottom. I snatched my enchanted cloak, my sword, my dwindling bag of coins and jewelry. Carefully, I removed the last, tiny bottle of Flight that I had left. I hastily donned everything, keeping the bottle in hand. Then I checked the window.

I didn't see Quinn outside yet. Hopefully, the arrogant duke had detained him a moment. But I wasn't willing to chance anything. I eased open my window and slid out onto the shingled roof. The pitch was steep, but I only needed to go a few yards for clearance. I teetered forward, like a newborn calf, trying to keep my balance.

A figure moved down in the yard, just as I brought the bottle of Flight to my lips.

A curse rang out over the inn yard as I leapt toward the sunset, the wind whipping at my skirts.

A smile stretched across my lips as I turned my head to watch the spy master pass Marcus, whose jaw had dropped in shock, and run toward the stable.

Fool.

Did he think I'd escaped four years ago by using common means—

My thoughts faltered as Quinn Byrne emerged on the roof of the stable and took a flying leap into the air.

Sard.

I whipped my head forward and willed myself to go faster.

There was no way I was going to let him catch me. No way I was going back. I closed my eyes and flew right toward the sun.

Let the bastard go blind trying to catch me, I thought.

After the sun slipped below the horizon, I dove into some clouds. The wet chill clung to my skin. I couldn't see, but I pressed forward. I had to make it to Cerena's cottage. A few minutes there and I'd disappear again with a completely new body. I'd beg a spelled disguise out of her, even if I was short of coin. I'd no doubt I'd been her best customer for years.

Fear chilled my bones deeper than the wet clouds that clung to my skin.

Thunderation!

Was that how he'd found me? Did he know about Cerena?

I hadn't been to her in months. I'd gotten two spelled disguises the last time I'd seen the hedge witch. She hadn't even seen the newest face I was using. I hadn't told her I'd been working at Kylee's. The fear eased a bit. I was being silly. Paranoid. Kylee's was a common way point in the Cerulean Forest. I'd chosen it for the gossip.

I hadn't heard anything I'd been hoping for. But I'd heard plenty. I'd heard endless complaints about Duke Aiden and his lackadaisical management, his lean coffers, and his penchant for entertaining guests from the kingdom of Gitmore, the sworn enemies of Evaness.

I'd been planning on sending a dove home, to let my best friend know about the Duke's tendencies. But, with the spy master complication, any communication would need to be put on hold.

I ducked beneath the clouds and swore. I'd overshot Cerena's. I decided to land and make my way back on foot, rather than chance running into Quinn Byrne and his grey eyes in midair.

I landed in a pile of blue leaves, the yellow leached out of their summer green by the brisk change of season. The scent of dry, cool fall weather drifted over me. I inhaled and smiled into the twilight. Fall was my favorite season. The early nights meant respite from work for the poor farmhands (the few customers I actually liked serving). Fall meant warm stew that filled your belly as you put your feet near a roaring fire, inhaled the blissful smell of woodsmoke, and let the chill and heat fight for control of your body.

A fox darted out of the trees near me and I froze. I stood stock still and stared around me. Tingling anticipation crept up my spine. Something was out there. The question was whether it was the spy master.

The wind trailed its fingers over my neck and I suppressed a shiver.

My hands crept to my sword, but I didn't unsheathe it. No need to draw attention to myself if the fox was simply escaping a predator.

My pulse raced, and I forced myself to breathe slowly and silently, as I'd learned in combat practice. I tried to use the adrenaline to remain alert. To stay focused. But the longer I failed to see anything, the harder that became. My hands started to tremble. My body had to release the tension.

Finally, when my hips grew sore from standing in the same position for so long, I decided the fox must have simply outfoxed another animal. I made my way through the woods to Cerena's cottage.

I opened the door without knocking to find a wedded group already seated in front of the fire with my old friend. Three men and a woman swiveled their heads to glare at me.

"Excuse me," Cerena stood from her wooden chair and gave me the stink eye. A proud old woman with wavy silver hair and a limp she disguised well, she was the best hedge witch for a hundred miles. Not good enough for my ultimate goals. But good enough to be of use.

I responded to her glare by putting my thumb and fore-finger together in a circle, in the hand sign we'd agreed upon years ago, so she could identify me.

Cerena's eyes widened but she turned to the group. "One moment. My … cousin needs a room for the evening. Let me just get her tucked away and we can continue."

Cerena hurried me down the hall and up some rickety stairs. "You have the worst timing."

"I'll be out of your hair quickly."

She rolled her eyes. "That group down there are lower nobles. Your appearance here is going to cause chatter."

"Then I'll take to the woods for a bit. No problem." I shrugged.

Cerena rolled her eyes and opened the door to her bedroom. I shut it behind her as she opened the trunk where she kept her most potent spells. The spelled disguises that I desperately needed. "How many this time?"

"How many do you have?"

"Three prepared and I got a little creative with them. You know how you asked me to see about animal transformations. I worked that out. But …" she trailed off and held out her hand.

I sighed. I slipped my hand into my bag. The coins I had made at Kylee's wouldn't buy one disguise, let alone three. But with three … I'd be good for nearly a year. My hand clenched around a necklace. It'd be a dead giveaway, but I had to have those spells. "I need to trade this time."

"Trade?" her lips curled back. "You know I don't do trades."

"I know you're sick of fertility spells." I jerk my head toward the stairs. "Let me guess, they want a girl."

Cerena snorted. "Of course, they do." The birth ratio in our country had been five men to one woman since the curse a thousand years ago. Every family group sought daughters like they sought gold. Because daughters would be worth gold, when sold to the right husband group.

She tucked the spell bottles into her pocket.

I pulled out the necklace. I let the rubies catch the moonlight. Let the diamonds wink at her.

Cerena's eyes widened. "Where'd you get that?"

"The palace—"

"They'll string me up if I'm found—"

"Melt it down. Sell the stones separately. It wasn't the queen's. It wasn't stolen."

"How—"

Bang. Bang. Bang.

I glanced over my shoulder. The front door downstairs creaked under someone's vicious pounding. I had a good idea whose.

Cerena's eyes turned back to mine and narrowed. She eyed me up and down. "Who's after you? And why?"

I stepped up to her and placed the necklace in her hand. I heard a crash that could only have been the crash of the front door slamming open and hitting the wall. The family group's exclamations drifted up through the wooden floor slats.

"Please," I begged her.

"Who's after you?"

"The palace spy master."

She handed me one bottle.

"Why?"

I glared at her as footsteps pounded on the stairs. "Because I refuse to take the throne."

I pried a second bottle from her shocked form and raced to the window as the door to her bedroom burst open.

I dove through the glass and twisted open a bottle as I fell. I put the vial to my lips as I met the spy master's eyes.

Cat, I thought.

And then … I landed on four paws.

CHAPTER TWO

I cursed myself as I ran. Cat? That was the best I could come up with? What shite! Why not mountain lion? Wolf? Wolf would have been a better choice. Yes, as a cat I was small, but I wasn't well equipped to deal with the forest's wild animals. And stupid magic. I hadn't been specific when I was falling and shouted out an animal.

I glanced down at my four paws and saw they were all brown. But my legs were sarding grey. Light grey. Like a Siamese cat. Might as well have tied a flaming torch to my back. I was pretty sure moonlight was reflecting off my gorgeous bright grey fur as I dodged through the bushes. I would be ridiculously easy to spot. And I was stuck in this form until the spell wore off or someone reversed it. I wouldn't be able to get to my sword, my money, or my clothes until then. They were all … I wasn't really sure where they went. I'm sure the mage master had told me what happened to objects during a spell like this, but I hadn't thought I'd needed to listen. Stupid younger me.

At least I matched Quinn's eyes. Those piercing, arresting, storm-cloud eyes. I wondered how long he'd been pursuing me. This was the first time in four years he'd gotten close. At least, it was the first time I knew of. I wondered if he would chase me through the forest. I stopped to eye a nearby tree. Maybe I should climb and watch. Better than running all night. I could conserve my energy and watch where he went, then skulk off in the opposite direction.

I stopped at a promising massive oak. Twitching leaves set my nerves on high alert and sent me skittering up the trunk.

Plonk.

I fell backwards.

Apparently, climbing was an acquired cat skill, not an instinct.

I tried again. This time my claws latched on tight. I hugged the tree with all my strength and gradually worked out how to sink one set of claws at a time in. It was slow going up the trunk. I'd just reached the first branch when I heard a twig crack behind me. I shivered and lowered myself to clutch the branch in front of me.

From the bushes, a bobcat emerged. Its ears were pitched forward, listening. The cat's lanky limbs stalked through the trees.

I couldn't help a low hiss.

The bobcat immediately paused.

For a second, I wished that Quinn would come this way. The spy master's tromping would scare off this beast. And I wouldn't have to huddle here, shivering, cursing my stupid territorial cat aggression.

I crouched lower on the branch and tucked my tail around me.

That sliver of movement gave me away. One minute, the bobcat was on the ground, the next minute my wide eyes were facing its open jaw.

"Sard!" I tried to say. All that came out was a howling mewl.

I backed away but lost my grip and started to tumble sideways.

My stomach jerked upward from the fall.

Strong jaws latched onto the loose skin on the back of my neck.

My body swung back and forth like a pendulum.

I'm a sarding saddlegoose, I thought. I'm going to die eaten by a wild animal. 'Here lie the bones of Princess Bloss, heir to Evaness. Princess Peacemaker. Cursed beyond reason. And stupid enough to be eaten by a cat. A bear? Nope, you heard it right. A sarding cat.'

I cringed and rolled myself into a ball the best I could as the bobcat shuffled back down the tree with me.

My heart beat a million miles a minute.

To my shock, the cat didn't rip into me once he reached the forest floor. Nope, he set off at a trot.

Shite, I thought. Is he a she? Is she a mother? With a den of cubs? Am I going to be torn apart by dozens of inexperienced tiny sharp teeth? Hell no.

I swung my legs and tail and wildly and flung myself around.

The bobcat bit deeper into my skin but stopped before making me bleed.

Panic flooded my veins at that response. That was not a normal predator's response.

I swiped at the bobcat's head, and landed a blow, scratching its nose.

The bobcat shook me. But didn't end the annoying little kitten.

Sard it all, my brain whispered. I don't think this cat is a cat.

The spy master must have taken Cerena's last spelled disguise. He must have seen me transform into a cat and chosen an animal strong enough to catch and keep me.

Quinn Byrne was smarter than I'd anticipated.

Clearly, he had orders to bring me back alive. He had no idea what torture awaited me at the palace. Or maybe he just didn't care.

After all, I was his betrothed. He was one of the four knights my mother had chosen for me.

If he didn't bring me back alive, he'd never ascend the throne.

With that in mind, I swung my body around. I extended my claws and buried all four paws in his jugular.

ॐ

Quinn dropped me.

I rolled along the dead blue leaves, skittered to my feet, and ran. I didn't spare a glance backward. I didn't think I'd killed him, but I'd definitely done serious damage.

I hope I didn't kill him—I quashed that thought.

The spy master would have ended my quest and damned me and the kingdom.

The hill ahead was dotted with boulders and I dashed up it, hoping to find someplace to take cover.

I scooted into a narrow cleft between two rocks and found myself in a small cave, a tiny, cat-sized tunnel that burrowed into the hill. It was perfect.

I settled in, determined to wait a few hours, or a few days, if that was what it took. I'd wait until I couldn't scent that bobcat any more. And then I'd continue my quest for the wizard. The one man in the seven kingdoms who might be able to change the price of my magic.

I curled my tail around me and watched the opening of the cave, gradually drifting to sleep.

My best friend featured in my dreams frequently. That night was no exception. Even as a cat, I felt a tinge of longing.

Connor had grown up with me at court; the son of Duke Doyle, who ran the largest market for exotic good in Evaness, Connor had been my intended for my contingent of knights from the moment I was born. But I'd only grown up knowing he was my best friend. My confidant. The beautiful boy with the dark curls and winning smile. The maids had started calling him 'lady-killer' at age six, when he'd bribed them with sweets and compliments.

He and I had been inseparable; we'd been boisterous and obnoxious little shites who ran rings around the servants.

My governess had nicknamed us "peas and carrots."

The first time she'd done that, Connor had stood at his desk and thrown a quill at her. "We're like bread and honey!"

He'd been so offended she'd called us vegetables. I suppose, to eight-year-old boys, there's little more disgusting than being compared to a vegetable. I smiled and stretched in my sleep as I relived that memory. He'd gotten smacked with a ruler for that one.

Slowly, my dreams morphed into a more recent memory. The last memory I had of Connor.

He'd hovered above my naked body, sweat collecting on his neck.

"Are you sure?"

I'd loved his growly voice at that moment. Normally so sweet and happy, eighteen-year-old Connor was the joyous one at court. Every noble loved him. They couldn't help it. He brought a lively energy into the room with him. His mouth always stretched in a smile.

That night, he hadn't been smiling. He'd looked almost angry. But I'd known he wasn't angry. He'd been physically trying to hold himself back. To keep from mauling me after I'd teased him so mercilessly all day.

I'd pressed my breasts against him during dancing lessons, swiped my hand 'accidentally' over his manhood when I passed in the hall, even sat on his lap during a minstrel's performance that evening. He'd endured it all with nothing more than a flash of heat in his eyes. Then I'd drug him down to the summer garden, to our secret spot.

For the first time, I'd peeled off my clothes in front of him, enjoying the way his eyes had bulged and his jaw went slack. It had sent a delicious tingle down my spine to my core.

Because with Connor, unlike with anyone else in the world, I'd known his reactions were for me. Not the crown.

"I'm sure. My coronation and our wedding are the day after tomorrow," I'd told him.

His eyes had lit up at that. "I know. I can't wait—"

"I want you first. Before that. Before—" I hadn't mentioned the others. I hadn't even met Quinn Byrne then. My marriage was a political arrangement. The only consolation had been that I would love at least one of my husbands.

Connor's eyes had darkened with understanding. He'd opened his mouth to argue, but I'd cupped my breasts in my hands and drew his attention to them.

"Anything you want, Bloss Boss," his eyes had dilated.

"Kiss me. Everywhere," I'd ordered.

"Yes, my queen." He'd smiled at my command and taken to his task with reckless abandon.

He'd trailed kisses down my neck and dipped his tongue into the hollow of my breast bone. He'd bladed that beautiful tongue of his and traced hot spirals onto each breast, ignoring my nipples until I begged him, ordered him, and finally grabbed his face and shoved it where I'd wanted it.

Only then had he suckled me, flicking his tongue back and forth, drawing out the sweet agony.

"How are you so good at this? Who've you done this with?" I'd gasped, wrenching his head up so I could read the truth in his blue-green eyes.

He'd blushed. "No one. But I've watched. A lot."

I'd arched an eyebrow at him. "How?"

He ducked his head to pop my nipple back into his mouth. He'd sucked it briefly before rubbing his body along the length of mine and whispering, "Your secret corridors. I love to use them to spy on the nobles."

I'd burst out laughing. "You would."

He'd given a little shrug. "My spying's all for your benefit anyway. All of it."

"Even the dirty bits," I'd grinned.

He'd winked. "Especially the dirty bits. Otherwise, I wouldn't know how to do this."

He'd trailed his fingers down my belly and then side to side along my thighs. Gently, softly, he'd started to circle my opening, spiraling again. His spirals had gotten smaller and smaller until—

A noise startled me awake. I jumped and hissed, hitting my head on the top of the cave.

What the bloody hell?

Men's voices echoed around me. It took me a moment to realize that my small tunnel led to a bigger cave.

Cautiously, I trotted down my tunnel, hoping against hope that Quinn hadn't followed me here.

As the tunnel widened, I slunk toward the shadowed side. Firelight started to flicker along the cave walls as my tunnel opened onto a large cavern. A group of men crouched in a middle area free of stalactites. A fire jumped and flickered at their feet. The smell of roasted rabbit permeated the space. I fought off a cough brought on by the smoke cloud that hovered over the top half of the unventilated cavern.

The largest of the men, a man with a patch over one eye and a rough looking scar on his arm, stood. He spoke. "His orders are to bring the beast under cover of night. He says it will automatically be drawn toward the princess."

The man holding the spit, a scrawny middle-aged fellow, scoffed. "It's all well and good for him to say that. Ain't it? But I've seen those things. The monster's more like to rip out a hundred heads than get the right one."

"This is his plan."

"Well let him drag it 'cross the border then. An' let him try to keep it hidden. An' let him—"

The big man stepped closer to his complaining companion. His arm swung like a hammer. I heard the *thwack* of his fist smacking down. The scrawny man wobbled where he stood. Someone else scrambled to scoop up the spit, so that their dinner didn't burn. Scrawny fell back on his butt, dazed.

"Anyone else have a problem with the plan?" Big guy glared at his companions. One by one, they shook their heads no. "Good. Then in a few weeks, we should be rid of Princess Avia."

My heart leapt into my throat. Fear buzzed along my spine. These men were planning to attack my little sister. The new crown princess. I skittered backwards. I turned and ran blindly back up the tunnel.

I could hear them toasting behind me.

"To a new day for Evaness!"

Bile rose in my stomach. They were sick men. Twisted. Maybe it was just talk. Maybe. I tried to calm my beating heart. But cat reflexes don't react too well to logic. My heart raced. Every nerve in my body pushed me to bolt. My instincts screamed that these men were serious. These men were dangerous. They were going to kill my sister.

I tripped. Rocks skittered down the tunnel behind me.

"Someone's here!" I heard one of the rebels yell.

Sard.

Now I didn't just have a spy master chasing me. I had a rebel group, too.

CHAPTER THREE

I tumbled down the hill into the night and took cover under some bushes.

I sniffed desperately, trying to separate the smells that assaulted my cat nose.

I smelled bear scat somewhere nearby, and instead of revolting me, it just sent a warning tingle to my toes.

Don't walk there, my senses whispered.

I heard boots tromping around the hills behind me. I crouched lower to the ground, desperate to catch Quinn's scent.

Warm and wild, slightly musky, his bobcat smell hadn't been the worst thing. I twitched my nose to the north, seeking.

There. There it was.

I shot out of the bushes and through the fallen blue leaves, not caring how much sound I made.

An arrow whizzed overhead.

A *boom* sounded behind me. Like those rebels had set off an explosion spell.

My ears rang, and my balance was thrown off. I stumbled sideways, though I didn't slow my pace. I couldn't.

Sard.

Those shites were serious. Beyond serious. This couldn't be a small operation if they had the funds to pony up for spells like that. Even the royal palace only used explosion spells for war.

Avia. They are gonna hurt Avia. Go!

I pushed my cat legs to go faster, pushed the nose to keep on Quinn's trail. When it turned left, I tried to turn so quickly I ended up rolling head over tail into a thorny bush.

I landed right at the feet of a very angry bobcat, whose neck wounds still showed a trickle of blood.

The cat's eyes flashed, and his big paw batted at my head and pushed it down into the leaves.

I let him. I held very still as his sharp ears caught the sound of the rebel's hunt in the distance.

His eyes flickered back to mine and held.

I twisted slightly until I showed him my belly.

His nostrils flared, and he gave a huffy cat breath at that. I wasn't sure if he was pleased by my submission or annoyed he didn't have the excuse to hurt me.

If we'd been human, I would have told him what I'd heard and bolted. I'd have told him, kicked him in the nards, and run for my life.

But we weren't human. I couldn't talk.

I had no choice.

I was going to have to let him bring me in.

Quinn the bobcat leaned down and nudged me with his nose until I rolled onto my feet. Then he scooped me up by the scruff and turned east, heading toward the dawn, the castle, and my sister.

۶

Five hours past sunrise, we arrived at the palace. I expected Quinn to go around to the soldier's entrance. But he trotted toward the main gates. He crossed the moat, letting me dangle over the water once, just because he could. The huge oversized portcullis loomed over us. Wagons traveled in and out, carrying laundry and foodstuffs and nobles.

Shite. He was going to reveal me here. In front of everyone.

Because everyone knew enchantments couldn't be brought in to the castle of Evaness. No spells could make it past the barriers at the gates. An invisible shield protected the castle, set up by one of the great wizards who ruled centuries ago. The shield removed all mage spells and revealed all true human natures. No hidden poisons, no spelled disguises, nothing made it past the gates. Only the royal family and palace mage could use their magic inside.

Quinn shifted me in his mouth. He batted me with his paw until my body spun to face his furry chest. He walked calmly up the bridge, ignoring the villagers and servants who screamed and fled at the sight of a spotted bobcat.

He dodged a soldier's arrow.

My heart pounded, and I fought to keep from trembling. Yes, the arrows concerned me. But the gate did even more.

Why this gate? Why not one more private? Why reveal me in front of everyone?

And then it hit me. He was here to humiliate me. Much as I had humiliated him.

I hadn't thought much of it at the time, but now I was sure Quinn was angry. I had run from the palace two days before my coronation. The day after he'd been announced as my fourth husband.

His father had just won a major naval battle. My mother had seen me as a fitting reward. My husband group had lacked an Admiral. Quinn had been on that path.

I remember mother telling me, "One who controls the sea controls the land."

I had bit back an argument about the sky at the time. No one had controlled the sky since dragons had been vanished after the last Fire War. I'd just nodded my head and let her tack on another man. I'd already planned to leave at that point anyway.

The only thing I'd known of Quinn Byrne before I'd run had been his name.

The timing was pure coincidence. I'd seen the chance to escape and leapt at it.

I very much doubted the spy master believed in coincidence.

I closed my eyes as he neared the portcullis. We just had to pass it to encounter the shield.

Think of Avia. Think of Avia. You have to warn her. Let him do what he wants so you can get to her, I told myself.

My back was shoved against a frozen stone wall. My eyes popped open in surprise. My body twisted and shifted and grew to my natural human size. Quinn's grew at the same time, until he loomed over me.

My breath caught in my lungs. I hadn't truly appreciated just how handsome he was. But now that those tempting lips were inches from mine, I couldn't help but stare. Particularly when one of those lips curved upward in a smirk.

He was hot. And not in a drunken I-haven't-been-touched-in-four years way like Abel or Marcus. Quinn was tall and lean but muscled. His arms boxed me in against the stone wall. For a second, the image of them boxing me in on a mattress flashed through my head. The stubble that covered his jaw made me want to rub my hand and face along his. Perhaps changing into a cat left lingering instincts. I'd only ever used the spelled disguises to go human before.

Yes. It's definitely cat instinct. Not attraction, I told myself.

I was smarter than that. He was the enemy. His job was to bring me here and keep me here. My job was to warn my sister and escape again to continue my quest. Not to wonder if he was rough or gentle in bed.

I glanced at those grey eyes. Rough. They definitely screamed rough. My thighs trembled at that thought. And for a second, I was glad I'd run before I'd seen him. He'd tempt the devil into sweetness. Half-elves were dangerous that way.

Quinn grabbed a lock of my hair and twisted it around his finger.

Welcome home, wife.

I started. It was as if I'd heard his voice in my head. No. I was overtired. We had traveled through the night.

If his stern face had anything to say, it wasn't welcome home. It was: I sarding hate you.

I looked away to gather my wits and saw the staring crowd.

Quinn pulled my attention back to him when his body pushed into mine, and even though we'd regained our clothes, I felt every hard inch of him pressed against my stomach.

Part of him didn't hate me, at least.

I nearly made a bawdy joke about him holding me at sword point. But the expression on his face made me pause.

Maybe I should apologize first, I thought.

"I—"

Quinn didn't let me speak. Instead, he held a finger to my lips. He ran his hand over my long brown curls, then up my neck, sending shivers of delight and fear down my spine. He traced my brow and the underside of my hazel eyes. His fingertip was warm, and a stark contrast to the fall air.

My skin came alive at his touch. Heat pooled in between my legs. I forgot myself for a moment and pressed into him.

I forgot he'd only meant to use me to show his prowess. His catch. To rub in my nose the fact that I'd been captured. That the spy master had been successful.

He turned me into a simpering barmaid. Stupid, temptingly handsome man. And me, the idiot, acting like we were lovers.

Quinn stepped back, taking my wrist in what might have been mistaken for a protective gesture.

But I knew better. It was a shackle.

He turned me toward the courtyard, where nobles and servants and soldiers had all stopped what they were doing. They all stood stock still, staring at us.

I'm sure I was a sight, disheveled, in a servant's black dress, one that was too big on my naturally slender form. At least Quinn wasn't much better. His outfit still had hay sticking out of it from the barn at Kylee's. His nose still had the cat scratch I'd given him. I couldn't see how his neck had fared.

Quinn marched toward the front doors. I struggled to keep pace with his long legs. There was no way I'd let him drag me through my own courtyard like some criminal.

No sarding way.

People's eyes followed us. The silence was deafening.

"Princess Bloss?" a woman's voice called out.

I turned to see Lady Agatha, a snotty and entitled woman who'd spent far too many years fawning over my mother.

"Yes?"

"What happened to you?" she put a hand to her chest in mock horror. Or maybe it was real horror. For a woman who'd only ever worn silk, perhaps a woolen dress was horrific. Still, she was only asking to satisfy her own nosy curiosity. Not out of any concern for me.

"My husband and I were just copulating in a field. You should try it sometime." I winked at her as Quinn jerked me up the stairs.

He didn't give me enough time to enjoy the way her jaw dropped down like a door with a broken hinge.

But I did hear him mutter, *I hope your mother thinks you're as funny as you do.*

I met his eyes as two servants opened the double doors to the castle.

"Don't worry. She won't."

Quinn kept a death grip on my wrist as he led me to the right, not to the main throne room, but to a minor receiving room used for groups of foreign dignitaries. Still pretentious. It still held five thrones on a raised platform. But it was a smaller, more intimate level of pretension.

The room was empty.

Quinn halted in the middle of the room and stood silently under the main chandelier. He didn't go to the bell-pull to ring for servants. He didn't call for anyone to come. He must have assumed that the gossip from the courtyard would ensure my mother and sister found us. Not to mention, my three other husbands.

I sighed. Husbands. That was the lie my mother had put out when I'd run. That we'd all secretly married, and they'd secured their positions as my knights. It had been whispered about that we'd been too eager to wait for the formal ceremony. What with the threat of dragons looming and my intention to seek out and kill the last of the monsters ... that last bit had dulled any gossip about my impropriety.

Why my queen mother had invented the lie instead of simply handing my husband group off to my sister and declaring her the crown princess immediately, I didn't know.

"So, what are you gonna do about all those rumors that I was off hunting some made up foreign dragons?" I tried the conversational approach with Quinn.

It didn't work. He didn't even look at me.

Unlike before, when at least I felt tension rolling off him, felt him give in to the thrill of the chase, there was nothing. It was like I was talking to a big, grey stone wall.

Fine. Sard you, too, I thought. Until I realized that he might have been waiting for me to apologize.

It might end up the only moment I ever had with him alone. The palace was always full of eyes and ears and I'd rarely gotten a moment's privacy growing up.

Was that why he didn't call anyone?

Shite.

I at least owed him an apology. I was sure he hadn't wanted the match either. To be told two days before a wedding? Even if the bride came with a crown, that was a lot to take in.

I sighed. "You know when I left, it had nothing to do with—"

"You're back!" Avia strode into the room, her skirts sweeping over the mosaic floor, her face as hard and brittle as iron. Four years had changed her. My sister wasn't the gawky little twelve-year-old I remembered. She was sixteen. She looked taller. Leaner. And she had bags under her eyes so deep they could have been craters.

"I—"

She pulled the crown off her head. My crown. The crown she'd been forced to wear after I'd run. She studied the rainbow array of gems. Then she flicked her wrist. The crown flew at me, smacking me in the chest.

I took a step back as it rolled on the floor and Quinn stopped it with his foot.

"Take it. And them," she snarled gesturing behind me. She grabbed her red skirts and swept out of the room before I could respond.

She was a little bit angry with me.

Understandable. I can handle that, I told myself.

I turned. Behind me were the three other men I'd been promised to. The men I'd abandoned.

Their gazes were cold, hard, and unforgiving.

Even Connor's.

My childhood best friend, my first kiss, my first love, Connor stared at me the way I'd seen him stare at my mother.

It almost looked like anger and disgust warred beneath his blue-green eyes.

That stung. And not a little. It stung like I'd walked into a hornet's nest. Which, perhaps I had.

I shrunk back. I knew I'd missed sending that last dove to him, but I'd sent so many before. I'd written him nearly every month of my absence. Sometimes more. He'd never written back, but obviously, I hadn't expected him to. The palace was full of eyes and I didn't exactly ever provide a location. But I didn't expect the vitriol from him. Not from my sweetling.

Connor mussed his brown curls and shook his head at Quinn, as if asking why the spy master had bothered to bring me home. Then he turned and stalked to a shadowed corner of the room, outside my line of sight.

That dismissal pulverized my heart, smashed it into tiny little bits of dust.

Connor! I cried out in my head.

But I hadn't been raised to be queen for nothing. I kept a mask of calm on my face. And turned to face the other two men.

Ryan was a tall, dark-skinned god of war. Some women at the inn had liked to compare men to drinks of well water. "He's a half-dipper." Or "he's a sludgy sip." Most of the comparisons were insults. But once in a while, they'd say a man was a sweet sip of ale. Frothy and fizzy and fun at night. If they'd have seen Ryan ... he would have been a glass of wine. His looks made women sway like drunks.

He had deep chocolate eyes, lashes women would kill for, and a goatee. The man was also six foot five and stacked. His muscles had muscles. Part of his heritage as a part-giant, I suppose. Giants were known for their strength. Ryan's human side accounted for his brains. And with the combination, it was no wonder he'd worked his way up to be a general in the Evaness army.

Before I'd run, I used to sneak into the back of the practice arena and watch him from the shadows with my lady-in-waiting. He had always practiced without a shirt. And when I'd been a gawky teenager, he'd already been in his mid-twenties. He was eight years older than me. He'd been the cause of my sopping underthings on more than one occasion.

We hadn't really known each other. He'd been called out on patrols, or to supervise the borders, or whatever else. I'd been stuck inside the palace. And eight years was a lot when I was eighteen. I hadn't known what to say to him. Ever.

I discreetly scanned Ryan as he glared at me with crossed arms. He stood in his traditional breeches and boots. He'd clearly just tossed on a white shirt as he'd come in from the practice yard. Four years hadn't diminished his physique. If anything, he looked bigger. Definitely meaner. Or maybe that was simply the emotion he hurled at me.

"Why are you here?" he got right to the point.

Of course, he would. Ryan had never been one for niceties. That had been Connor. Ryan was more likely to punch you than talk through issues.

Of course, he was also a bit of a braggart. Before I'd left I'd heard talk he'd gotten my name tattooed onto his body after we'd been intimate.

I stared into his brown eyes as memory of that lie flared.

"I came to check on your tattoo, darling."

"Frigid witch," he stormed forward and yanked me away from Quinn.

He pulled me up against him, and though I could feel the violence shimmering in the air, I also felt the heat of his body and see the beads of sweat pouring down his muscles from whatever workout my arrival had interrupted.

His scent made my throat go dry. It was wood shavings and male musk. If he'd been a god of sex, I'm pretty sure I would have volunteered to be a virgin sacrifice.

But he wasn't. He was a man who led our army and dealt out death in daily doses to the kingdoms nearest.

My stupid female hormones would do well to remember that, I scolded myself as my feet dangled in midair.

"Why the hell are you back, Bloss? Why now?" he growled.

I licked my lips. "I came to warn Avia."

Ryan dropped me. I fell onto my crown. It stabbed me in the hip.

"Ow!"

Not one of the men moved when I cried out.

I deserved that.

I pushed the crown aside, leaving it on the floor. I wasn't here for it, anyway.

"I overheard a plot to kill my sister."

My eyes flickered from one man to the next. Their only response was silence, though Ryan's chest heaved like he wanted to attack me.

"A plot?" he scoffed.

"Yes. They are planning to send a beast after Avia. The group was after me. So was Quinn. I thought him the lesser evil. So I let him catch me."

The men's eyes flicked to Quinn and he nodded, then shrugged.

I didn't know what the shrug was about. Or why he didn't speak.

Judging by the gleam in his eye, he was getting a kick out of watching the awkward hatred in play.

No one said anything after my statement, and my eyes finally landed on my last husband.

Declan McCarthy was a halfling. Half-human, half-fae. He was the bastard son of the Sedarian queen. She'd had him when her husbands were all abroad with the navy. No one knew exactly who his father was, or what type of fae he was, other than powerful. And too sarding smart. He used to speak like he was a walking book, with long sentences and technical words that could put me to sleep in an instant. Originally, Declan had been sent over to minimize the bastard child's interaction with the real heirs to Sedara's throne. But his adeptness had caught my mother's eye. Helped him make her list.

Declan was handsome, in his own way. He had blond hair and ice blue eyes. He didn't make my heart ache like Connor or make me cross-eyed with lust like Ryan. He definitely didn't have that edge of dangerous aggression and amusement that drew me to Quinn. Declan was … safe. He would have been the perfect gentleman. If I had married him instead of running away.

But I hadn't. And four years was a long time. For all I knew, he'd grown into a monster.

Declan pushed back his blond hair and stared down at me with pensive blue eyes. "What beast?"

I was startled he actually spoke civilly to me. "I'm not sure."

"What group is sending it?"

"I'm not sure."

He tilted his head and gave a smile that sent ice down my veins. "So, you ran four years ago, have diligently avoided capture, and suddenly appear here to warn Avia about a supposed plot against her. A plot for which you can provide no details?"

"I—"

"Send her to the dungeons." Declan jerked his head at Quinn, who locked his hand around my upper arm.

"Either you've suddenly become stupid, or you have an ulterior motive," Declan stated.

"Or," Connor's voice rang out of the shadows, "maybe someone's found a way to get around the shield. Maybe she's not Bloss at all."

CHAPTER FOUR

Quinn yanked me sideways, but before he could drag me off, my mother's personal butler, Jorad, appeared.

"Her Majesty, Queen Rella, would like the Crown Princess Bloss to attend to her in her chambers."

"Her chambers?" my eyes went wide. "Why's she in her chambers?" My heart skipped a beat and my face grew pale when Jorad didn't answer.

Mother never stayed in her chambers. She was always up before dawn and worked long into the night. Meetings. Audiences. Meetings. Repeat.

I'd expected her to appear and berate me. I'd expected my fathers to trail behind her like ducks, like they always did, and shake their heads in silent disappointment over me.

Something was horribly wrong.

I kicked Quinn in the knee, surprising him enough to release me, and I ran. I ran through the palace, buzzing past servants and around maids with mops and laundresses carrying curtains and sheets. I ran past nobles, and dignitaries, and anyone in my path until the way became a blur because worried tears filled my eyes.

I stopped in front of my mother's chamber, biting at my cheeks and blinking back the moisture in my eyes. I could not cry in front of her. A queen could not cry. A queen showed no emotion.

Ryan skidded to a halt behind me and had to reach over my head and put an arm on the wall to prevent himself from crashing into me. His hulking form would have smashed me to bits if he had.

Behind me I heard a click as a secret panel opened in the hallway and Connor and my other 'husbands' poured out of a hidden passage, muttering and cursing.

I took a deep breath, trying to steady myself. Ryan didn't say anything, just loomed over me, watching. The look in his eyes was pensive, calculating. He was weighing my emotional response and what it meant.

I could see the question in his eyes. Why would the woman who'd run from her family give a shite if something was wrong with her mother?

Sard. This is why my mother said no crying.

My hands shook as I turned the handle and pushed open the door.

Mother lay in her giant four poster bed, her hair plaited in a braid that reached her waist. The velvet covers were drawn around her waist and pillows propped up her back. A small lap desk was pushed to the side of her and overflowed with paper. As if she was working from her bedchamber. As if this were a normal event.

Was she that ill? Was it serious?

My heart beat a mile a minute as my eyes roved over her.

She was thinner than I remembered. Her hair was streaked with grey. Her lady-in-waiting clucked somewhere but the woman left the room at the flick of my mother's wrist. For the first time in my memory, my queen mother smiled when she saw me.

"Bloss. I'd heard you returned. Well done," mother nodded at someone behind me.

I supposed Ryan and the others had followed me into the room. I didn't turn to look. I was still in shock.

Shock turned to anger. She was acting so calm about my return. So normal.

I saw her hand tremble against the bedsheets, though she tried to hide it.

That wasn't an emotional tremble. It didn't stop. She ended up burying her hands in the blankets to conceal her weakness.

My shock transformed into fear, and fear shape-shifted into an angry bear raging inside of me.

"What the sarding hell is going on?" I stomped further into the room. Ryan maintained his place two steps behind me. "I haven't heard any talk about you being sick."

She laughed lightly. "I can't be ill. I have one missing daughter and another that's two years away from being eligible to marry and take the throne."

Those words blasted like a cannonball through my stomach. "Below the belt," I snarled.

"Is it? I thought I only spoke truth."

I seethed. She was always good at cutting me, at throwing me off balance and forcing me to use my power. It flickered in my stomach even now. I shoved it down forcefully.

No. I left that all behind, I told myself.

She watched me through slitted eyes, waiting to see how I'd respond. When I'd left, I'd been a scared little princess. Now? If this was the inn, I'd have cursed her to high heaven. So that's what I did.

"You only speak half-truths, you black-souled she-witch. And you know it." I growled.

Out of the corner of my eye, I saw Ryan take a disbelieving step backward.

I'd just cursed the queen. No one cursed the queen. Not only that, but four years ago, I would never have said that. When I was eighteen, I'd been mother's plaything, her puppet.

Aw, shite, I thought.

He was gonna think I wasn't myself. That I was some kind of magicked spy.

But my mother grinned. "Grown up a bit have we? Think you can spit vitriol at your monarch?"

"Someone should. You surround yourself with enough ass-kissing fools."

"Your Majesty," Connor's voice interjected. "Are you certain it's Bloss?"

She arched an eyebrow. "She looks quite a bit worse for wear, but … Bloss, what did you do to your tutor when you were three?"

I rolled my eyes. "I bit his nose so hard they had to stitch it."

"And when Avia was nine and you were fifteen, what was the horrific fight in your chamber about?"

My cheeks grew pink. "I refused to let her stay there at night any longer."

"Why?"

She was trying to embarrass me. The bitch. But I'd seen so much in my time outside these walls and I wasn't easily embarrassed. I'd seen men caught with their trousers down tripping through the streets as they chased after their furious wife. I'd seen a man who'd fallen through the slats of a rotten privy and had to yell for help and be towed up by six villagers, a woman going to the doctor for boils on her … Whatever mother asked me, it couldn't be worse than that.

I squared my shoulders and looked her straight in the eye. "I pushed Avia out because I was too old ..." I trailed off, not wanting to say more.

"Too old to comfort your scared little sister?"

I swallowed. "I was a teenager."

My mother slowly folded her hands in her lap. Finger by finger, letting us all just watch her like mice watch a cat who's paused in toying with them. There was no hope she'd let me go. No hope she'd let it drop. Not when the tension level ratcheted up several levels and she could feel it. She reveled in these moments. She always had.

"The night before you left, what did you give Connor?"

My eyes widened and flitted to Connor's. His seafoam colored eyes were just as wide as mine. He seemed shocked, too. I didn't ask how she knew. But she did. She always knew.

I worked very hard to keep my hands from curling into fists. But my fingers flexed in anger. On instinct. I wanted to punch her in the mouth.

Behind me, Ryan let out a low growl as he saw my stiff back and realized the implication.

Mother had chosen Ryan for me when I was sixteen.

He'd been twenty-four then. Eight years my elder, already an officer. A local boy who'd come to the castle and 'made it.' I'd never questioned why she chose him then. I'd been overwhelmed. He'd been a dreamboat by all accounts. Part of the naughty fantasies I'd whispered with my lady-in-waiting. But sometimes fantasy was better than reality. Reality had scared me.

Ryan had approached me the night after the announcement. I'd been walking back to my rooms when he'd grabbed me from behind, like a thief, and stolen into an unlocked room. He'd pushed me up against the wall, dragged his hand along my hip, and whispered dirty things in my ear. Things that I'd been too naive and cowardly to take him up on as a teenage virgin.

I nearly laughed at that memory. His little whispers were nothing to what I'd seen in the months I'd worked in the counting house at the back of a brothel. But back then, I'd been too dazed by his looks and too scared by his words. I'd run.

Ryan's hand clamped down on my shoulder as I faced my mother. His fingers dug into me painfully.

I bit my lip and tried to decide what my mother's goal was. The answer to her question would divide them. They were meant to be a team, four knights who protected different aspects of the realm. She'd selected them to operate that way. For their differing but complementary abilities. Answering would mean war amongst them. I might be furious at her. But she'd also raised me to be tactical. She had a reason. "Why are you doing this?"

"Which of them did you write to while you were gone?"

I heard muttering behind me as the men whispered to one another.

Ryan's hand nearly crushed my clavicle. My knees bent under his weight and I had to struggle to remain upright. Pain rippled down my arm like flames. I pushed his hand away and took another step toward my mother.

"Why are you stirring the shite?" These men were perfect leaders. She'd chosen them.

They'd never be able to rule divided.

Did she expect me to use my power to end this? Sard her. That was only temporary. The barbs she threw could not be repaired by fleeting magic.

Before I could determine the method guiding her madness, her eyes flickered to the side. Her maid had returned with the castle mage, Wyle, and ten soldiers in tow.

My mother nodded toward me.

"Do it now."

The soldiers surrounded us. Declan, Connor, and Quinn were herded closer until the armored guards formed a circle around us.

The mage, Wyle, sprinkled a ring of ash and salt around us. He lit a candle and burned a sage leaf.

And then he muttered a spell in an ancient language.

He ignored me when I interrupted. My mother ignored me when I shouted. The guards ignored me when I tried to break through their circle. My idiot husbands ignored me and followed their queen's orders even as golden circlets appeared and glowed on our wrists.

I finally kicked the soldier in front of me, walloping his crown jewels. He fell forward and I jumped on his back, intending to launch toward the doorway and out of the room.

But Wyle's chant ended just as I jumped.

And an invisible tether yanked me back.

I hit the ground.

Stars were an understatement. I saw supernovas. The vertigo was so bad, I turned on my side, in case I needed to puke.

Not a single person moved to help me up.

Gradually, the room stopped spinning. When I was able to make my way to my feet, I turned to my mother.

"What in the sarding hell was that?"

"That was a bonding spell. From now on, you must be within five feet of one of your husbands at all times."

CHAPTER FIVE

*T*he soldiers and the mage filed out, leaving only myself and four stunned men facing the queen.

"You can't do this!" I screamed.

"I can and I have. You will accept your lot in life, Bloss. Your foolishness has gone on long enough."

"Foolishness? To try to find a—" the geas (the spell that prevented me from speaking about my power) cut off the string of curses I wanted to say and the end of my sentence.

I turned to stomp away but I found myself stopped by an invisible wall. I glanced down. The golden circlet on my wrist glowed faintly.

Rage threatened to engulf me. That circlet felt like a bear trap that had clamped down on my arm.

It sparked panic in me. Riotous panic that spread like fire. Quick and hot and choking.

I closed my eyes and breathed. In and out.

If I were at the inn, I would have cudgeled her to death with a soup spoon. I let that image play through my mind for a moment to quash the panic.

"Bloss, your kingdom needs you," my mother called behind me. "Now that you have returned, your husbands can help you grow reacquainted with your kingdom. And I can die in peace."

I turned back to my mother, to meet her eyes as mine filled with angry tears. But I held onto my control. Not a single one slid down my cheek as I looked into her lined face.

"You have another daughter. Avia will be a great queen."

"Perhaps," she gave a half-nod. "One day. I cannot wait that long."

"So you condemn me—"

Someone's hand clamped over my mouth. A hard chest pressed against my spine for a millisecond, before I was released.

I looked sideways to watch Ryan moving back to his place. "Sorry, Your Majesty," he addressed my mother with a slight bow. "I found the condemnation comment a bit offensive."

My mother grinned. "As did I, General." Her grin faded, and her lips straightened as she glared over at me. "The kingdom comes first. Always remember that. All of you.

Declan, perhaps you might be able to escort my wayward daughter to her chambers? She needs to bathe and change out of those filthy maid's clothes."

My eyes widened at the implications. He'd be within five feet of me at all times.

My nostrils flared. I ground my teeth together and glared at my mother.

But Declan started to move. When I didn't immediately follow, all three of my other husbands took several steps backward. The spell yanked on me, and I stumbled.

Declan snapped. "Come on."

I had no choice but to follow him. But as I left the room, I gave my mother a single finger salute.

She wanted to sard with my life?

Just wait.

She would rue the day. I'd make her hand that crown back to my sister so fast her wrist snapped. Then I'd make sure Avia was safe. I'd get rid of this gods-damned curse. And I'd disappear into the forest again.

As we marched down the hall, Ryan turned to Declan. "Find out who's right. That's an order."

Declan's eyes flashed with heat at the cryptic comment. He and Ryan paused and exchanged a long look. There was something in it. Some underlying tension.

"Are you going to come?" Declan asked.

"Not with you." Ryan answered.

Declan bit his lip and gave a nod. He started walking again, a little faster.

"What the hell was that?" I asked.

No one answered.

At the first split in the hallway, Connor sped off without a backward glance.

Declan did not lead me to my chambers. He led me into a hallway in the royal wing that I'd never been to before. The knights' hall. The hall where my fathers had resided. The hall where my so-called 'husbands' now slept.

The Queen's husbands had moved to her chambers now that she was so ill, so they could tend to her. It was what my grandfathers had done in their day as well.

Once my mother passed, my fathers would be sent to the cliffs. A knight existed only so long as he was bound to his queen. The archaic, matriarchal laws of Evaness didn't allow former knights to remain in the palace. Too much room for confrontation. To have authority and lose it— that was a hard battle. No. Knights were destined to end their lives with their queen.

I brushed away the dark thought and focused on the present. I had too much to worry about without becoming maudlin and depressed.

I looked instead at the portraits lining the walls of the knights' hall.

"Why are you taking me here?" I asked. I had to trot to keep up with the pace Declan set. My other husbands peeled off one by one, in other directions, but Declan continued down the corridor. He didn't answer me until he came to the very last door at the end of the hall.

"I have work to do," Declan's jaw ticked as he held open the door for me, begrudgingly polite.

"You heard my mother. The queen cannot be denied," I rolled my eyes.

"Your maids will be able to assist you here," he turned and led me into a room that was full of sumptuous blue velvet and brown leather.

"What if I don't want to be assisted here?"

"You think I give a damn what you want?" Declan took a step toward me, his boots scraping along the stone floor. This close, the smell of parchment and ink radiated off of him. It was the sort of scent that made me want to curl up near a fire and read. Of course, not with him next to me.

"Of course, you do. I'm apparently your precious wife," I shot back.

Declan's frigid eyes warned me to stop. They were little bits of frozen blue sky and they hailed down hatred and disdain. "You're a coward, Bloss. I don't know why Quinn bothered to bring you back."

I hardly knew Declan before I ran. We'd studied together. But he'd been so far ahead of me in analysis and tactics … we hadn't been friends. So why did his words pierce me like arrows? Why did they make my heart ache? Because they were true.

But harsh truths never made me reflective. They made me want to fight. I stomped Declan's foot and when he lifted it from the ground and was off-balance, I pulled his hair. As if I were five.

That was a mistake. Despite his scholarly ways, Declan was still nearly six feet tall. He grabbed my upper arms and shoved me. I fell to the ground. When he stomped to the bell pull, the curse yanked at me until I was forced to crawl along behind him over the stone floor.

"Ass!" I screeched.

Declan merely smirked and straightened his hair as his butler scurried into the room. The butler halted when he saw me but knew better than to ask.

I plotted Declan's untimely death as he addressed his butler.

"My wife needs a bath. Have one set up near my desk."

"Yes, Your Highness."

"I'd like a privacy screen," I threw out as the butler made to leave.

The man turned back but didn't face me. He faced sarding Declan. Declan shook his head.

The butler was out of the room before I could argue.

I seethed, standing and turning to Declan again. "What was that?"

Declan smirked. "We have a bet going. I'm simply taking the opportunity to settle the matter." He strode past me toward a massive desk that sat underneath a twenty-foot arched window. The desk was covered in scrolls and missives. An ink pot and quill stood neatly in one corner. As Declan pulled out his chair, I was again forced to move closer to him.

I waited, but the servants were taking their time bringing the tub, my maids, and the water. They were probably all quite intimidated by the disagreement between Declan and I, and were waiting out the fury, so that they wouldn't bear the brunt of it. That's how they'd been after my mother and I would row when I was younger, anyway.

I tapped my foot impatiently. But eventually curiosity won out. I had to ask. "What's the bet?"

Declan's mouth curved into a half grin just as the sunlight shot a beam onto his face. He looked breathtaking in that moment. I had to remind myself he was a know-it-all triptaker who'd find fault in everyone short of my mother. An ass, who'd just called me a coward.

"The bet …" he turned slightly in his chair and let his eyes wander down my figure, "is whether or not you're horribly deformed. Down there."

My eyes widened, and my jaw dropped. "What?"

"Ryan's put twenty pounds wagering you have a cock."

My head exploded. This? This is what they thought? I opened my mouth to respond but Declan cut me off.

"You see, Ryan can't think of any other reason you might have refused him. Of course, before today, none of us knew that you'd given yourself away—I believe that will change any payouts. Connor wagered pretty heavily against the cock." Declan's eyes flickered between mine, as if hoping to catch me out. But I was so caught up in my fury at this wager the men made, I couldn't focus on anything else.

Declan shrugged. "Now, Quinn has theories about other deformities. Scars, diseases. He gave the most detailed description out about blue waffle disease."

A whore's affliction!

My hand flew to my mouth in horror. "That's a lie!"

Declan turned back to his papers, as if dismissing me. "I suppose we'll see, won't we?" He grabbed a letter opener and sliced open a missive. He acted as if our conversation meant nothing. As if the years of speculation about me were of little importance.

I rubbed my brow as servants brought in the tub and filled it. It gave me time to think. These men hated me. Tried to explain my departure by way of disease. Treated me as a joke. I'd tried to give them the best chance at life. And I was a joke to them. My mind hardened. Connor. It had to be him. He knew all. Or as much as I could write about with the geas blocking me. He must have instigated this hatred against me.

My face turned to stone as the last of the steaming water was poured into the tub. If he hated me, then fine. There was little I could do. I'd known when I'd left that it was a possibility.

I ignored the full body ache and the hole that opened in my chest at the thought. I would not be some heartsick fool. I'd done what was best for him. If he'd torn up my letters and hardened his heart, that was his choice. But to mock me with the others? Encourage them to think such awful things? That was beyond the pale.

I stripped off my dress and ignored Declan's speculative gaze on my pale skin; his eyes lingered on the freckles on my arms from the summer I'd spent in the fields, the soft curves of my breasts, and the dull red of my nipples. I stepped into the water, facing him, letting him look his fill. "You see? No cocks. No disease. No extra limbs."

I circled slowly in the tub so he could see the back as well, letting water slosh onto his stone floor. When I turned forward to stare at him, I think he gulped. "I'm clean. Not quite virginal. But not the monster you'd hoped." I ground my teeth together as I said that last bit.

I sank into the heated water and pretended Declan wasn't there, that his eyes weren't riveted to my body.

I leaned my head back against the side of the copper tub and sighed. I let the heat sink into my bones and wash away my fear for Avia and the disbelief my stupid husbands had about the threat against her. How could I convince them to help? I had no idea. I pulled up my emotions one by one: my anger at my mother, my husbands' anger at me, my frustration, the desperate trapped feeling of being back in the palace … I pulled each emotion up and then let it go, like the swirls of steam from my tub, disappearing into the air. Emotions wouldn't help me solve the problems I had.

Queens used strategy. Not emotion.

I'd save my sister and give her the crown, break this curse tying me to four men who clearly hated me, and leave again. I'd figure out how after I'd enjoyed the first hot bath I'd had in four long years.

⟨

*I*t must have been an hour later when I looked up from the water. My fingers had shriveled into prunes and I was delighted by that fact. Begrudgingly, I cleaned my skin, refusing to call a maid in. I washed my hair and my face. But my back was a struggle.

I heard Declan muttering as he poured over a giant ledger. "Sixty-two and one-hundred-four. Nine-thousand… that can't be right. I'll need to send the auditor." He made a note in a hand-sized notebook next to the ledger. He reached up and ran a hand through his blond hair, straightening it for the eightieth time. "They should try barley next year … rest the wheat field …" his muttering as he worked was equal parts endearing and annoying. I'd forgotten that about him. When I'd known him, half his muttering had been in Sedarish. And, being a self-conscious teenage girl, I'd thought he'd been muttering about me.

"Have you always talked to yourself?" I asked as I used the sponge to reach the middle of my back. Of course, this made me arch forward.

Declan turned toward me and his eyes immediately fell to my chest. I raised an eyebrow but he didn't move his eyes away. "It helped me practice the language. Now, it keeps things clear."

"What province are you looking at?"

"Ranwalf. Reviewing a request from Duke Aiden. He's scheduled for a visit …" he went back to muttering under his breath at the ledger.

"Is he behind on payment?"

"Why the interest?"

"I happened to run into Quinn and Duke Aiden together. The duke's rather fond of pissing away his tenant's hard-earned gold."

Declan muttered something about women and their gossip.

"Excuse me?" I leaned toward him.

"He cheat on his wife? He or any in his husband group?"

"Daily."

Declan waved the quill at me. "There you have it. He scorned his wife, so she'll ruin him for other women by saying he can't manage his funds. Common tactic. See it at court all the time."

"His wife's too busy raising her sixth son to be bothered with his whoring," I countered. "I've *seen* him lose thousands."

"Well, Ranwalf province must have thousands to give then. Because they're paid up on taxes. He's coming for a visit to discuss crop rotation."

I scrunched my nose. "Deadly boring."

"Unless you realize that wheat goes for five times the rate of barley. He wants a second year of the wheat crop. His weather is fantastic for it." A tinge of the nerdy scholar came into Declan's voice as he spoke.

I bit down on my lip to avoid calling him 'adorable' and end up scorned and silenced.

He continued, "With the right calculations and application of power, I could do it—"

"What?"

"Magnify their minerals. The trick would be where I could take a reduction—"

He turned back to his calculations and a stream of mutters poured forth. I pondered his words for a bit. My mother hadn't only chosen Declan for his brain. His fae heritage gave him the unique ability to multiply things. He could turn one chocolate cake into one hundred, as he'd done on my seventeenth birthday, before he'd learned I hated chocolate. I'd wanted a vanilla cake, but Declan's power came at a price. Whatever he multiplied, he had to choose something else to divide. That year, he'd chosen vanilla.

"What would you divide?" I played with the sponge, floating it over the surface of the water.

"I was thinking quartz. I'll need to research the implications. But ..." Declan trailed off as he bent under his desk to grab a book from a stack I hadn't noticed previously. Bending over gave me quite the view for a moment. I think he might have realized it, for he popped up quickly and bumped his head on the edge of the desk.

I grinned leaned against the tub, "You know, back when we had lessons together, I always thought you were cursing me during arithmetic."

"If I'd known what a cunt you'd turn out to be, I would have," Declan turned to grin at me. But it was a bitter grin.

It soured the endearing effect his embarrassment had on me.

I snapped back, "Well, you were supposed to be the genius. You should have figured I'd leave. Guess my mother's impression of your intelligence was wrong." I wink at him as I raise a leg to wash my foot.

"Yes. I should have refused appointment to your husband group."

"Appointment? You mean honor."

"I mean appointment. I wasn't given much choice."

"Makes two of us."

"Is that why you left?"

"I left so I could find a wizard to get rid of my ... cock," the geas almost tied my tongue and that was the best I could get out. I punched the side of the tub.

"Is that so? Because Quinn put money on that one as well."

I threw the sponge at Declan. Unfortunately, the bastard ducked. The sponge splatted against the window and Declan grabbed it and tossed it back at my head before it could do much damage to his precious papers.

He shook his head at me, looking like a disappointed school teacher. "You're an idiot. You expect me to believe that you actually returned to help your sister, when you can't even take that basic question seriously?"

"You expect me to take men seriously when they've wagered gold on my body parts?"

"You're impossible." Declan turned back to his desk.

And for some reason I panicked. It felt symbolic, his turning his back. Like a door was closing, an opportunity flitting away. I felt a sudden, urgent need to win his trust and get his help. If anyone could figure out the geas, and my reasons for leaving, it would be him.

"Wait."

He turned back and raised his eyebrows. Our eye contact became intense. A staring contest as I willed him to take me seriously. "I'm complex. I'm a riddle you need to solve."

"What do you mean?"

"I can't say."

He rolled his eyes. "If you're going to be that way—"

"No." I stood, rivulets of water flowing down my body, dripping from my fingertips.

Declan seemed to leave his seat without thought, also standing. His gaze traveled over my body.

"I mean, I *can't* say."

His blue eyes narrowed in thought and focused back on my face. "Is this a word play?"

"No." But his sentence sparked excitement. "I mean, there are words I cannot say. Important words."

We shared a long moment, weighing one another. I wasn't sure if he believed me. I tried to wait until he nodded or gave some acknowledgment. Some sign of trust. But a chill crept over my body and shivers set in, and still, he said nothing.

"They forgot a robe and towels," I noted, as my teeth chattered.

"I'll ring for them," Declan took a few steps toward the bell pull before my knee slammed into the edge of the tub, yanked by the curse. He was too far away.

"Stop!" I climbed out of the tub and limped over to him, a stream forming on the floor beneath me and running down the cracks in the floor. I rubbed my knee and moaned.

Our eyes met and Declan's eyes almost looked playful. Like he was holding back a laugh.

"You think this curse is funny?"

"It's a spell."

"It's a curse. My mother wants us to hate one another."

Declan's brow arched.

"More. She wants us to hate each other more. She never wants us to have a moment's peace."

The amusement faded from Declan's face. "I think we've already got the hatred figured out."

"Sard you. Just give me your shirt for a towel."

"What?" he balked.

I took a step closer and put my hand on his arm. "Give me your shirt."

Heat flashed in his eyes for a moment. And then it was gone.

"No," his words made me second guess what I'd seen.

But my instincts screamed that I was right. My mind flashed back to the look Declan had when Ryan gave him an order in the hall. There'd been tension there. Sexual tension? I decided to test it. "Declan McCarthy, you give me that shirt right now, or so help me—"

"You'll what?" his whisper was breathy. Yeah. Some part of him liked it when I bossed him around.

I narrowed my eyes. "Are you willing to find out?"

"Yes."

"Stand still and face that wall," I growled.

To my surprise, he did.

I stalked around him as if I were going to his bed to grab a sheet. But as soon as I was behind his back I grabbed my long hair and pulled it forward over my shoulder. I leaned toward him, putting my hair as close to his back as I could without touching. Then I twisted. A waterfall erupted from my hair and drenched Declan's backside.

"Ah!" he jumped.

I didn't give him a chance to retaliate. Bastard wouldn't give a lady his clothes? Well, then his clothes would get ruined.

I tackled Declan to the ground and sat on his back. Then I rubbed my sopping body over him like a cat. I pressed my chest to his back and ran it up and down. I ran my legs over his pants. When he reached his arms back to grab me, I balked.

"Don't you dare touch. Put your hands here." I tossed his hands straight out on either side of him and scooted up to straddle his torso. I leaned into his back and pressed his palms to the floor. "Stay."

Declan complied, out of shock or arousal, or maybe both. I got my front side dry, but my back was still drenched from my hair.

I decided to press the point.

"Turn over, Declan." I sat back on my knees so he could.

When he did, his face was flush. His eyes were dilated. His breathing was rapid and shallow. "Now, you can give me your shirt, or you can—"

"Sard you," he breathed.

"I didn't offer that as an option."

He didn't laugh. Neither did I. I stared down at his ice blue eyes. I noticed the tiny frown line between his brows that he got from reading his ledgers and muttering at them day after day. My fingers went to smooth it down of their own accord before I caught myself.

I'm teaching him a lesson, I had to remind myself. Feeling the heat of his body underneath me made it hard to remember that.

Declan's eyes roamed my body and I decided to see just how far I could push him.

I grabbed Declan's right hand. I turned his palm so it faced away from me, so he couldn't cop a feel. Then I dragged his arm down my back slowly. I rubbed his forearm everywhere. I grabbed his left arm and did the same for my legs, dragging his arm up my calves and over my thighs, along the ridge of my ass.

And as parts of my body grew drier, other parts grew wetter, particularly when I felt his bulge pressing against the crack of my ass. I hadn't had a man's hands on me, caressing me, in so long. Declan didn't speak, but he was panting by the time I was done.

I leaned forward as if I was going to kiss him. But I simply patted his cheek with a wicked grin. I stood, looming over him, letting him see my most intimate part. "Fine. Forget the shirt. I'll air dry the rest. But I warned you." I stepped back.

"You did," he propped himself up on his elbow. He didn't look like he minded being freezing and wet at all. In fact, he gave ample attention to my chest, indicating he didn't mind me being freezing and wet either.

"You are supposed to be the gentleman of this group."

"Gentlemen are only polite to ladies," he sat up and shrugged, pulling off his soaked shirt and wringing it out.

"We've established I don't have a cock," I argued as I tried very hard not to stare at the dark blond happy trail leading south. Declan most definitely had a cock. One that was at full mast.

"But we haven't established that you're a lady."

"Then what the hell am I?"

"A puzzle. A riddle I need to solve."

My eyes met his. A buzz filled my stomach. Like bees had invaded. Or was it butterflies?

"Put the shirt on and I'll ring for some new clothes." He tossed his shirt to me.

As I pulled it over my head, I asked, "So, um, does this mean that you believe me? About coming here to help Avia?"

Declan pulled the rope and leaned against the wall, watching as I struggled to straighten out his soaked shirt and cover up important bits.

"No. I don't believe you at all."

I spun toward him, aghast. "But—"

"I think you have an ulterior motive. And I'm gonna find out what that is."

CHAPTER SIX

Declan resumed work and didn't speak to me or look my way as maids dressed me and did my hair until I was mother's perfect doll again. My hair was curled in ringlets. My eyes were lined in kohl. Emeralds glittered at my neck and a plunging neckline showed off my modest cleavage to its best advantage. My billowing, hunter green skirt was lined with lace made by the pixies in Cheryn. I picked at the padded, long sleeves of my dress. Even more than the circlet in my skin, the sleeves felt like cuffs. They reminded me of every day I'd spent with my mother, in training to take up my place as monarch.

I rubbed my arms and stared out Declan's window. After his declaration, we'd come to an unspoken agreement: ignore one another.

He didn't trust me? Fine. Forget understanding the geas. Forget my curse. That wasn't important anyway. I didn't need him to know me to accomplish my goals. But I had no idea how I was going to achieve any of them. I wish my mother had cursed me to be within five feet of my sister at all times instead. Then I could protect her.

When Ryan arrived to "hand off the prisoner," I'd almost been relieved.

Until he had led me to the outdoor practice arena, where his soldiers used wooden swords to hack at one another.

"You haven't finished this for the day?" I sighed. It was late.

Ryan glared down at me. "Those of us who actually do our jobs, instead of run from them, have a lot of work each day."

I bit my lip. So this was it. I was to be dragged from job to job with each 'husband' until I died a slow death from hatred and boredom.

"May I—"

"No."

"You didn't even hear what I—"

"Didn't need to. Your job is to provide water."

"Water carrier? Surely you have a servant—"

"Surely you can do this simple task?" Ryan cut me off and hauled me, far too easily, over to a giant barrel of water. Nearby stood pewter tankards. Ryan dropped me into the dirt and yelled toward two of his fighters. They came closer and he started correcting their form.

"Elbow up and out," he pulled a squire's arm until he was satisfied with the angle. With a nod, his two fighters continued their practice bout. He leaned against the wooden fence separating the fighters from the crowd and I forced myself to keep my eyes on the soldiers, and not the tight fit of leather pants on Ryan's ass.

"Think you could be a little gentler? He only looked fourteen," I scolded.

"Sixteen. And he's about to be sent on patrols. He needs it."

"Patrols where?"

"Don't pretend you care."

I gritted my teeth. I didn't want to fight with him in front of his men, but I was getting sick of being accused of not caring simply because I'd left the throne. They had no idea how much I cared. I cared more than anyone for Evaness. I cared enough to give it up. Jackanapes.

"Hopefully not too close to Rasle. I heard they're in for a hard winter. Lotta folk try to sneak through those woods. They'll raid our farms and villages for food like they did two winters past," I went for conversational as I filled up a tankard.

Ryan glanced down at me. "And how'd you hear about that?"

I shrugged and turned back to his men. "One of the girls at the brothel I worked at—"

Suddenly, my feet hovered two feet off the ground. Ryan's furious face was level with mine. His glance was acid. My insides shriveled and puddled on the floor.

Shite. I bet he made grown men keel over with that look. The other armies wouldn't stand a chance.

He marched me to the weapons room, disregarding the tankard I still clutched in my hand.

He slammed the door closed behind us and dropped me to the ground. Water sloshed all over my dress.

"The last man that got his drink all over me got what was coming to him," I warned as I scowled down at the sopping fabric. Really? I'd just gotten dry.

Ryan's hand came around my neck. I felt his fingers flex. He shook me slightly, but he didn't clamp down. It was clear that he was using every bit of restraint he had not to snap my neck. His brown eyes bored holes into me. "What the sarding hell do you mean, you worked at a brothel?"

I held up my hands, placating, though my heart was racing. He could snap me in half. In quarters. He could probably crack me so many times that my bones would be splinters. I worked hard to keep a wobble out of my voice. "In the counting house. In the back. I touched the coins. Not the customers, oh delirious one."

Ryan closed his eyes and huffed a breath. His fingers flexed on my throat and I felt my windpipe constrict before he let up.

I gasped for breath as he slowly pulled his hands away from my neck.

As soon as his hands were down, I walloped him with the tankard. Fight or flight took over. And the past four years, I'd trained for fight.

"What the—"

I didn't give him a chance to recover. I smashed the tankard into his nose just as the two soldiers he'd been training walked through the door.

Ryan's hand closed around my arm, neutralizing my weapon of choice. So, I reverted to the age-old standard kick to the nards.

"Gah!" he roared, pulling me into a bear hug so tight I could hardly breathe. He used his massive thigh muscles to trap my legs and lifted me from the floor, so I had no leverage. I could feel every inch of his bulging pecs against my back. His arms felt as large and hard as tree branches. If he just lowered my body a few inches, my ass would be aligned with his—

"What's wrong with you?" he growled in my ear.

I didn't answer, since my blood was pounding too hard in my ears to hear anything clearly. My neck still spiked with pain. My windpipe still wheezed with each breath.

His hands shifted, and my power flared. I tried to push it down, but my adrenaline had spiked. It was too high. I couldn't control it. I could not stop the surge of power that ripped through me, ready to protect me. Like a cannon, or dragon fire, the glowing green pulse of energy blasted from my body.

"Sard!" I screamed, as the pulse touched each of the men in the room. Their expressions changed, dulled; vacant smiles grew on their faces like dandelions. False, weedy happiness invaded their systems. A sense of calming peace. My power. My curse. Because forcing peace on others had a price.

Pain ran up my arms like fire and I felt the skin burst apart on my forearms. Deep, trench-like wounds opened under my sleeves and blood soaked them.

"Ahhh!" I howled, cradling my wounded arms.

Ryan dropped me and tilted his head, a dopey, puzzled expression coloring his features. His thick lips hung open.

Behind him, the sixteen-year-old soldier stared at the weapons like they were mounds of gold. He looked stunned, or amazed, or … "Feels like a sex hangover," he elbowed his training partner. "You know. That moment right after when you still can't quite see straight?"

Ryan snapped out of his daze a bit at that, and moved in front of me. It almost felt protective. But I wasn't sure. My sleeves were soaked. The extra padding my mother had sewn into my gowns wasn't equipped for this kind of blast. I wasn't equipped. I felt light-headed. And not in the good way the men did. Not from peace magic. From blood loss.

I stumbled. I would have fallen face-first onto an axe if a pair of arms that were not thick as tree trunks hadn't scooped me up and turned me around. I stared up into Quinn's grey eyes as he clutched me to him.

"My sister. I need my sister. Take me to Avia."

I slumped forward and let the spy master carry me away. I could only hope he'd bring me to my family and not showcase my weakness to the world. I could only hope he hated me slightly less than my other husbands.

CHAPTER SEVEN

I faded in and out of consciousness as Quinn carried me through the palace. He cradled me against his chest. And though he was a relative stranger, and I was at my most vulnerable, I felt safe in his arms. This warm feeling and a dull memory of being rocked filled my mind. And then a strange song. One I didn't remember ever hearing. It was beautiful and lilting. Had one of my wet nurses sung it to me? I couldn't remember as I faded into oblivion.

When I came back to reality, Connor walked next to Quinn.

"She fainted? She always faints," Connor shook his head, and the brown curls I loved so much swayed against his forehead.

I didn't always faint. He just didn't happen to know about the blood-letting side effect of the peace power, a power my mother liked to publicly claim could 'tame dragons.' No one knew. Stupid geas.

I didn't hear Quinn's response, but I felt him hold up my arm.

"She's bleeding!" Connor let out a string of curses.

I shook my head. I had to swallow several times before I could speak. "Just a little. I need Avia." Shite. Even that much speech left me gasping, short of breath.

"Where the sard is Ryan? Why didn't he heal her?" Connor roared.

Declan's voice drifted from somewhere. "You know how he gets. He has a patrol tomorrow. He can't go on a rage bender. Let me see."

I pulled my arms in as tight as I could and turned into Quinn more, hiding from their prying eyes. If my mother knew they'd seen, I'd be done for. "I'm fine. Stupid mistake. I need Avia. Only Avia."

Quinn didn't respond, just continued down the hall. I heard a smash somewhere behind me. But my eyelids flickered closed before I could figure out if it was Declan or Connor smashing things. Maybe it was Ryan—

The next time my eyes opened, I was nearly naked. I only wore a shift. But I was in a bed and covered by sheets. My arms were bandaged, and it felt like the bleeding had stopped, but they still throbbed dully. And I was cold. I yanked at a down comforter that had been near my waist, pulling it up to my chin.

As my eyes adjusted to firelight and candles, my sister leaned into view. She had apparently perched in a chair at my bedside. Which was her bedside, as I took in the details of the room. She'd always been a fan of rose quartz and tapestries full of handsome minstrels. Avia had a book and a cup of tea on a side table next to her chair. Her hair had been plaited into braids and she was in her night robe. So I supposed I'd been out for quite a while.

"You're the absolute worst! Worst person in the sarding world. You leave me with your shite husbands, trying to pawn those asshole old men off on me. Leave me with *mother* and that stupid crown. And then you come back! And you don't even have the decency to let me wallow in my hatred! You get sarding hurt! So that I *have* to care!"

I bit back a smile. "I'm sorry, Squawk."

She stood and slapped my stomach, the effect muffled by the comforter. "You should be. Worthless shite sister. And don't call me that."

"You'll always be Squawk to me."

"I'm sixteen—"

"Still squawking like a gull, too."

"I do not squawk," Avia squawked as she sat back in her chair with a humph.

I decided not to push her further. She had helped me, after all.

My eyes flickered around the room as I fingered my bandages. It looked empty. Other than the flickering candles scattered about the space, there were no signs of life. I didn't see them. Not one stupid husband.

"How'd you do it?"

"Do what?" Avia raised her brows, but her look was too self-satisfied for me to believe she didn't know what I was talking about.

"How'd you get rid of them? The shite husbands. Did Her Majesty lift the curse?" I sat up in bed, pulling the covers around me.

"Of course not," Avia studied her nails, preening, dragging out the moment.

"What then, oh wise and most gorgeous sister?"

"The pet name is dead," Avia pointed a finger seriously at me.

"Absolutely," I half-lied. We'd see how genius her solution was before I killed the name off entirely.

"I had Quinn wait in here and made Connor go to the next room, behind the wall. Then I sent Quinn away. I told him they'd need to take shifts a room over while you recovered."

"I could kiss you right now. I didn't know what I was going to do … how'd you explain what happened?" As one of the few people in the world who knew the price of my magic, she'd been put under the geas of secrecy too. My mother had even placed the geas on my fathers. No one could reveal my vulnerabilities.

Avia shrugged. "I didn't have to say anything. Ryan made assumptions. Thought you'd scraped against one of the weapons. Or … something about a dented tankard?"

"I smashed him with one, so I guess—"

"Long as they don't know the truth …"

I leaned back against the headboard. "I wish they did. For their own sakes. I know why—"

"After what happened to your dad, mother's protective," Avia kicked her feet onto the covers, smacking my thigh in the process.

I sighed.

Avia and I spent a long moment, both staring at the flames in her fireplace, both of us trying not to remember what had happened to my biological father.

"Why'd you leave?" she finally asked.

"To find a cure."

She turned, and her eyes met mine. Hers were wet with tears, her lashes clumped together. She must not have been repressing the memories quite as well as I had. "I miss our dad, Lewart."

"Me too."

"He always snuck up on me in the hallway. Did you know that? He'd always jump out and scare me. To keep me on my toes."

I laughed a little. "No, I must have been with the tutors when he did that."

"He was wonderful."

"He was."

"I wish he'd found a cure. A way to stop this."

"Me too." I swallowed the lump in my throat at that selfish thought. He'd tried. Once he'd known I had the same powers he did, he'd tried.

"Did you find a cure? Is that why you're back?"

Avia looked so young and vulnerable in that moment, with her tears and her braids and her hope-filled expression. I held out my arms and she scurried into bed beside me. She left the sheet between us but tugged the comforter over herself and snuggled into my arms. I was brought back to childhood. To the many nights she'd fallen asleep in my bed claiming she had a story to tell me, or that she'd seen a shadow monster in her room. She was only sixteen, still just a child. I hugged her tighter and stroked her hair.

"I wish I'd found a cure, sweet girl. I wish. The wizard I hunted is apparently as mythical as the dragons are now." I planted a soft kiss on her forehead.

The sheets became damp. Avia had started to cry again.

"Does that mean … I'm still going to have to become queen?" she whispered.

Her broken tone cracked my heart. I didn't want to answer. But I'd never lied to my sister. Not about anything serious. I couldn't lie. But I could answer in a way that was more comforting. Less intimidating. "I've gotten better at controlling my power."

"But today—"

"Was a mistake. I'll do better." I pulled her even closer. "I'll do better. And I'll help you. Train you and protect you. So that you'll be ready."

At that last, she let out a sob. "I don't want to be ready." She clutched at me.

"Sweet girl, I hope you never need to be." But she would. Because my father's fate was to be my fate. And today only proved that four years of control could be wiped away in a single instant.

I let her cry until she had no more tears. And I held back my own. Because this was about her. I held her and let my hopes of a quick solution and quick escape go. Instead I focused on how I'd felt when I was her age. A teenager, unsure of everything, too scared to test my mother, intimidated by the world and its expectations of me. At least I'd had Connor then. A companion to lighten the journey. I'd left this poor sweet girl alone with the burden of a kingdom on her shoulders. And four headstrong men who'd clearly not taken the time to reassure her.

They'd be hearing about that tomorrow.

My little Squawk drifted off to sleep and I started to join her. But as I stared at the flames in her fireplace, strange thoughts entered my head. I imagined it was Quinn next to me, not my sister. I imagined that I was surrounded by his arms and that his soft breath fluttered like a feather against the skin of my neck. I imagined safety and warmth and companionship. I imagined him whispering, "It's all right, Dove. I'll protect you."

I closed my eyes. Clearly, the blood loss was making me delusional. I curled up and pushed the hallucinations and my worries away as sleep overtook me.

CHAPTER EIGHT

*T*he sun and the maids rudely awakened me.
After my injury, I'd have loved a lazy day under
the covers. But queens do not rest, my mother always
said.

So, just after dawn I was up and prodded and poked until
I was fitted into a red brocade gown with a high neck and
told that a morning tea for the nobility had been planned
to welcome me home.

Of course, Her Majesty summoned Connor and I to her
rooms for a briefing before that. We had to have our story
straight, after all.

Connor appeared in Avia's doorway just as my hair was
fitted into a silver tiara. His dark brown curls were
slightly messy, and I had to hold back the urge to fix them.
He wore a light blue shirt that matched his eyes and offset
his tan, and breeches that were form-fitting under his
leather boots. In other words, he was the perfect picture.

Everything I'd remembered and loved but grown up. With sexy stubble.

I gulped when I saw him. Every bone in my body ached to hug him.

But his eyes avoided mine and his lips thinned as he offered me his arm. He was cold and stiff as he escorted me to my mother's chambers, though he smiled and nodded to everyone near us. He looked like my best friend but didn't feel like him.

Maybe I'd deluded myself thinking the letters would be enough. They clearly hadn't been. Though our arms touched, it felt like there was a wall between us.

I opened my mouth to ask what was wrong nearly a dozen times, but there was always a courtier or a servant or someone within earshot. I'd seen the slightest word turn into a whirlwind of gossip within the palace. And I didn't want that. Not for him.

Instead, I also focused on those around us, giving little waves to the nobles and nods to the servants we passed on our way to the north wing. It felt wooden, and fake, when I wanted to flip off half the people I saw for how they treated their tenants.

Lady Aster shot her race horses rather than let them retire to the meadows or be used in the fields. She got a tight-lipped grin.

Countess Orunta and her husband group were known to raise taxes on mead so that they could build themselves luxury ships. She got a weak wrist wave.

A dozen times, I spotted open doors. I really wanted to yank Connor into a room and let him yell at me until we were alright again. But I'd have to curb the barroom brawling techniques I'd gathered these past four years. I was certain the incident with Ryan had already caused loads of gossip. I couldn't let it get worse.

When we reached my mother's rooms, Connor held open the door.

Inside, my mother and one of my fathers, Peter, sat together on the bed. He fed her breakfast. It was a sight that was endearing, but also a testament to how weak she truly was.

I lifted my chin. She'd never want acknowledgment of her weakness.

I waited as Peter lifted a cup of tea to her lips and helped her drink.

Declan's mentor, Peter, was the most patient of my fathers. He'd always been the one to teach me things as a child, from math to archery. He'd never spoken a harsh word to me. Always carried a sweet in his pocket. He was a scholar and a softie.

After he dabbed at my mother's lips with a napkin, she shooed him away, gathering her bright green dressing coat closer to her rail-thin body.

I broke form and ran to Peter and gave him a quick hug. He'd grown larger around the middle since I'd seen him. But his eyes were just as kind as I remembered. He hugged me back and placed a quick kiss on my forehead. "You're in trouble, you know, Blossie."

I nodded against his chest. "I know."

"Your mother needs you. Evaness needs you. No more running."

I nodded; I didn't tell him I'd come to the same conclusion last night.

Peter left the room, taking my mother's maidservant with him. Apparently, my mother and sister had become more accustomed to demanding privacy in my absence. I had been the only one in my family to kick out every servant in my chambers when I'd been younger.

I smiled at mother. "Queen Gela, what will you do if you need to blow your nose and no servant is here to help you?"

She rolled her eyes, another first. Her out-of-character choices nearly made up for Connor's coldness. He hadn't moved from his spot since we'd arrived.

"Was that an eye roll? Did you actually express annoyance?" I clapped. "Mother, I'd have poisoned you five times a day when I was younger if I'd known it would loosen you up."

She gave me a deadpan stare. "Tactless."

"It's my best quality."

She shook her head, "Let's focus, shall we? Bloss, when you left, you started in the woods and back-country mountains of Cheryn. You chased two dragons that were sighted by various locals, a purple stinger and a red heathen. But the cave complex over in Cheryn is quite intense. You spent eight months exploring the caves but lost the dragons."

"What about Cheryn's diplomats?"

My mother smiled. "Just after you left, I had Connor send word that you'd be traveling the area, seeking to contain the dragons, which some of our northern sheepherders spotted. So, you were granted royal passage. You were even invited to the Sultan's annual feast but, unfortunately, you were in the caves at that time, and weren't able to attend."

"How generous of him to extend the invitation," I said wryly. "Considering the fact that before I left, he accused us of flooding the international market with cattle in order to drive down his prices."

My mother raised a brow. I couldn't tell if she was pleased that I'd remembered the state of affairs before I left, or annoyed I'd referenced leaving so casually. "Sultan Raj has since become quite an ally. One of his sons has been sent here, in fact. So, please behave accordingly."

"When did he arrive?" I was startled. I was certain that I didn't have the right diplomatic skills to handle the all the going's on at the palace. I was dreading this tea.

The favors and rumors at court changed by the hour. They were always impossible to keep up with. I was certain to offend at least three people that morning. But, in terms of major events and political maneuvers, I tried to keep my ears open. I should have heard about the sultan's son coming to visit.

"He is traveling now. He arrives in three weeks, and shortly after his arrival, we will host a welcome ball."

I held in my groan.

That means corsets. I hate corsets, I complained internally.

Mother continued, "The last two years, you spent in the northern wastelands of Macedon. You've been out of touch with most of civilization, only interacting with the occasional ice-fishing caravans that travel through there. That explains your outrageous behavior yesterday." Mother gave a cutting smile. "You've been quite accustomed to violence and fending off the attacks of those heathens and we expect it will take you awhile to readjust to polite society. I do believe the palace healer called it hysterical stress syndrome."

I seethed. But I bit my tongue. The fact that I wanted to throw her tea in her face only proved her point. "I shall do my best to adjust as quickly as possible."

"You will also need some remedial lessons regarding current affairs as well as to be briefed on each of the nobles residing in or visiting the palace. I'll let your husbands schedule those."

"I want Avia to join me."

Her lips thinned. "She is not, and has never been, the crown princess."

"She is and will be our queen," I countered. "She'll need to know a lot for whatever husbands she takes on, because you clearly have not reassigned—"

"Why would I?" Mother countered.

"Because I can't—"

"You can and will. This is your birthright and duty." Her speech was ruined by the fact that a short little hair popped out of her braid and fell into her face.

I didn't comment on it. Or her argument. We'd had the same argument in circles since she the moment she'd begun selecting the men for my husband group. It was an argument I couldn't win. No matter the fact that I was right.

I decided to concede the point to a sick woman. Or at least agree with what she factually had said. "You're right. It is my birthright."

Her eyes narrowed, expecting the follow up argument.

I bit my tongue in order to swallow said argument.

When she was satisfied, Mother continued quietly, "If need be, your knights can always tell the world you've spotted another dragon."

I froze. My heart stopped in shock. That was not something she'd said during any of our arguments. Ever.

She stared straight at me, steady and strong and … I saw a glimmer of affection in her eyes. Perhaps a hint of tears.

It was the only time I'd ever heard her acknowledge my death was a real possibility. Perhaps facing death herself had changed her.

My heart swelled with gratitude and pain at the same time. It felt like I was flying and falling in the same moment. Or as if I were lying in bed, during that dizzy second between waking and sleeping. "You mean it?" I asked, voice trembling, as I took a step toward her.

She pulled a piece of parchment from her stack. "I have a report of yet another sighting right here."

I walked the final steps to her bed and took the sheet with a shaking hand. It bore Quinn's seal and the current date.

My mother's lip quirked up in a grin. "When you control the flow of information darling, you get to determine what information should flow. And after four years of accepting such tales, and seeing you again, if anything ever—"

"Thank you!" I hugged her tightly, pulling her into me and crushing her bones against mine. "Thank you," I whispered in her ear. "Thank you. That's all I ever wanted."

She nods. "I know. I know now. Because it's all I want. But it's too late for me and mine."

A tear dripped down my cheek.

"Oh, no, none of that," Mother wiped the tear away and gave me a tight smile. "Queens do not cry."

I swallowed down the rest of the tears, giving her a stiff nod.

"Your Majesty, you can't mean this! You're going to let her run again?" Connor stomped to the edge of mother's bed and glared down at her. "You can't allow it! She'd just said she wouldn't leave and now you're going to let her? She can just walk away again?"

I turned to mother and whispered, "I need to tell him."

"No," she cut me off immediately.

"I need to explain—" I said it louder, hoping that if I addressed the queen, but said it within Connor's hearing, that the geas might be foiled. No such luck. My words were cut off.

"We don't need your lies, Bloss. But the people need a steady hand. Your Majesty, don't—" Connor argued.

Mother clapped her hands, summoning her lady-in-waiting and cutting off any further argument.

I clenched my fists and leaned close to her ear, pretending to straighten her pillow. "You have to let me tell—"

She held a piece of parchment in front of her face, as though she was reading. "No. It's not safe."

I leaned toward her, even as her maid and Connor both hovered close. "Why not?" I whispered.

"Because they don't love you."

I pulled back.

There was nothing I could say to argue with that.

CHAPTER NINE

When we left Mother's chambers, Connor was fuming. Livid. The sunshine boy had turned into a solar flare.

"I'm not planning to leave," I told Connor, hoping that reassurance would help resolve the issue.

"I'm not planning to care if you do," he shot back.

"This is only in case of ... dire circumstances," I whispered as a chambermaid passed us.

"Like the dire circumstances last time?" Connor snarled. "What were those? Was there an assassination attempt on you? Just like your little sister now? Is that your go-to conspiracy?"

"No."

"War? A plague? No. Wait. You actually did hear reports of dragons?" he whispered savagely.

"I fell in love with you. Those were the circumstances." I snapped.

His jaw dropped.

But he didn't look happy. Or relieved. Or anything positive. He only looked shocked.

Suddenly, Connor snatched up my hand and tucked it forcefully into the crook of his elbow. He leaned close and fingered my curls.

His face radiated fury, but his posture looked like the doting husband from behind, as three tittering noble girls trotted past us on their way to the tutor. Giggles drifted down the hall behind them.

Connor didn't acknowledge my words as he began leading us at breakneck speed across the palace. As the chief diplomatic arm of the crown, Connor generally knew where everyone was. Which also meant he knew where everyone wasn't. We wove through the halls seeing only the minimum of people, until we rounded a corner and nearly tumbled into Lady Agatha and her portly son, Willard.

"Good morning!" Lady Agatha was decked out in white pearls and a white dress that matched her white poof of hair. The only spots of color were the rouge in her cheeks and lips. Next to her pristine outfit, poor Willard looked a mess. His manservant missed a spot shaving, so he had a little patch on one cheek. His shirt was partially untucked.

"Morning Lady Agatha, you look just gorgeous," Connor turned on the charm.

Lady Agatha's holdings were vast. She and her husbands held ranch lands to the northwest and raised cattle, which fed many of our soldiers or were traded with the country of Cheryn.

"It's a beautiful day, isn't it?" I showed my teeth at the mother and son, but I wasn't quite certain I'd smiled. I think my fake smiling skills had grown rusty during my four-year stint outside the palace. I took a deep breath and tried harder to mask my hurting heart.

I grabbed Connor's hand and interwove our fingers, partially because I needed his social grace to cover me in this moment and partially because I missed him that much. His hand stiffened in mine, but his face remained a mask of propriety.

"Not many beautiful days left! My old bones can feel it. The winter will be here soon enough." Lady Agatha eyed our hands, as expected. "And you two look just as thick as thieves once more. Easy to pick up where you left off?"

"Four years later, and I'm still stunned each time she walks into the room," Connor's look was easy, but I recognized the tightness at the edges of his mouth. It wasn't a compliment, but a cut. Connor was always able to find a way to say he was fine when he wasn't. He was raised by a family who made their fortune from sales. You had to read between the lines with him. Because he would always find words to say what he truly meant. Stunned.

Was he shocked I came back? Or stunned like a man who's been smacked in the head? Dazed and hurt? He expected me to leave again, that much was clear in mother's chambers. So, I supposed dazed and hurt each time he saw me would be accurate.

I stretched my 'court-smile' further and fought the tears that came to my eyes. I'd destroyed the most precious thing in the world to me. His affection.

Connor sniffs lady's underthings.

I blinked and stared at Willard. Did he just say that? But the mousy fellow was scuffing his shoe on a crack in the floor. Lady Agatha smacked him. "You know my Willard has always spoken fondly of you, don't you, Princess Bloss?"

I brought myself back to the conversation, struggling for an appropriate response. I came up with, "As I have of him."

Lady Agatha grinned, so my answer must have been decent enough. But Connor's eyes narrowed slightly.

I ignored both of of them as we continued to the large banquet hall where tea had been set out at a table long enough to seat forty.

Lady Agatha prattled something to Connor and I used the moment to think on what I'd just heard. Or thought I'd heard.

I touched my free forearm, feeling the bump of the bandage beneath. Maybe my brain was still rattled from losing so much blood yesterday. That made more sense than Weeping Willard making a snarky comment about Connor. Willard had been the kid clinging to the tutor's legs as the rest of us had waged the wars of childhood with flying ink pots and spitballs.

Lady Agatha smacked Willard's arm and he jumped. "Didn't you just say yesterday how happy you were that Bloss is back?"

"Yes. Yes. Mmhmm," Willard rubbed his elbow and scooted slightly away from his mother.

"I know the pair of you are excited by the reunion, but can I steal your bride for a moment, Connor? Girl talk, you know," Lady Agatha linked arms with me.

Connor let go of my hand. He clapped Willard on the shoulder as if they were old friends, draped an arm over the awkward man, and led the way to a table nearby, where breakfast was laid out and steaming. It was close enough that it wouldn't activate the distance curse and drag me across the room, but far enough that Connor escaped Lady Agatha's attention.

In other words, Connor left me with the snottiest but wealthiest noble in the palace on my arm. Alone. A woman I'd always avoided like the plague.

Sarding Lady Agatha! Really, Connor? I grumbled internally.

Immediately, a mental image of Lady Agatha naked and kneeling on the floor came to mind. Her paunchy husbands surrounded her and she had them each lift a bare foot. She grabbed the closest foot and gave a long sniff. Her body shuddered … as if stinky feet were orgasmic. She sniffed another.

What in the shite hell?

"—were thinking that you might need additional help, what with the current issues with Sedara."

I shook myself. Something was happening to me. I was having delusions. Hearing voices. Seeing things. Did it relate to my power? Had my father seen these things?

"—with Willard. What do you think dear?"

Lady Agatha had droned on this entire time. I had no clue what had been said.

"Of course," I responded, smiling widely. Shite. I hoped she hadn't asked for me to declare war.

"I'll have the steward arrange for a meeting time for the two of you tomorrow."

A meeting? I could handle a meeting. I caught myself before I sighed in relief.

Lady Agatha patted my hand and walked away, but as she did, another mental image flooded my mind. She was still naked, still on her knees. This time one of her husbands held a leash. *"Bark for me!"* he snapped. *"Aarf!" "Aarf!"* she yipped.

My faced turned eight different shades of red as I tried not to burst into laughter. If this was delirium, if this was how my death came, I'd gladly take it.

I inhaled and calmed down. Then I stepped into the fray. I smiled and repeated my mother's false story ad nauseam, complimented the women's dresses and the men's hair and bit back insults regarding the paltry provisions half of them made for the farmers under their care. Those issues would come up soon enough.

Connor stood next to me, touched my shoulder when he passed, smiled at me when someone asked about my return. He was a wonderful actor. But there were no secret moments. He didn't link our pinkie fingers or whisper sweet things in my ear to make me blush. He always used to let me know what I meant to him in little moments.

I was back. I was staying. I was staying for Avia at first. But Mother had given me a way to protect Connor. Protect my husbands.

I looked at Connor, laughing over some joke about corn and 'seedy' men that had been said a thousand times before. But his laugh was so pure. So beautiful. He lit the world around him.

I'd thought of Connor every day for four years. I'd written him. On nights when I'd wanted to quit my quest and give it up and go home, I'd pressed on. Because of him. When a Queen dies, her knights go with her.

I could never condemn Connor to that fate.

For years, I'd worried and planned and searched for ways to keep him alive.

My mother had given me an out. A way to cover for my husbands if something happened to me.

As I watched Connor, I realized I had to use the same tenacity I used on my quest.

I had to get him to fall back in love with me. Because life without him was not an option.

I decided to start small. I crossed his path more than necessary, just so I'd have an excuse to trail my fingers over his back.

With the curse, I'd have thought we would have had to stand side by side, but with the crush of nobles so eager to speak with the newly returned princess, it was quite an effort to stay near Connor.

When one of the more beautiful courtiers flirted with Connor, I gave in to my natural jealousy and hugged him, planting a kiss on his cheek right in front of her. Mother would scold me later about decorum when she heard. I didn't care.

I gushed about him and his prowess with a bow when I spoke with several noblemen planning a hunt. They invited him to join and I pestered and teased and cajoled him until he gave in with a begrudging laugh.

"Please! I haven't had venison in ages! I've been stuck eating half-frozen fish up north."

"You don't need me to eat venison."

"That's true. Why do I need you again?" I winked saucily. "Oh, I remember."

The other nobles laughed uproariously and one of them said, "Just like newlyweds again."

"Maybe we should lose our wife to a dragon hunt for a few years, huh?" They laughed.

Connor leaned in and whispered in my ear. "Your mother will kill you for that comment."

I shook my head. "She doesn't want me dead." I reached a hand up slowly and touched his curls. Heaven. I'd dreamt of this.

"Maybe I do."

I leaned back and searched his eyes.

He meant it.

I had to fight the chasm that opened in my chest. I deserved this. I deserved his hatred. I'd have felt the same.

"Have you tried to feel if I'm telling the truth?" I whispered.

"Has it occurred to you that your feelings don't matter to me anymore?"

I dropped his hair. I gulped. "You're right. They shouldn't."

I took a deep breath, regretting that I'd let it come to this in a public place. I wanted to collapse on a bed and cry. Or under the bed, as I'd done when I was a child and needed to get away from the prying eyes of the maids.

I grabbed Connor's elbow and turned to the first person on my right. I needed a distraction. The first person I saw was the ambassador from Sedara, Declan's home country. Meeker had been our ambassador for years. He was a short, bushy-haired old man with a thick accent and he was quite upset that a pegasus team had been shot down and captured in Cheryn. The two countries had been poking one another for the last five years, often trying to drag Evaness into their conflict.

"Two injaared animals. And they won't evaan speak to us. Probably they are breeding them as we speak," he swigged his orange juice as if it were spiked. "Those bastaards will do anything to steal our magic."

I didn't ask why Sedara had sent a pegasus team to fly over Cheryn. It was easy enough to guess. It had either been an aerial attack or a spy mission. Either way …

"I'm sure we could speak to the Cheryn ambassadors about the release of your pegasus. Connor is an excellent diplomat," I smiled widely. "He's always had a golden tongue."

A picture of Connor's tongue between my thighs appeared in my head and I stiffened involuntarily. Then his tongue turned to gold. And dragged his jaw down so his face smacked the floor. He tried to swallow, but the golden tongue grew longer.

"Are you alright, darling? She had a hard day yesterday. I'm not certain she's feeling better," Connor turned my face to his and flashed a warning with his eyes. He gave my hand two squeezes.

That was our signal. Shite. I'd said something wrong. And then my brain had gone and fritzed, seeing things. I restored my face to calm. "Just a little light-headed. Probably tired from travel."

"Travaal will do me in. Gives me the shits, too," Meeker nodded at me. "Go get some raast, Princess. I'll talk to your man here about the horses and those blimey baastards."

I was being dismissed from the conversation. As if I was nothing. Not the crown princess. As if this conversation were for men.

I bristled and opened my mouth to argue, but Connor swept me into a hug. "Shut your mouth and let me fix this shite you stirred up. Sedara's already been hard enough to calm down recently because of some stupid stolen chains or something. Damn Bloss. Setting me up as the go-between for countries on the brink of war? Really? I'll get another sitter summoned so you can ruin someone else's morning." He snapped for a page and told the boy to summon Declan.

Was I that bad? I *was* hallucinating …

Quinn appeared at my side mere seconds later. Had he been in the room? I hadn't noticed. Shite. One day at the palace and one little injury and I'd become passive. Next thing, I'd forget to have my food tested for poison. Wonderful. Not to mention whatever I'd just said.

Maybe Connor was right. Maybe I'd ruined his morning.

The picture of Connor letting out a giant trumpet fart filled my mind. I had to shake my head to clear the image.

Quinn offered his elbow as he escorted me out of the room.

We paused at the door, so that everyone could turn and bow. I gave them all a smile and a nod.

"Can you take me to Avia's chambers, please? And can we somehow repeat the set up from last night? So that one of you can work in the next room and I can rest? I really don't feel well."

Quinn nodded briskly. He walked me straight down the hall. Unlike Connor, he didn't stop to acknowledge anyone. He didn't smile. He just strode with purpose, cut through the crowd. He had shite to do and no time to be bothered. When I'd been younger, I'd have been scared witless about offending someone. But after several hours of mindless chatter, it was refreshing. Freeing.

I held onto his arm a little harder than I'd intended as I realized that. But he didn't seem to mind. Quinn closed his big hand around mine and he pulled me into his side.

It was odd. I almost felt happy.

Here.

In the palace.

With a stranger.

When we reached Avia's door, I pushed off Quinn's arm. "Thank you."

He escorted me into her bed and helped me sit. One of her ladies-in-waiting helped pull off my slippers and get me under the covers.

Declan dipped his head in the door shortly after I laid back.

"Same routine as last night?" he asked.

"Yes, please," I called, and Quinn nodded.

Declan ducked out and I heard the door next to ours creak open.

Quinn stared down at me while he waited for Declan to get into place.

"Thank you," I mumbled. "I'm not sure what's wrong."

Quinn simply quirked up one side of his mouth in a half-grin and turned. He marched away with the same silent confidence he always had.

My eyelids fluttered closed as I waited for Avia to get back from lessons. And dark, naughty dreams drifted over me. I was naked, in a bedroom, standing on a plush rug. Ryan was behind me, his large arms wrapped around mine. He palmed my breasts and held me upright as

Quinn kissed his way up my right leg, dragging his pointed tongue along the sensitive nerves on my inner thighs. Connor and Declan watched, hands on their dicks. Quinn's mouth was just about to reach the pinnacle of my thigh when hands started shaking me.

"Are you okay?" Avia's voice cut through my dream. "Why are you asleep so early?"

I cracked my eyes. "You just ruined an amazing dream." I pushed her hands off my shoulders.

"You shouldn't be having amazing dreams mid-morning. What's going on? And why are you in my room?"

"I think I lost too much blood. I've been seeing things all morning. Also, my room is in a tower. We should switch. I can't pull the man-behind-the-wall trick in my room."

"What?"

I rubbed my face and stretched. Then I sat up in bed. "What part are you asking about? Rooms? It's logical."

"No. Why are you seeing things? What things are you seeing?"

"Well, weird things. I spoke to Lady Agatha—"

Avia groaned.

"Yes, I know. But the point is, I started seeing her naked. Barking and stuff. And then I said to someone else that Connor had a golden tongue and suddenly I was picturing … his tongue turning gold. Or random stuff. Like Connor farting, loud."

Avia cocked a brow. "Were all of the things you imagined dirty or embarrassing?"

"Um … yes?" I had no idea where she was leading.

She sat on the bed so hard I bounced. "Lean forward," she commanded.

"Why?"

"Just do it."

I complied. She dug her hands into my hair and started to tug.

"Ow!"

"Be still."

"What are you doing?"

"Just a moment … ah! There!" She yanked a piece of my hair triumphantly.

Unfortunately, that piece was still attached to my head. "Ow!"

Avia didn't apologize. She laughed instead. "Quinn marked you."

"What?"

Avia fingered a small bead knotted into my hair. She held it up in front of my face. "You didn't research the spy master who was after you? The one you were supposed to marry?"

"What research was I supposed to do in a wheat field or tavern disguised as a commoner? It's not exactly as if they're publishing tomes on him," I retorted, snatching my hair out of her hand and examining the bead. It was a small brown bead and blended perfectly. If Avia hadn't found it in my tresses, I'm not sure I'd ever have noticed it. It could have passed for a small knot.

"You know Quinn's mute," she said.

"No. He's arrogant. Too smug to talk to the townspeople. Rubs his air of mystery in their faces. Just expects them to know who he is," I muttered, thinking back to the complaints at the whorehouse in Tera. They'd also complained he'd never spent any coin with them.

"He's mute."

"He's not. I've heard him," My eyes shot to hers.

"You what?"

"I heard him speak when we first arrived. He called me wife."

"Are you sure this wasn't in your hair then?"

"We'd just transformed, so I doubt it." But I gnawed my lip. He'd fingered my hair. Had he placed it then?

"His power is thought transference. He can send his thoughts to you. And pick up on any thoughts you project loud enough," Avia grins. "Its price is his voice. He just tries to put on a mysterious air."

Her words caused my stomach to drop like a stone. A million images from the morning shuffled through my brain. The naughty thoughts. The dirty words. "That fat-kidneyed ass. He's been putting dirty thoughts in my brain all day. I thought I was delirious."

"Really?" Avia's eyes glittered with mirth. "So, you pictured a naked Lady Agatha barking during tea?"

"All morning."

She burst into laughter. "Ah! Of all your husbands, he's my new favorite."

I rolled my eyes. "Take him."

"Oh no. I don't want to deprive you."

"Deprive me of what?"

"The joy of revenge."

A slow, evil smile made its way across my face. There would most definitely be revenge. I'd make Quinn Byrne suffer more than any spy he'd taken to the dungeons below. I went to the bell-pull next to the bed and rang for a maid. When one appeared, I gave her a grin. "My sister and I will need wine and glasses. We have some planning to do."

Avia hopped in place and clapped her hands. "I love when you turn into the evil villain."

I shook my head and looped my arm over her shoulders. "Not the villain. The avenging angel." I winked. "Now, let's plan a man's downfall."

CHAPTER TEN

*T*hree glasses of wine later, Avia held quite a list in her hand.

She wrote the latest option with flourish, twirling the quill as she underlined it three times. "That's it! Damsel in distress!"

I rolled my eyes and kicked my leg across the arm of the chair I sat in. "I still think lice in his undergarments is a good idea. Think of the crotch itch!" I closed my eyes and smiled, imagining Quinn having to wriggle through a state dinner, having to dance in front of others in the ballroom. I'd dance three dances in a row with him, just to keep everyone's eyes on his hands. To draw out every time his knee twitched from the urge to scratch. The sort of twisted bliss that only comes from planning revenge filled me up. I floated around in it, a sea of evil fantasy.

"No." Avia ruined my moment. "That could come back to haunt you. Too much. Damsel wins." Avia stretched out on her plush pink rug in front of the cozy little fire her maid had stoked when the wine had been delivered.

Unlike Avia, I couldn't curl up on the rug next to the fire. I was restricted to the far wall so that I'd stay within five feet of one of my husbands, whichever one had 'wife watch' currently. I'd tired of the bed and so Avia's manservant had dragged over a chair for me before she'd shooed him away again. It wouldn't do to have him overhear the princesses' nefarious plans. Quinn might get word.

I jolted up in my chair. "What if he's reading my thoughts right now?"

Avia scrunched her brow. "I don't think that's how it works."

"You don't think. But you don't know. He could be. Blast!" We'd have to scrap all our plans. I'd need to improvise then. And come up with something new. Something better than yellow dye slipped into his tub water to stain his skin. Better than the teas hedge witches made for older men who still wanted to service their wives. Sard it all. Three hours of work gone.

I sighed. I wished I could pace freely, but I could only take two steps before turning around. This stupid five-foot spell kept me walking in a circle. I had to resort to chair acrobatics in order to move. I hooked my feet solidly around the chair leg before arching my back over the other chair arm and leaning back so that my hair swept the floor. "I'm going to have to improvise."

"You can still improvise with the damsel idea. We didn't decide exactly how it would work."

"That one seems the hardest to pull off."

"Why? Acting helpless? That's not hard."

"Maybe for you," I retorted. "Some of us have actually worked."

Avia's threw her quill at me. If the feather on the end hadn't been so large, it might actually have reached me. Instead, it drifted down softly to land near her feet.

I laughed, "You're quite vicious, aren't you?"

"Shut it," she sat up and planted her hands on her hips. She took on the voice of our old nanny. "If you open that mouth one more time, Bloss Hale, I'm going to ask the healer to sew it shut. And if he won't, I'm sure the hedge witch has a potion for it."

I groan, "Remember how fierce that woman could look, even with that mole?"

"The one on her chin with the hair sticking out?"

"Yes! She should have been laughable. But she was completely terrifying."

Avia laughed. "I always thought she was a hedge witch herself."

"Ooh, maybe she was."

"Or maybe she was a princess in disguise like you."

"Maybe."

"What was it like? When you were gone? What was it like as a commoner?" Avia sounded wistful. I glanced over at her, with her legs tucked neatly underneath her and her hands clasped in her lap, she looked like an eager student. Just like when she used to ask me what it was like to be born with powers. Only one in every hundred humans or so were. My mother hadn't been. Avia wasn't born with power. Some of my fathers had powers.

My mother had insisted each of my husbands be gifted with magic. They had been carefully selected for their powers and their capabilities to protect Evaness.

I pondered Avia's question and my answer carefully. How could I sum up the four years I'd spent on my own? The struggle to hide and survive, to blend in, to quickly adapt to new situations, to always be on the alert ... I didn't think she'd accept exhausting as an answer.

Before I could decide what to tell her, the fire spiked and a log rolled out of the fireplace.

"Ah!" Avia jumped and ran to grab the poker, so that she could roll it back in.

But the log didn't stay still. It wiggled. The log had a tail. And four little legs ending in claws.

I fell off my chair. My hands and knees smacked the floor as I flipped head over heels. I scurried to my feet just as the flaming monster touched the rug Avia had been sitting on.

Whoosh.

The rug burst into flame.

"Sard! It's a fire salamander!" I screamed.

The flaming lizard flicked its tail and then ran, directly at my sister.

Fear turned my stomach. I felt light-headed. Sick. No! Was this the creature? The one I'd heard about in the forest? Had someone sent this thing after Avia? "Run!"

My sister turned on her heel and ran, her blue skirts billowing out behind her, chocolate curls streaming through the air like ribbons as she rushed away, screaming.

I tried to run toward her, but the stupid distance spell yanked me backward. I landed flat on my back, hitting my head. Hard. I clambered to my knees, woozy. Where had Avia gone?

I spotted her at the far end of the room, waving the fire-place poker wildly.

The salamander was scuttling toward her like some evil, enchanted living torch. Its nose touched the edge of a tapestry and flames shot up the wall hanging. Smoke started to coat the ceiling in an ominous black cloud.

"Move! Move!" I screamed. I grabbed the nearest thing I could find, my empty wine glass, and threw it in between them. The glass shattered on the floor, startling the creature for a moment.

Avia darted toward me. "We need water."

I glanced at the pitcher on her washing table. It was across the bed. I leapt onto the bed, hoping I could reach without —I strained. My fingers were just shy of touching. Sarding distance spell! I screamed at the wall. "Come on!" But whoever was behind the wall moved the wrong way. I was dragged backward over the bed.

I looked toward her servants' entrance. The creature was scrambling toward us. Where were Avia's handmaids? Why hadn't anyone come?

Shite. Another rug was set ablaze.

I scrambled all the way off the bed and shoved Avia behind me; I pushed her toward the far wall. "Go through the secret passage. There's nothing but stone there still, right? Nothing can burn?"

"But—"

"Do it!" I shoved her again, not hard enough to trip her, but hard enough that she ran as I'd said.

Avia activated the secret seam the palace mage had created by tracing her finger over the stones. A door handle appeared. She pulled open the door and turned back, "Come on!"

I didn't bother to tell her I couldn't, that I was tied to a stupid husband on the other side of the wall who was clearly oblivious to our screams. I was too busy staring at the sarding living flame darting toward her. The animal was clearly fixated on her. That's exactly what those men had been plotting. They'd said the beast would go straight for her—

Fury rose in me like a storm. I fought against it. I couldn't react the way I had with Ryan. I couldn't blast power. This was one tiny creature, not a part-giant. My heart didn't care. This thing had threatened my little sister. I reached out my hand. I'd never tried to stop a creature before. Only humans. I struggled internally to control the dose. I pushed out a small pulse of peace and the lizard swayed, as though dizzy—

The door burst open.

"What the hell is—" Declan's scolding tone cut off when he saw the fire.

Avia froze in the doorway of the secret passage.

I looked back at Declan and yelled, "Multiply sand!"

At the same time, he called out, "Water!"

It was as if someone dumped an entire rainstorm on us at once. The water gushed down in sheets. The fires were doused, and the orange fire salamander went limp; a little hiss of steam escaped him as the fire on his body went out. The water swept him up in a wave. Rather than let him disappear, I scooped up the little monster. He was still so hot he burned my hand.

"Ah!" I dropped him back into the puddle. And, as if he were a sentient creature, not simply a stupid lizard, he ran right for the fireplace and scurried up inside the chimney.

I turned slowly to Avia. Her hair was plastered to her face. Her brown eyes were wide and fearful.

"Are you okay?" I asked.

"I've just been nearly burnt then drowned. I think I need a minute."

"Fair enough," I turned back to Declan, who had taken a few steps forward and now stood at my side. I looked up at him, his straight, perfect blond hair was bedraggled. His grey velvet coat was ruined.

His eyes met mine and he held them for a long moment.

"I'm fine—" I started.

"Why'd you say to multiply sand?" he asked. As if that question were the most pressing thing despite everything that had just happened.

"Because it can smother a fire. Of course, I didn't realize you'd go overboard and fill the entire room—"

"That salamander was still actively on fire."

"I had calmed him down. He was still."

"Really?" Declan raised a brow. "The room's contents suggest otherwise." He eyed the ruined tapestry and the two burnt rugs.

I glared at him.

"Back to the sand," he dismissed my anger as if my emotions were unimportant. "What specifically made you recommend it?"

I shrugged. "When I was in the village of Lucha, I saw an execution by fire. At the end, they used sand to douse the fire instead of water. Kept the wooden pillar from rotting. Easier clean up and re-use, the village executioner said."

"The future Queen of Evaness takes advice from executioners?" Declan asked.

"He knew what he was talking about."

"He did?"

"They have a lot of pillaging from Rasle's mountain clans. When winter closes in, Lucha has a lot to handle."

"Did he say what kind of sand, or the quantity to fire ratio?"

"You are not asking me that."

Declan looks startled. "Yes, I am."

"The type of sand is irrelevant. Right now, we need to change. We need to get this room cleaned up. And we'll need to keep this all very discreet."

"What? Why?" Avia pulls me around to face her.

"Because I think someone let that salamander in here on purpose. I think you were just attacked."

CHAPTER ELEVEN

*R*yan walked into the room. "You won't believe what happened. There's a huge pit that opened up in the courtyard. As if a giant hand scooped up a ton of sand. What the hell—" he stepped around the puddles that dotted the floor. "What happened in here?"

"Fire salamander. I had to decrease the sand to make more water in here. The blighter must have tried to get out of the cold." Declan replied as he stripped off his soaked coat.

I couldn't help admiring how his white shirt clung to his body, even as his words stung. I'd just said I'd thought this salamander had been sent deliberately, hadn't I?

I met Declan's eyes. "You think a fire salamander scaled four floors of palace walls, bypassing the many warm cozy fireplaces on the lower floors and just happened to end up here?" I glared at him as Avia's lady-in-waiting and maid appeared.

They shrieked, and immediately hustled my sister out of the room to bathe and get re-dressed so she wouldn't 'catch her death.' I waved them off when they offered me the same. I was too furious to deal with servants. There was no coincidence here. That salamander did not just wander in.

Ryan's eyes flickered between my anger and Declan's dismissive head shake. His lips quirked in amusement.

"Don't go turning a salamander into a dragon," Declan said over his shoulder as he walked toward the door. "They sneak in during winter."

"It's not winter yet."

"It's not an attack. It was a tiny salamander."

"Queen Matha was killed by a poisoned frog," I shouted.

"Queen Matha was killed by her own idiocy," Declan turned at the door. "Who kisses a frog?" He nodded toward Ryan. "You get our lovely wife for the afternoon. Watch out. Connor says she's a walking disaster."

"I'm not the one who flooded the palace."

"No, you're the one who was screaming her head off over a tiny reptile the size of a twig."

I clenched my fists. I really wanted to grab the wine bottle and hurl it at his head. But Avia's personal servants were already streaming in, silently and efficiently cleaning up the disaster. I could've hit one of them.

Declan disappeared.

"Ass." I closed my eyes and breathed through my nose. It didn't reduce my fury.

Neither did the sight of Ryan when I opened my eyes.

He was openly grinning down at me. "Afraid of a lizard?"

"Don't," I threatened.

Ryan smiled wider. He scooped me up into his arms facing him. One forearm became my seat as he used his other hand to drape my arms around his shoulders.

"I can walk, you know."

"I know," his deep voice rumbled. "But what if you see another flaming lizard? Or an ant?"

I smacked him. But his body was warm and I was soaked. Plus, I had a view of the top of his sculpted pecs peeking out from beneath his shirt. I decided not to argue too hard against this arrangement. Still, I had to say something. "Last time you had your hands on me, you were trying to kill me."

"I was trying to stop you from killing me."

I shrugged. "Semantics."

He laughed, and the laugh vibrated against my pelvis. If I hadn't been so cold, it would have done very naughty things to me.

"You're angry a lot," he commented.

"I don't like idiots."

"Declan's a genius—"

"He's an idiot. All the furniture in that room is ruined. If he'd used his power to dump sand on selected areas just to smother the fire, it could have been swept up. The few burnt items could have been taken out. He flooded the entire room, like he has no control over his blasts at all."

"I don't think he's ever had to use his power for an emergency situation before," Ryan shrugs.

"Really?"

"Unless a hoard of locusts is an emergency, he mostly deals with crops and livestock—"

"We should change that."

"We?" Ryan shook his head. But he didn't comment with all the servants surrounding us.

I knew what he was thinking though. I leaned in and whispered, "You'd rather lose an eye than work with me, right?"

"Exactly."

I sighed, and Ryan began to walk with me in tow. Instead of going into the hall, he ducked into the secret passage that Avia had opened up. He shut the door behind us and proceeded to walk down the dark stone hallway with confidence.

"You know these passages well? Visit my sister a lot?" I asked, curiously. My mother hadn't released these men

from their contracts to me. But I'd been gone four years
…

Ryan barked a laugh. "Yes, I snuck down to play tea-party with her often. Of course not. Didn't she tell you?"

"Who? What? Who's supposed to tell me what?" I asked. I tried to search his deep brown eyes for answers, but I could hardly make them out in the darkness of the tunnel. Only the occasional stream of light from a spy hole lit our way.

"Darling wife, that mother of yours is quite the strategist."

"If by strategist, you mean controlling, conniving battleax, I'll agree," I spat back out of habit, more than anything. It was true. She was a conniving wench. But with mother's recent gift, I didn't put sting into those words. Not the way I used to.

Ryan laughed again, and this time my lady parts did react. "That's exactly what I mean. From the moment we signed our engagement contracts, we've all been unable to 'find release' with any other woman. The spell was woven into the paper, and the binder placed in the ink. Or so Declan seems to think." Ryan's tone was reflective.

I went into shock. Utter shock. My stomach was gone. It dropped out somewhere on the floor and was left behind as Ryan began to climb the circular staircase leading to my tower room.

"You're sure?"

"Yeah."

"But, we ... you signed that contract when I was sixteen." That was six years ago. Six *years*.

"Yes," Ryan's voice is soft.

"No wonder you hate me so much."

"You think that's the only reason we hate you?"

"Of course not. But it's got to multiply the hatred. Two, three times? More?" He didn't answer. I didn't really expect an answer. "No wonder you were angry when I said I'd been at a whorehouse—"

He chuckled. "Livid. I don't think angry covers half of it. I thought your mother had only made the spell one-sided. To think, you'd run off for four years, that you'd been with other men. I wanted to rip you in half."

"I thought you'd break my bones into matchsticks."

"I might have tried." He pulled me closer. "But it wasn't one-sided, was it?" his voice hitched, revealing how much my answer mattered.

I thought back to Marcus and Abel. We'd kissed. They'd groped. There had been nothing even close to release. And, looking back on it, I'd been so drunk at the time, but there had been a strange compulsion to leave. I'd thought I was simply going to puke. But maybe the stomach churning, gut-wrenching feeling had been the spell. I'd certainly never wanted to repeat the experience. No matter how they'd begged.

I tightened my arms around Ryan and whispered, "No. It wasn't one-sided. I had no idea about that spell, though. If I had—"

"Don't lie."

I took a deep breath. He was right. He was being honest. Vulnerable. I had to be, too. It was only fair. "I still would have left. But I would have tried to break that spell before I went. I would have tried to set you all free. I never meant to make such a mess of things. I honestly thought it would help."

"Why?"

I leaned into Ryan, resting my cheek on his chest. Though his body was hard, it was strangely comfortable. I felt his heartbeat against my cheek. It was steady. He wasn't angry right now. He was curious. Anyone would be, if their fiancé ran away. He deserved some form of explanation. Especially now that I knew exactly how much he'd suffered.

But how could I answer him? What could I say with the geas blocking me? I spoke slowly and carefully, testing the words as I said them. "You have the power to heal gently, without pain. But it makes you rage. Quinn can speak to others' minds but loses his voice. Declan can multiply something but must decrease something else for balance. Connor can feel others emotions but then loses his head to depressing thoughts. What about—" But the geas wouldn't let me finish the sentence. Somehow the spell knew I was too close to revealing my nature.

Sarding hell! I wanted to scream. My insides bunched up in emotion and frustration. "I can't—I can't—you need to talk to Declan. I can't say anymore. It won't—" The geas cut me off again. This time a tear of frustration did slide down my cheek.

Ryan fell silent.

"More spells?" his question seemed to echo off the stones.

My mouth opened, but words wouldn't come. I grabbed his hand and held it to my lips so he could feel the movement. I hoped that would show him I couldn't say. That I was trying, but that I couldn't talk.

He didn't question me further. I hoped he'd heard the honesty and the frustration in my voice. I hoped he didn't just dismiss me as Declan had. I prayed someone would be able to puzzle me out. Because that was the only way my knights and I could have an honest discussion about why I left. And why they needed to prepare for a life that probably wouldn't involve me.

Ryan finally reached the secret door to my tower room.

He set me down and ran his hand along the magical seam. The handle appeared, and he held open the door like a true gentleman.

I went through and walked into my old chamber for the first time since I'd run.

Everything shone and sparkled; there wasn't a speck of dust. The lavender and cream motif I'd had as a teenager was still there. The murals I'd commissioned of unicorns and dragons when I'd been a young girl still adorned the walls. The faint scent of rosemary tinted the room. My favorite smell. The staff had been busy. They must have cleaned and aired this room out upon my arrival. I trailed my hand over my favorite reading chair and made my way to the arched window by my bed. The sill was lined with glass bottles filled with potions every color of the rainbow.

I walked over to the window and ran my finger around one of the corks. I picked the bottle up and smiled. An old label, written in my eight-year-old scrawl stated the potion inside was for 'giggles.' I watched the swirling purple mist inside. The potion was long expired. I doubted it would even make me grin, let alone giggle. Not to mention that I doubted my eight-year-old self had gotten the measurements for the potion exactly right.

Hedge witches had an exacting job creating spells. The tiniest thing going wrong could ruin a spell. It was a very precise practice. Declan probably would have been wonderful at it. I'd never been. The palace mage had tried to teach me the basics. And I'd only ever just muddled through those lessons. I'd experimented plenty on my own, and plenty on Avia until the day I'd given her giraffe-like purple spots. But I'd never had the knack. It had been why I'd been so dependent on Cerena and the other hedge witches I'd met in my travels.

"Don't you want to change?" Ryan gestured at my sopping dress. He'd already removed the shirt I'd soaked and hung it over the fireplace screen to let the fire dry it out.

"Yes," I answered, though I wasn't answering the question Ryan asked. Since I was eight, all I'd wanted was to change. Ever since my father had died and I'd realized how much danger each day was.

I sighed and put down the potions as Ryan approached.

"Got any love spells in there?" he joked, waving a broad, dark arm at my collection. His biceps and triceps flexed as he moved his arm and I swallowed hard.

"Yes. Probably five or six. Little girls are quite obsessed with them."

"Show me one."

I picked up a jar with that had turned a moldy green. Brown clumps floated around inside. "This was one attempt."

"That looks awful."

I laughed and shook it. "Definitely not an appealing sort of love."

"Looks like more of an obsessive peeping tom potion."

"Or a creepy old man foot-licker."

"Foot licker?"

"Quinn's been planting perverted thoughts in my head about feet."

"Ha! Good for him. Definitely foot-licker potion." Ryan took the bottle from my hands and his fingers brushed mine. My hand tingled from his touch.

He was touching me a lot today. Why? He hated me. Had the six years driven him that crazy with lust? Did he need it so badly he'd even stoop to seducing me? The woman he hated more than any in the world? And if that was his goal, if that was what he needed, who was I to refuse? What was I to do? Turn him down? Make him suffer more when all he'd ever done was sign a contract? Maybe said some naughty words?

I studied Ryan's face. His black hair was shaved close to his head. His brown eyes were hard but lined with curled lashes that softened him, made his face almost pretty. That was the only soft part of his body though. I had to swallow carefully as I lost my train of thought looking at him. I turned back into the sixteen-year-old girl who'd fanned herself with her hand when he'd walked off the practice arena, a sweating mess without a shirt, with back dimples that peeked deliciously out of the top of his leather pants.

Ryan touched my arm and jolted me out of my thoughts. "Why haven't you put love spells on us?"

The question jarred me, like I'd been thrown from a horse. "What?"

"Your mother seems to love to seal our fate with spells. You're back, right?"

"Yes."

"Quinn said he heard you were staying." Ryan didn't ask, but the question lingered in the air.

"Yes."

"You could just spell us all to be in love with you."

I reeled back slightly, a bit horrified. "Why would I do that?"

"To make this easier on yourself."

My lips thinned. "Is that what you think of me?" His lack of an answer said more than enough. "Well let me ask you something, Ryan O'Sullivan."

"Hale. Ryan Hale. We're 'married' remember?"

I ignored his sarcasm as I shoved my finger into his chest. "Did you spell your soldiers into following you? Or did you earn it?" I waited, and let that sink in. "I earned your hatred. Fair and square. By a stupid, impulsive choice that I happened to think was the right thing when I was eighteen. That hatred's mine. I'll earn your respect, too. One day, I'll earn it. I've spent my entire life trapped by magic and Mother's stupid spells. I'm not about to use magic for something as idiotic as a love spell that wouldn't even work on you stubborn bastards."

"Why not?"

"Hedge magic has limits. You have to be open to it. Unlike mage spells—which are higher level and can sard you over completely—thank you, Mother. Now if you'll excuse me, I'm turning to ice."

Sard it all. He thought I was as bad as my mother? I brushed past him toward the wardrobe and grabbed out one of my dresses at random. I sort of hoped the distance spell would make him trip after he'd been such an utter ass. But no such luck.

He followed right behind me. I started unbuttoning my sopping dress in front of him, ignoring the perusing stare he gave me. A second ago I'd considered letting him use my body. Then he'd had to go mention spells. If he thought I was that much of a bitch, was there any way this could work? Maybe not.

My fingers were stiff from being cold and wet. I struggled with the buttons on my wet dress. After five buttons, they refused to work. I tried and tried again but the next button in line refused to budge.

"Need help?" Ryan asked. His voice turned husky.

"I think they sewed this button on wrong," I complained, trying again. My fingers slipped.

"Here." Ryan gently moved my hands away and pulled on the button. It slid free on his first try.

"Thank you," I said, avoiding eye contact. Humiliating. I felt like a dalcop. Being undressed like a child by a man who thought I was heartless enough to make him a spelled plaything.

Ryan's hands were surprisingly gentle as he released button after button and slowly slid the gown off my shoulders. It puddled on the ground beneath me.

His breath caught as he eyed my cold, hard nipples through my chemise. The white fabric was soaked and did nothing to hide them. Ryan's eyes dilated. His fingers fisted in my chemise and he slowly pulled that over my head, knuckles scraping every inch of skin along the way.

I shivered but not from the cold. A tiny part of my mind wondered if Ryan would actually have been gentle with me our first time. I'd never know.

When the chemise was gone, Ryan took my hand and led me over to the fire. "Get warm and dry first." He stood me in front of the fire and tossed his warmed shirt over me. He yanked the hem down and fussed over straightening it, as if that mattered. But it let his fingers brush my thighs.

I gasped involuntarily.

Ryan met my eyes and his look was hard. Almost scary. "You want to earn your way back, Bloss? Without love spells?"

I nodded.

"Then drop to your knees."

I watched his eyes closely. He had been pushed and pulled and played like a puppet by my mother. Maybe to earn his trust, I needed to let him pull my strings. Let him take charge for once. Let him be in control instead of controlled. I slowly slid onto my knees.

Ryan looked shocked right out of his dominant persona. "You did it. I didn't think you'd do it."

I quirked a grin at him. "Unlike my sixteen-year-old virgin self, the idea of a little rough play, dirty talk, or a finger in my ass doesn't scare me."

"That's what made you run that night?"

I put my hand on my heart. "Didn't even know that ass play was a thing. I swear. I thought you'd meant to tear me apart."

He laughed and held out a hand. He yanked me to my feet. I was shocked. My mouth had been level with his cock. I'd been certain he'd been about to take advantage of that fact.

"Honesty gets you out of the mood?" I questioned.

Ryan winked at me and gave another booming laugh. "No. But we have an audience."

My father Johann stood in the doorway, avoiding looking directly at me. He ran a hand uncomfortably through his stiff grey hair. "Your mother needs you. She said it was a political emergency."

Shite.

CHAPTER TWELVE

I threw on a pale green dress, which Ryan buttoned for me.

"I can't believe I just said the words 'ass play' in front of one of my fathers," I groaned.

"If I have my way, you'll say a lot worse things than that," Ryan winked.

I rolled my eyes as I slipped on dry shoes, though part of me hoped he was serious.

We ran through several secret passages in order to get to Mother as quickly as possible. When we had to take a sharp turn and go down some steps, I nearly fell. Ryan latched onto my hand and stopped me from tumbling face-first. And he didn't let go. It might have been wonderful under other circumstances. I might have taken it as a sign. Read something into it. But he grabbed my burned hand.

"Ow!" I pulled away from him.

"What's wrong?" he stopped and pulled my hand toward him. Not that he could see anything in the dark passageway.

"The salamander burned my hand."

"Of course, it did. Here," Ryan put his large hand over mine. His was so big that both my hands might have fit into his palm. A dull pink light emanated from his hand.

And my burn disappeared.

"Your magic is pink," I marveled.

"Shut your mouth about that," Ryan's voice was strained. "Not the time to make fun of me." I could feel his hand clench over mine. He trembled with restraint, trying not to crush my fingers when that's what his body urged him to do.

"Sorry. Here." I pushed the tiniest pulse of peace I could manage. Lime green light lit his features for a moment, and the twisted expression on his face relaxed.

He sighed. "Thanks."

"Not a problem," I replied, pulling my sleeve more securely over my wrist, where a small gash had ripped open the moment I used my magic. "Was it enough?"

I think Ryan nodded in the darkness. "Yeah. First time I haven't had to punch a wall."

I didn't quite know what to say to that. "Well, shall we?"

"Yup."

We made our way quickly to the hallway where mother's room was located. That was as far as we could go within the secret passageway. The Queen's Chamber had to be entered through the door by everyone but herself. Ryan opened the seam on the spelled door and let us into the hall.

I blinked, my eyes adjusting to the light, only to find his hand extended toward me.

I looked side to side to see if someone was standing nearby. Or behind me. I pointed at Ryan's hand. "Is that for me?"

Ryan grabbed my hand and yanked me toward him. He started walking to mother's door, pulling me along. "Shut up and follow."

"Yes, sir."

Ryan's eyes glittered as he glanced back at me. "You'll be saying a lot of that later."

"You don't hear it enough all day from your men?"

Ryan reached Mother's door but didn't open it. Instead, he pulled me close. He leaned down and whispered into my ear. "None of my men say it while they're on their knees, about to suck my cock."

I nearly came undone at his words. My eyelids fluttered. My thighs tightened in anticipation. Ryan had always been the dream of masculine hotness. But paired with this little dominant streak? Intoxicating. I was about to be drunk on lust. But I couldn't let him know that. Not just yet. I wanted his trust first. Then his lust. So I pushed back. "And you think I'm going to do that? Get on my knees and suck you off?" I trailed my breath over his neck, teasing.

His grip on my hand grew tighter. His other hand grabbed onto my hip and squeezed. "Pretty sure you already showed you were quite willing."

I grinned and pulled away. "We'll see."

"You have six years to make up for," he growled. "Since the night I signed that damned contract."

I leaned my back against the door and gripped the handle. "I know. But I don't only plan to make up for it on my knees. I've learned about so many different positions from those girls at the brothel. You'll have to be more creative than that."

I winked and pulled open the door to mother's room.

Ryan's chest heaved from the caveman lust he had to suppress. I was a soaking mess. All my body wanted to do was go back to my chamber and let him toss me around on the mattress. The thought of Ryan pinning me down nearly made me convulse. I had to close my eyes and swallow before taking a step forward, clearing my mind, and approaching the Queen at the far side of the room.

My fathers surrounded her. Gorg, the stiff-neck ruler-wielding, rule-following spy master who used to punish even my smallest offenses with a rap on my fingers; Peter, the knight with a heart of gold who'd taken on Evaness' economic matters; and Johann, Ryan's mentor in our war games.

My mother stopped whispering with Johann when I reached the foot of the bed.

"I was summoned." I waited.

Mother looked back and forth between myself and Ryan, who'd stopped uncomfortably close behind me, nearly pinning me to the bed frame. Her eyes may have been pleased at that, but it was hard to tell.

"There is a problem with the entourage from Cheryn."

"Problem?" I asked. My mind flitted to robbers or carriage breakdowns on the road.

"The visit was initially arranged to introduce Sultan Raj's son, Abbas, to your sister. He's twenty-five, with four younger brothers. They're in need of a wife."

My stomach revolted but I kept my expression neutral. I didn't want Avia to leave. If something happened to me and we could explain away my absence, it wasn't a big deal. But that was a gamble. What if we couldn't explain my absence? What if, at some point, people stopped believing I was hunting dragons? What if something happened to me publicly? Evaness would want a new queen. But I'd expressed that opinion countless times. Each time I'd been rebuked.

I waited for mother. She liked to allow tension to build sometimes. It helped her feel in control—that was my theory, at least.

"Abbas is apparently traveling with two hundred pegasus fliers."

My neutral expression dropped. As did my jaw. "That's an attack force!" Cheryn was an aggressive country, sure. When djin and giants were half the population, it was bound to happen. But we'd had a decent treaty with them since I was eight. Since the last Fire War.

"Apparently, additional forces have been gathered at the border, awaiting some kind of signal."

I had trouble breathing. Unconsciously, I leaned back into Ryan. He put his hand on my shoulder to steady me. And he didn't remove it.

"Why is this the first we're hearing about this?" Ryan demanded. "I didn't have any reports this morning."

"They were just spotted at the border half an hour ago," Mother said.

Johann turned to Ryan and grimaced. It made the scar on his cheek wink like a dimple. "Apparently, they've been slowly moving troops dressed as civilians to their border towns for months. This is not some hasty maneuver."

My eyes flickered between Johann and my mother as they shared a look. And suddenly, everything clicked.

"What do they want? Have they made demands?" I asked.

"None," Gorg answered, his face as hard as granite.

I bit back a smile. They all played their parts so well.

"I can't believe this. Should we prepare for invasion?" Ryan turned to Johann.

"No," I responded, before my father could answer. I gazed straight at my mother. She stared steadily back, waiting to hear what I'd say. I took a deep breath and went with my gut. We'd planned for contingencies and scenarios like this for as long as I could remember. She'd always taught me to divide the work. Give everyone a job in a crisis so they have no time to panic.

I applied that strategy. "We wait. We receive Abbas cordially. The ball is still on. In the lead up and during the ball Connor and his diplomats can feel him out. Quinn's spies will tell us the difference between what Abbas says and what they see."

I glanced up at Ryan. "You can tell the local militias to assemble using Quinn's contacts. I also believe the ambassador to Sedara is angry at Cheryn. Perhaps, Declan could speak to him, with Connor's help. Feel out their interest in an alliance. If Sedara seems agreeable, Ryan, you'll need to go to Sedara yourself to ensure coordination in case this gets violent. While we house the pegasus fleet, we can feed them sycamore seeds to give them muscle tremors and make it difficult for them to fly. That will effectively remove them from the equation and keep this to a land battle."

I turned and glared hard at mother. "Avia stays here. She starts training for my position immediately."

"What?" my fathers all turned to stare at me. Ryan's hand clamped down on my shoulder. I didn't look at him.

"I thought you were staying," Peter said.

"If war breaks out, I'm the biggest target. I'm also likely to —" the geas cut me off. I just pushed past it. "We need the second heir. She needs to be prepared."

There was a long moment of silence. Then a single clap. My mother smiled at me from her bed. "You see? I told you all that four years wouldn't lessen her strategic thinking. She's still sharp as a whip."

I didn't smile back. I'd never liked these tests or her methods. Instead, I gave her a sharp nod. I didn't bother to tell her that her look to Johann had given her away. In a true crisis, my mother never made eye contact. Connor taught me that about her. Even when we'd been eight, before his powers had fully developed, he'd been incredibly perceptive.

"Where did the pegasus poisoning come from?" Peter asks.

"Spent some time on a farm with horses," I shrugged. I turned back to mother. Now that I'd passed her test, I wanted to discuss real issues. "This morning, a fire salamander was in Avia's room."

"Declan's told me," Queen Gela responded.

"The creature ran after Avia and only Avia. I'd like extra guards on her."

"Abbas will take that as a personal offense when he arrives. He'll think we don't trust him."

"I'd like a woman who works for Quinn on her then."

Mother nods. "Done."

I swallowed a smile and gave her a nod of thanks.

"Good. Well, I believe I have a long list of current events to catch up on."

"Yes, and the royal dressmaker will be visiting to help create your ball gown."

I curtsied and Ryan bowed and we left the room.

Back in the hallway, Ryan ran a hand over his buzzed hair. "She always test you like that?"

"Since I was nine."

He blew out a breath. "Damn. I thought that was real."

"We're supposed to treat it as if it is. Once or twice, she's given me a real scenario and enacted my advice."

"What happened?"

"Considering the first time, her lesson was that my actions cost lives … nothing good."

At the corner, I could see Quinn leaning against a wall, nonchalantly reading a letter. But I had no doubt he'd been listening, probably to every word in the Queen's chamber, too. He pushed aside his black hair when he stood and slipped the letter into an inner vest pocket.

"Hale," Ryan grabbed my arm and stopped me.

"Yeah?" I turned to look up at him.

His face was earnest. "If you think Dec needs practice controlling his powers, I'll help."

I held his eyes. I heard his words. But it seemed like his eyes said even more than his mouth did. He was offering to help me. Me. The bitch who'd left him high and dry for six years. "You're sure?"

He nodded. "Better for him anyway. If something ever happened. He should be prepared. Right?"

I couldn't help the smile that flitted over my face. "Thank you ... sir."

Ryan groaned and threw his head back. "You're evil."

"Suppose you'll have to punish me ... sir."

He laughed. "Quinn, get over here and take Bloss away before I drag her back to my room and keep her there for a month straight."

I leaned up on my tiptoes and pressed my hands against Ryan's chest, "If you did that, I'd miss Abbas' visit completely. No ball. I vote for lock up."

Ryan laughed and pulled my hands off, passing them to Quinn. "You're gonna kill me."

Quinn took my hands and spun me out and then back in, as if we were dancing. He pulled my back to his chest, his bearded cheek rubbing against my cheek, arms entwined with mine.

Ryan walked off, smiling and shaking his head.

Hello, wife. Quinn's sultry mind-voice flitted through my head.

I twisted so I could meet Quinn's eyes. "You are in trouble."

He grinned. And his grey eyes sparkled with mischief. *So are you.*

"What? Why am I in trouble?"

You agreed to consider Lady Agatha's son, Willard, as a suitor.

CHAPTER THIRTEEN

"*B*ut ... but ... I'm already 'married,'" I whispered as a healer swept down the hall toward my mother's rooms. My eyes followed the man as he slipped inside. She hadn't looked bad when I'd seen her. But she wouldn't have told me about her discomfort anyway. The man wasn't racing. I'd just seen her. I convinced myself it was a routine visit and turned back to Quinn. "If you all are bound to me ... I thought no one could be added after a marriage ceremon—"

You don't have to speak out loud to me, you know.

Oh.

With the bead, you can just think something ... and project it.

I pictured Quinn prostrate on the floor, bowing repeatedly to me. *Like that?*

You're more creative than that, I'm sure.

I closed my eyes and imagined Quinn draped in fur, with homemade paper bunny ears clipped into his hair. He sat on Willard's lap. The chubby man bounced him on his knee and handed him a carrot. "Suck it," Willard demanded.

Quinn laughed silently, his shoulders shaking. *That was a good one.* His hand stroked mine as he moved me to his side and tucked my hand into the crook of his elbow, so he could escort me properly.

"I've had the unfortunate privilege of seeing something similar in real life," I forgot to speak in my mind.

Thank you for sharing that trauma with me. I'll treasure it forever.

I was furious at you this morning, you know. I thought I was delirious. We both paused to nod at Baron White admiring a painting as we went through the main gallery.

I know. Why do you think I avoided you until now?

I pinched the skin near his elbow and he started but didn't pull away. I sneaked a glance and he was still grinning. That shite. I'd get revenge on him.

Did you hear everything Avia and I talked about?

Do you mean, will I be making my manservant test all my bathing products? And clothing? And brushes? And food? And double check under my saddle for tacks? Yes.

Damn it all. I hate you a little bit.

No, you don't. He glanced down at me, eyes filled with amusement, and something more.

That something more sent a shiver of nervousness down my spine. I wasn't quite sure why. Goosebumps rose on my arms as Quinn stopped walking.

He brought his hand up and stroked my cheek with the backside of his fingers. *I've waited so long to talk to you.*

Yes. Four years. He'd shown up to the castle and found no bride. *You hate me for leaving, too. I'm sorry. I swear, I didn't know my mother would block you from other relationships. I never knew. Ryan just told me. I wouldn't have let her do that to you.*

Bloss—

I'll find a way to get you released from that spell. I promise. Just give me a few days—

Bloss—

I— my thought was cut off. Because suddenly, Quinn's lips skimmed mine. My heart galloped like a war horse. *WHAT?*

He gave the slightest peck at the corner of my lips and pulled back to meet my eyes. *I don't want to be released from that spell.*

If he hadn't been holding onto me, I might have fallen to the floor. His words left me dazed. So much so that I forgot to speak in my thoughts. "Oh. Really?"

You're adorable when you're flustered.

Queens aren't adorable.

You aren't a queen yet, Dove. You're just my reluctant princess. Now, go turn down Willard. Tell him four husbands are more than you can handle. But do it politely, please. Make a concession or two.

Quinn pulled open a door handle I hadn't even noticed because I'd been so trapped by his damn irresistible eyes. He opened the door and released my arm in the same moment.

Don't you have to come in? I cocked my head.

Just stay near the wall so poor Willard gets the illusion of privacy. I think he might be about to piss himself. An image of Willard in bright red breeches with a wet spot over his crotch popped into my head. Willard reached his hands together to cover it and his lips popped into a little surprised circle.

I bit my lip and shook my head, but my eyes danced with mirth. *You're awful,* I told Quinn.

I know.

Willard was already in the room and he stepped forward to bow and kiss my hand. He was wearing bright red breeches. I had to swallow a smile. Quinn was on point.

"Your Highness, thank you so much for taking the time to see me. My mother was so pleased when you agreed to this meeting the other day," he mumbled, coming forward as Quinn pulled the door shut behind me.

I noticed his hair was thinning as he bowed over my hand. Not that thinning hair mattered in arranged marriages. But, my mother had seemed to happen to find handsome men for me. I'd never thought too much of it, busy as I'd been planning my escape. But, for a second I wondered how many other candidates she'd turned down. I was sure Lady Agatha had approached her. Willard was the lady's only child. She'd never been able to carry to term again. This couldn't be Willard's first attempt to attain knighthood. So ... why now?

"Lord Willard, we've known each other since childhood."

"Yes, Your Highness," he squeaked. He looked to his left, away from me. A bead of sweat rolled down his forehead. And he breathed through his mouth.

I blinked, reminding myself to keep my face neutral. "Your family is very important to this kingdom. You're very important."

"Thank you," he gritted his teeth together, and his face turned an odd blotchy red.

Was he embarrassed by a compliment? I wouldn't have been surprised if Quinn's prediction about the piss came true. I tried to take a surreptitious step back. "Your mother has suggested you be added to my contingent of personal knights."

"Yes," Willard wheezed.

"This suggests your family has needs of a very delicate nature, that you'd like the crown's help, but perhaps ...

you feel those needs won't be met by someone who is only your monarch. Are your lands in danger?"

I said be polite!

I ignored Quinn and focused on Willard's uncomfortable fidgeting. His eyes flashed to mine only briefly. Defiance and a bit of anger seemed to flicker there, though his nervousness quickly outpaced other emotions.

"Willard. I've been married four years and have obligations to my current knights. They have been kind enough to wait for me as I tried to put the country's needs before our own. I cannot accept you into my contingent—"

Willard gulped and wiped his forehead with a handkerchief.

I took his hand and continued, "But I would like to offer you something else. Something that will allow you to trust me. I'll offer a mage oath."

Willard gasped.

Inside my head, Quinn swore. *I said turn him down gently, not offer the kingdom's secrets on a sarding platter!*

Good thing I haven't been to any briefings yet to learn those secrets, I replied. *I'm four years behind on confidential information.*

A picture of a dog and her suckling pups popped into my head.

I hope you mean clever bitch, I shot to Quinn.

Was that dog doing tricks? He sent a new image of a dog with glowing red eyes.

Ass.

Never said I don't like evil bitches.

I focused back on the paunchy man in front of me. Willard pulled out his handkerchief again and patted the rolls in his neck. I think the kerchief might have stuck inside one of the rolls for a moment. I averted my eyes and waited for his response.

"I … I will have to ask—"

He was going to ask his mother. Adrenaline flooded me. I couldn't let him do that. Lady Agatha would be furious. We'd end up with a rift between the crown and one of our major nobles. I had to get Willard to agree. Sweeten the pot, as the whores would have said. Or 'Make the offer irresistible, so they can't see the consequences for the glittering gold beneath their eyes.' Those were Mother's words. I moved until Willard met my eyes. "Truth for truth, Willard. You and I. No mothers involved. We can go before the palace mage and have him bind us. Right now. And after you reveal whatever truth you need my help with, I promise, I'll do whatever I can to help seek a solution. And I promise to be discreet. No one else need know."

The breath whooshed out of Willard. "Oh, thank God." He squeezed my fingers and dragged me into a full body hug. That was when I could finally smell the stench of his nervous sweat. "Thank you for saying no," he whispered.

"Um … any time?"

He chuckled and released me. "I do apologize, Your Highness. I meant, thank you for finding an alternative."

I shrugged and smiled. "Well, our tutors did always call me a little genius." The term they'd actually used was gnat.

But Willard coughed out a polite laugh.

I held out my hand so Willard could escort me to the mage's tower. "Shall we? I hope you don't mind, but one of my husbands will probably escort us to the tower … they've been a bit attached since I've returned."

Willard took my arm and for the first time since I'd known him, puffed his chest. He pulled open the door and led me into the hall. "Well, now, seeing as they married the class genius, they should be."

I genuinely laughed. I think it was the first joke I'd ever heard from Willard.

Quinn pulled himself away from the stone wall he'd been leaning against. He let Willard continue to escort me, giving the man a respectful nod. Willard doddled along with a grin, content to show his family's solidarity with the royal family via a public stroll through the palace.

Quinn flanked my other side, obviously staring me up and down despite the other nobles hovering nearby. *Dove. I didn't know you were a genius. I'd love to pick your* brain *later.* His gaze landed on my ass.

His naughty implication sent a rush from my nipples to my mound. *Who says my brain is open for business?*

The catch in your breath and the look in your eye, he countered.

I shot him a naughty grin, elation bubbling in my stomach. This was what I'd always hoped marriage would be. Banter and inside secrets. And laughter. But then I wondered ... was it a trick? Was Quinn toying with me? Was he going to turn angry like the others? Get me close only to push me away? Show me what it had been like for him? Being abandoned?

Quinn's fingers brushed mine. *No tricks, Dove. I promise.*

I stared up into his grey eyes. *Really?*

Really.

My knees went weak. My heart went haywire. And my feet gave out. I tripped on the edge of a rug. "Oh!" I nearly pulled Willard over with me. Luckily, Quinn grabbed me and yanked. Willard's weight on my other arm nearly ripped me in half until Quinn reached over and helped Willard to his feet too.

I turned to the pudgy man, whose waistcoat had rolled up over his middle. "I'm so sorry, Lord Willard. I wasn't watching where I was going. It was completely my fault."

Willard only smiled as he struggled to straighten his waistcoat. "Perhaps your knight should escort you, Your Highness. Since you can't seem to take your eyes off him."

I blushed scarlet, particularly as two noble ladies nearby craned their necks to listen to our conversation. Quinn just grinned and tugged me closer until I fit under the crook of his arm.

"Sorry, Lord Willard, I can't help it. He's been rather obsessed with me."

If only you knew. Quinn jerked his head toward a stairwell and the three of us began to climb.

Quinn and I quickly outpaced the portly Willard and when we had rounded yet another bend ahead of him, Quinn pulled me roughly against him. His hand traced down my back, and then he squeezed my ass.

"Whoa!"

Shhh. Quinn grinned, running his hands back and forth over my hips. He glanced over my shoulder and must have seen the top of Willard's head, because he led me into another sprint up the stairs. The next time he stopped, I was breathless.

You're insa—

Hush. He grabbed my face in both hands and bent until our eyes were level. His eyes … my chest got an airy, restless feeling. Like the wind was dancing between my ribs. I clung to him. *I think I'm hallucinating again.*

He smiled, his eyes simply flickering back and forth between mine as if he were drinking in every fluttering, girlish beat of my heart.

Can you feel what I feel?

Do you feel like you're flying?

I nodded.

Willard's head poked around the spiral staircase and Quinn yanked me upward once more.

You didn't answer, I scolded.

How would I know it felt like flying? Unless I felt the same thing.

I was already breathless from climbing. But his answer took my breath away.

Two seconds later, before I could process what anything might mean, we stood in front of mage Wyle's door. Quinn rapped smartly and then stood aside to let Willard and myself in. I went first, seeing as Willard was heaving like a messenger horse that had rushed down from Macedon.

"Hello, Wyle," I strode toward Wyle's project table before he could even take off the oversized goggles and gloves he had on. The table just stretched the limit of my distance spell with Quinn. I reached but couldn't quite rest my hand on the table.

"Your Highness," Wyle carefully set down the glowing orange beaker he'd been holding. He pushed his dark goggles up into his skull, which was lined with perfectly symmetrical white braids. His pointed elf ears twitched.

His large, almond eyes blinked as he adjusted to the daylight.

"What lovely concoction are you making there?" I asked, nodding toward the beaker.

"Not making," he sighed. "Extracting. Declan's asked me to help with research he's been doing into water contaminants."

"Oh," I quickly switched off that deadly boring topic. "Well, if you have a moment, Willard and I would like a thirty-minute mage oath binding." I turned to Willard. "You think that's enough time to explain everything?"

Willard, who had bent over and used a table to help support his gasping, just nodded and waved a hand.

"I, oh, well, it's been some time since … I'll just need to grab the book, Your Highness. Reference a few things."

"Absolutely," I followed him as Willard sunk into a wooden chair by the window. Luckily, the bookcase was right by the door. I heaved a sigh of relief.

Wyle hummed as he looked through his handwritten tomes, until he noticed I was right behind him. "Your Highness?"

I leaned close to him, pulling a book from the shelf to cover my intentions. I flipped the book open to a random page. An anatomical drawing of a penis, with all parts labeled. How fitting, seeing as I what was about to ask Wyle to do. "I want you to lift the spells my mother put on my husbands."

"All of them, Your Highness?"

"All … what do you mean all?"

"Long life, virility, good vision, safety—"

"Okay, fine. Not those. The one where they have to be within five feet of me. And the one where they can only physically be intimate with me and no other woman."

Wyle raised an eyebrow. "Really?"

I did not answer. I was not going to explain myself to the castle mage. "This is confidential, correct, Wyle? She still has the spell set on you so you'll explode if you betray the royal family's secrets?"

"I—I … she put a spell on me?" Wyle sounded indignant.

"Of course, she does it to all of us," I patted his hand. "Are there any other controlling spells on my husbands that need to be lifted?"

"Does a spell compelling them to forgive you count?"

Disgust flooded me. My hands fisted and I accidentally ripped the penis page. "What?! Yes. Yes, that would count, Wyle. Please dispose of that one, too."

"I might need to consult the Queen."

I tilted my head. I gave him the look I'd perfected to fend off every farmhand for three miles when I'd worked in a field three summers past. A look that had sent the farm boys running back to their mothers. "Or, you could undo them *without* telling her."

"Or that. Of course, that." Wyle gently extracted his precious book from my hands. He eyed the page I'd ripped and gave a tiny moan.

"Sorry I ripped your penis. I'll get it fixed."

"No need, Your Highness. I have a spell for that."

"Of course you do."

He petted the page gently, muttered something, sprinkled a bit of ash, and the book repaired itself. I only hoped his skills would be as successful with my husbands.

Wyle tried to hustle me over to the chair where Willard was sitting. But my mother's distance spell-curse wouldn't let me walk that far.

"Do you mind if we do this over here?" I smiled.

The two men blinked at me dumbly, though it should have been obvious to Wyle why I couldn't move.

"My skin has just been really sensitive the last few days. I don't think I should be standing in direct sunlight." I fluttered my eyelashes, feeling like an absolute idiot.

I bet you look like an absolute idiot.

Shut it.

Of course, the two men complied with the request of the crown princess.

Willard dragged his chair over and sat next to where I stood, absolutely reeking of sweat.

I secretly wished I'd also asked for a spell to deal with that scent. If I'd been my mother, I probably would have.

As it was, I watched Wyle link our hands. He squeezed two lemons and trickled the juice over fingers. Then he lit a rose on fire and blew it out before the flames reached the stem. Finally, he muttered a few words in a language I didn't know.

"Is that all?" I asked.

Wyle nodded, his goggles falling down his face to thunk against his chest.

I turned to Willard. "I'm the youngest daugh—" I couldn't lie and say I was Avia. The mage oath must be active. "Try to say you are from Sedara, please."

"I'm from—I can't," he marveled.

"Good. Now, Wyle, please leave us. Take whatever you need to complete those tasks I've given you."

Wyle's eyes opened wide, His mouth gaped. With his beaky nose and wild hair, he looked like a startled bird. But he knew better than to protest. He gathered some books and ingredients and was on his way.

I turned back to Willard. "You have the floor."

He gulped.

I shook my head. "We were in class together ten years, Willard. Just tell me."

"We aren't getting enough rain."

"Okay." I waited, carefully blinking away the 'sarding idiot' face my tavern wench persona would have given him.

"A lot of our herds—they can't breed without enough water. The grass doesn't grow without enough water."

I nodded. Alright. The magnitude of the problem was starting to make sense.

"We've asked Declan for some assistance. But the balance … we lose too much soil in return."

"And what are the astrologers predicting this winter for you?"

"They say it's unseasonably warm. They predict a dry winter."

So, the situation was only likely to get worse. "I am aware that your livestock provide a good deal of your income. Would you mind telling me what percentage?"

"I … my parents have found it the most profitable avenue. In the past." Willard couldn't make eye contact.

I sighed. "All of it, Willard?"

He looked up. His lower lip trembled a bit. "All of it."

Shite. I tried to keep a neutral face. "Any areas worse than the others?"

"Grazing lands near the Purl Mountain range."

"Near the border to Cheryn then?"

Willard nodded.

"Okay, start moving your herds south if you haven't already. I'll talk with Declan. See what we can do."

Willard nodded again.

I put a hand on his shoulder. "I'll figure something out. We won't abandon your family. Though I do suggest you put your foot down and make them diversify a bit."

He gave a broken laugh. "Put my foot down. Yes. Mother would love that."

"You're the heir, Willard."

"You're different. Than before you left," he observed.

I smiled gently. "Better, I hope."

"You seem more … sure of yourself."

"If by sure of yourself, you mean mouthy and defiant, then yes. Four years outside these walls taught me that I have to think for myself, stand up for myself. No one else can do it for me. No one else can do it for you, either."

He mopped his brow once more and stood. "Thank you, Your Highness. If you could help us out of this predicament, it would mean … a lot."

"I will do everything in my power. And I hope to prove you can trust me with issues like this in the future."

Willard started to turn toward the door, and I thought our conversation was concluded. But then he stopped, turned, pursed his lips. "Your Highness, um, if you don't mind ... did you actually see dragons when you were gone?"

Shite. Mother's cover story. And I was still bound by the mage oath. "No. I did not."

Willard's eyes widened. "But—"

I took a deep breath and fought down the fear in my chest. He'd shared his family's vulnerable state with me. "Willard, I haven't seen dragons since I was a child. Not since the last Fire War."

Bloss! Dammit! Don't.

"Then ... why did you leave?"

"To save Evaness, of course. From people who might unintentionally destroy it. People who are better off unnamed."

"Ahh," Willard nodded.

Good save.

"Were you successful?"

Willard's last question was like an arrow to my heart. I met his eyes and fought back tears. I had to answer him. But I couldn't let him see how the answer affected me. A queen had to appear in control. "No. Not quite."

Quinn swung open the door at that point, cutting off our conversation and any further confessions I might have made.

CHAPTER FOURTEEN

Q uinn hustled me down the stairwell, berating
me.

Then I spent the afternoon surrounded by tutors,
updating me on the status of each of Evaness' provinces.
That was how I spent the next two weeks. Reviewing the
provinces, our nobles and their alliances, then reviewing
the foreign countries and our current relationships with
each.

Sedara was our strongest ally, thanks to my 'marriage' to
Declan, bastard son of their queen. But, our relationship
with them had become strained over the past year.

Declan supervised me but didn't participate for the most
part. He sat at a separate desk, as far from me as he could
get, running his hands through his blond hair and staining
it with ink from his quill as he muttered about holdings
and livestock and tried to puzzle out the issues from
different provinces. Somehow, he did manage to listen

with half an ear. He'd interrupt my tutors if he disagreed with some fact or figure.

"Sedara and Cheryn actually have had at least twenty aggressive incidents over the past eighteen months," Declan interrupted the young man talking about the two countries. "Cheryn's sultan has sent pirates, stolen goods, been really aggressive. Only seven of those incidents are considered public knowledge. The remainder, I'll tell you about some other time."

My stomach fell. Twenty incidents? That was serious. I turned to him. "How about now?"

Declan glanced meaningfully at the ledgers he was working on.

I ignored him and turned to my tutors. "Please give us the room for half an hour."

The men bowed their way out, and I looked sharply at Declan, who sighed. "As you know, Sedara, has the strongest navy. That navy controls access to a lot of trade. Sultan Raj is ticked about that. Sedara's navy also controls the magical weapons made by the elves on the Isles of Peth."

I nodded. "Access to Peth's weapons made a difference during the last Fire War. It's how Mother survived." I clamped down on memories of running through the woods—of treetops that flickered like matchsticks, burning from the top down. I shook off thoughts of my fathers, herding me toward a royal safe house underground, away from the dragons that scorched the countryside.

Declan inclined his head in agreement. "I'm pretty sure Sultan Raj thinks elven weapons will make a pretty big deal in the next one, too."

Fear pulsed white-hot in my stomach. I didn't want to live through another war. Ever again. Chances of me surviving one were slim. I gulped and stared up at Declan. "When do you think that might be?"

He shrugged, unaware of my discomfort. "The confidential incidents this year have all been to do with attempts to steal elven weapons. Cheryn's only been successful once, that we're aware of. They stole a shipload of enchanted chains that bind the wearer. Force him or her to do as told."

A shiver ran through me. "And one of the princes of Cheryn is coming here … to meet my sister."

Declan sighed. "Yes. And that's all strange as well. Five brothers. One full djinn. The other four are half. And they're sending the eldest, but the least powerful brother. He supposedly only has super speed in his arsenal of tricks."

"Why are they sending the weakest prince?"

Declan shrugged. "Unsure. Unless they're sending him with a length of elven chain they think makes up for that weakness."

I meet Declan's eyes. "Shite. So, they don't really want an alliance? Quinn's people are going to search each and every one of his bags. No one is to accept anything from them. Nothing. What kind of magical spells work with those chains? Do we know?"

Declan rolled his eyes. "There you go with the drama again. Is this the fire salamander all over again?"

I grabbed Declan by the collar. "I'd rather be insane than have my sister attacked or dragged off like some—"

"Calm down. Cheryn would need to ally with either Rasle or Macedon in order to launch an attack against Sedara. Rasle's queen and Sultan Raj don't get along, so no alliance will happen there. And Macedon's offended that Prince Abbas is coming here to court Avia, an underage princess, when their own princess is of age."

I watched Declan's eyes. The blue was soothing. I slowed my breathing as I held his gaze. "I'm scared for her," I whispered.

His hand reached up and stroked mine. "That's really why you came back?"

I nodded.

He gave a small smile. "I might, possibly, be starting to believe that. We'll look out for her, alright?"

Gratitude and relief swelled in my chest. "Thank you."

I had calmed down. But I didn't move. Declan didn't stop stroking my hand. He didn't break my gaze. My stomach began to buzz with nervous energy as I searched Declan's eyes. I wasn't sure if there was something there. Or I simply wanted something to be there. I took a bracing breath. I leaned forward slightly—

The tutors walked back in. And the moment was broken. Declan let go of my hand and dropped my gaze.

Disappointment blotted my vision when I returned to my seat. The words on the paper didn't make as much sense, nor the tutors' words. It was as though my ears were suddenly full of cotton.

Declan went back to his work. He seemed maddeningly unaffected. He didn't mention that moment again. Not that day. Or the next.

I didn't bring it up, except to relay the information about chains to Quinn and ask him to look into it. But sometimes, I snuck glances at Declan. Wondering, hopeful glances. He'd stopped hating me. Maybe, eventually, I'd convince him I was worth liking. At least a little.

"Princess Bloss?" an annoying tutor (whose name I'd forgotten) dragged me away from staring at Declan.

I returned to my studies.

Tutoring went on. And on. And on for days.

Every night, I was exhausted, because the tutors were told by my mother to give me crisis scenarios to ponder and solve. Every day I killed thousands of imaginary people. It left me wrung out, emotionally and mentally. Declan would hand my limp brain and tired bones off to one of my other husbands for 'wife watch' and go on his merry way.

If there was a formal dinner, I'd be handed off to Connor and his smooth-talking ways. I'd fumble my way through, trying not to offend ridiculously prickly court personalities; Connor would follow in my wake and clean up my messes. My four years outside the palace walls had—unfortunately for Connor—deteriorated my bullshite tolerance levels.

Two elderly noblewomen tittered on about the silk gowns they'd just ordered in from Rasle, our neighbor to the east.

"Actually, I know that the silk from Rasle is often woven out of false materials. Even spelled materials. You can test it by burning a strand. Real silk smells like burnt hair. Quite a few seamstresses have commented on how annoying it can be to think they're working with one material when—"

Connor grabbed my elbow. "Ladies, you look lovely this evening. Those gowns are magnificent. May I steal my bride for a moment? There's a gentleman clamoring for a dance with her."

He led me away. "Bloss—"

"What? Their dresses might have been silk, but—"

"Just compliment them next time."

"I'm awful at queening," I sighed.

Connor's lack of response only confirmed it. "Who am I supposed to dance with?"

"The ambassador from Macedon has a son visiting. He'd like to dance with you."

Connor brought me to a corner of the ballroom where Avia and a handsome young man were making small talk. As we got near, Avia let out a flirty giggle.

I did a double-take and re-evaluated the ambassador's son. He was tall and built. He had to be my age. At least six years older than my sister. Too old for her. Not to mention, mother would never approve of an ambassador's son. Too bad. He was handsome enough. He had wavy brown hair and dimples.

Suddenly, I saw him sweep Avia into a dip and kiss her. Then he swung her over his shoulder, pounded his chest, and ran out of the room.

I blinked.

Everyone was back in place, chatting normally.

Quinn was messing with me again.

Stop. Or I'll trounce you.

You can try.

Quinn's bullshite distracted me when I should have been listening to Connor's introduction. I suddenly found myself dancing with the man and I didn't even know his name.

"Alright, if I admit I was distracted by your dimples, will you tell me your name again?" I smiled.

"Mateo," he grinned.

"Mateo, I saw you talking up my sister over there. She's pretty wonderful, huh?"

He blushed. "Do all monarchs speak this way?"

"I'll probably get a lecture later. But … your impression?"

"She's very sweet."

"She is. She's also very fond of nicknames. When you next speak with her, please call her Squawk."

"Why do I get the feeling I'm being set up?" Mateo grinned.

"Because you are. But I do need to speak with your father soon about Macedon's interests here …"

"Are you blackmailing me into baiting your sister?"

"Maybe."

"Your Highness, I'm honored to be included in your schemes."

"As you should be. Oh dear, my knight's headed over. He'll know by my smirk that I'm up to no good. Quick, pretend I've been boring."

Mateo couldn't wipe the grin off his face. I, however, managed to look perfectly innocent as Connor cut in on our dance.

"What did you tell him?" Connor growled.

"Nothing. We simply discussed Avia."

"You didn't go making promises to consider him as a suitor like you did with Lady Agatha's son Willard, did you?"

"Of course not."

Connor rolled his eyes, made our excuses, and led me to Avia's room for the night. Once we were inside her chamber, he proceeded to ignore me. He went right to his pallet and right to sleep.

Whoever was spellbound to stay beside me was forced to sleep in my sister's new room with me. Her servants had moved her to a temporary room while her chamber was repaired. As far as I could tell, only the trusted servants for the royal wing knew about the change. But I'd grumbled and insisted on sleeping in the room with her. My husbands had not been pleased. Neither had Avia.

But no one had known how to handle me when I'd started screaming at the top of my lungs when they'd tried to drag me off. Insanity ploys have their advantages.

Avia had thrown a pillow at me the first night she'd given in. "You'd better not snore. And no naughty stuff with your husbands either."

She'd eyed Connor, the husband present that first night. Connor had turned his back on us, grabbed a stack of blankets, and made himself a pallet on the floor.

"My husbands would have to like me in order for there to be naughty stuff," I'd sighed as I clambered onto her bed with her.

Avia had grinned, "Oh, they like you. Some of them might even love you. But I think they're even madder than I am."

I'd hardly heard her last sentence. My stomach had dropped at the word love. And anxiety, curiosity, and obsession had sprung up. "Who do you think loves me?" I'd whispered. "What have you heard?"

Her brown eyes had sparkled as she shook her head. "If they aren't telling you, neither am I."

A whole round of tickle torture later, it seemed like my shite sister meant what she'd said. She hadn't squawked— first time in her life.

Connor hadn't joined in our tickle fight. He hadn't even looked up that first night. He'd read a book and then watched the flames in the fireplace before curling up to sleep.

He didn't talk to me whenever it was his night to stay with me. But Ryan and Quinn were both cajoled into playing cards with Avia and I, particularly after I promised to show them all the tricks I'd learned from the dealers at Kylee's gambling house. Those nights became far more pleasant.

I didn't give up hope on Connor. I knew I'd hurt him deeply. And I knew that his magic made him prone to depression. He could read the emotions of others, but then lost sight of his own.

Sometimes, when he slept, I crept out of bed, and stood over him, sending tendrils of peace to caress him. It was something he'd let me do when we were younger, but I knew he'd never accept if he was awake now. After I pulsed him with peace magic and bandaged my wrists, I always climbed into bed and watched him. It made the night full of wistful longing for me, full of memories, of sneaking Connor into my bedroom. Of hide and seek games with Avia that had devolved into hide and kiss sessions for us.

My eyes misted a bit, but as a memory of one particularly handsy kiss came up, Connor morphed into Quinn. And Quinn suddenly shoved the memory of me up against a wall. He dragged my yellow skirts up and slid his hands onto my naked hips.

Naughty girl. Did you not wear any underthings that day?

I had worn underthings that day. I was confused for a moment. Then I realized what was happening. *Get out of my head.*

Why? You were making me wild.

That was private.

No, Dove, what I'm about to do is private. And then the Quinn in my mind slipped to his knees and buried his head under my skirt. He breathed against my mound, placing a hand on either thigh. His tongue darted out and he gave each thigh a long, slow lick.

That's so real, I can almost feel it. I moaned.

Relax, Dove.

How is it so real?

Because half of lovemaking is in your mind anyway. Now, do you want to argue? Or do you want me to give you your first mental melt?

Yes. Please.

Quinn chuckled under my skirt but moved his face closer. I could feel his lips caress my slit. Back and forth, side to side, he barely touched me. But each touch sent a shiver of pleasure up my spine. Anticipation made me grow slick. And then he licked his lips and kissed my clit.

The torture was so good. But I couldn't take it. My real body was throbbing. My real hand slid down under the covers and pulled up my chemise.

Now, now. No cheating. This is my melt. You're giving yourself to me.

How did you know what I was doing?

You practically shout your thoughts, Dove. All the time. Now are you going to be a good girl and put your hand back up? Or should I stop?

No. No don't stop.

Then put your hands up by your head. And leave them there.

In my imagination, my hands were on a brick wall and I struggled to maintain my balance as Quinn's quick tongue went to work, lapping at my sex. In reality, my hands clutched the pillow and my feet curled. My hips lifted off the bed.

Quinn sucked my clit into his mouth and tugged on it, turning his head side to side gently. The suction made sparks shoot through me, and the extra tug turned those sparks into lightning.

"Ahh!" I screamed my release.

A hand touched my arm and shook me. "Bloss! Bloss! Are you okay?"

My eyes popped open. Connor's dark curls loomed over me. His expression was terrified.

My jaw dropped. I'd screamed out loud. In real life. Sard.

"I—I was dreaming."

Creaming.

"Dreaming." I was scarlet. Maybe even purple. I could not make eye contact with Connor. Not at all. "Sorry I woke you."

"It's alright. You're okay?" Concern colored his voice.

I nodded, biting my lip. Of all the times for Connor to worry about me. "I'm fine. Just a dream. Really."

Connor drifted back to his pallet.

I turned onto my side and punched my pillow.

I will get you back. For this and that other morning when I looked like an idiot.

I would think that tonight completely makes up for the other day.

Connor caught me.

That's not my fault.

I turned over on my side, grumbling internally. Quinn was right, of course. Connor catching me was entirely my fault. Didn't matter. I was still going to get him back.

I started to think of ways to get revenge that wouldn't give Quinn advance notice. I wasn't sure there was one. I yawned and my scheming faded. Quinn's magical mental prowess had done its job. I drifted to sleep in post-orgasmic bliss.

༄

The next morning, Connor handed me off to Declan and almost immediately, I asked him if we could go find Ryan.

Declan looked a bit bewildered by my request, perhaps because I asked while he was still finishing his morning coffee in his room. I gave him a winning smile. I wasn't sure that made any difference, but I knew I needed to start the day on a good note.

He made me sit and wait while he finished his drink, and combed his blond hair, and changed his vest.

While I waited, I told him all about Willard. And also about the spells. Declan was pleased to find out we now had a ten-foot radius. This made trips to the loo much less embarrassing for all of us. He was not as pleased to find out my mother had put a spell on him to make him inclined to forgive me.

I hoped my honesty counted for something. That I laid everything out on the table and said Wyle was unraveling the spells for us.

Finally, he was ready to take me to the practice yard. We found Ryan running drills with his men. They held staffs and swords and were running, thrusting, sweating, and overall looking very, very sexy. I had to peel my eyes away from the deliciousness. I think my orgasm last night had amped up my sexual awareness.

Ryan smirked at me. "Like what you see?"

"I'd like it better if you were out there shirtless."

That made his grin wider.

I sighed. "But they'll do. I'm with Declan this morning. I wanted to see if you wanted to help me out with that little project I mentioned to you."

Declan looked alarmed. He held up his hands a took a step back "Project? What project? You didn't say there was a project. I thought this was a handoff. I have work. If you want a solution for Willard—"

I clamped a hand over Declan's mouth. "That's confidential. And don't worry. We're just going to play with your powers."

Once Declan was calm, Ryan nodded to me. "I can help. Just let me go tell my captain."

Ryan sprinted off, zigzagging through the lunging, grunting, and groaning men.

You're randy this morning, Dove. Need me to do something about that?

Can you hear me from across the country?

With that bead, yes. How do you think I built my spy network to be so efficient?

I shoved down how impressed I was by that. *Leave me alone. I need to focus.*

Quinn sent me an image of a duck trying to mount another duck and continually falling off.

I burst out laughing. "Stop it."

"I'm not doing anything," Declan stared at me and shook his head.

"Not you. Quinn is in my head. Sending duck sex thoughts."

"Oh. Yeah, he can be a shite."

"Do you have a bead, too?"

"Yep. We all do. Just in case he's out and needs a contact back here."

Ryan ran back toward us. This time he didn't have a shirt.

I openly stared at his pecs, ogled his six pack, and let my eyes gaze at his happy trail.

"Did you lose your shirt between your captain and here?" Declan rolled his eyes.

"Nope. Quinn said Bloss was feeling naughty."

"Argh. Quinn, I'm killing you." I covered my face with my hands.

The mental image of Quinn running around me, waving a shirt and whooping like a wild man, appeared.

"What's he sending you?" Ryan leaned close and trailed my hand down his chest.

Oh Lord. I was about to combust from mental dissonance —the ridiculous mental pictures and the roaring lust. "What the sard am I supposed to do when you all gang up on me?"

"Just a little payback, Dearling," Ryan whispered, dragging my fingers up to his lips and kissing them one by one. He sucked my pinkie into his mouth just as Quinn sent me an image of a firework exploding.

I nearly exploded myself. I turned to Declan and grabbed his vest by the lapels. "Save me, please."

His eyes popped, and he reached up to pull my arms off of him. "Even if I wanted to help you, which—to be clear—I don't, what am I supposed to do?"

"Dump water on him, like you did the other day—"

"That will just make his abs glisten in the sunlight," Declan couldn't help the shite-eating grin that popped up on his face.

"Mercy!" I cried. "Give me mercy."

Declan took my arm out of pity and I led him out of the practice yard, glad to escape.

"Where are we going?" he asked.

"The stables," I replied. "We're going out for the day."

He nodded, and we walked in silence for a bit. Then Declan surprised me by saying, "Quinn sent us all an update on what happened last night."

My body heated up, like I was on a spit, over a fire. No.

"Yes, tonight, when it's my watch, I can't wait to see what you'll dream about," Ryan murmured.

I couldn't cover my face with my hands; a group of noblemen walked by just then, on their way to the practice arena. I had to fake a smile and a nod and maintain my composure.

Part of me felt like laughing. But the other part of me felt like crying. Because this either meant that my husbands were on their way to forgiving me, that they were joking with me and including me. Or it meant they truly and completely hated me and were determined to torture me. I wasn't sure which it was.

CHAPTER FIFTEEN

e reached the stables, which housed not only horses, but pegasi, bulls, donkeys, and two ancient horned gargoyles. Noble and servant children alike skittered in and out of the doors of the stable. It was a popular place to visit.

The beast master, Jace, was a grim, dark man with a jagged scar across his chin. He strode out the stable doors to greet us, a bag of apples in hand. He must have been feeding the horses.

He grunted at me. That was as much of a greeting as he ever gave.

Behind him, I saw three servant children pointing and making faces. Jace was both revered for his abilities with animals and feared for the scar on his face. He also had an uncanny sense of his surroundings. Without turning from us, he threw an apple backward, smacking one of the kids in the chest.

"Off with you!" he groused. The children scattered like mice.

"Morning, Jace. May we have three horses please?"

"How long a ride?"

"We'll be heading to Terra."

He nodded, gave a perfunctory bow, and disappeared into the stables. I heard another thunk of what could only have been an apple hitting wood.

"Get outta here, you mangy curs!" Jace bellowed.

Another group of giggling kids ran past us, one of them munching on a slightly bruised apple. I wondered then, if the apples really were for the horses or if Jace kept the treats for the children. The old hard-ass would never admit to it but … I bit my lip and resolved to send him a barrel of apples.

I laughed as the children ran down to the paddock and climbed the fence to watch the gargoyles stretch and run; I was as excited for my adventure today as they were for theirs. What I had planned was so much better than being stuck with tutors yet again.

"What exactly are we doing? Declan asked. "Terra's at least an hour away."

I shrugged. "Each fall, the farmers near Terra go into the hills and pick berries. Today is the first day of picking. I thought it would be a good opportunity for you to test your magic because it requires precision. And because you couldn't possibly drown anyone in the process."

"You did not almost drown!" Declan protested.

Meanwhile, Ryan grumbled. "I thought we would do something exciting. I thought we'd have him divide knives in half or something to help fend off an attack."

I rolled my eyes. "I'm pretty sure you think farming is exciting when food's brought to the table every night."

Declan laughed, "She's got you pinned, Ry!"

Ryan smacked Declan on the back. "Shut it." He turned to me, "What am I here for?"

"Isn't your family from Terra? I thought you might like the chance to see them."

Ryan groaned. "This is all a ploy to meet my family?" He pointed a finger. "You're going to try to get my mother to guilt me back into liking you, aren't you?"

"You liked me at some point to begin with?"

He bit his lip. "I didn't say that."

"Dec, Ryan liked me!" I threw out my arms and spun around. "Oh. Nope. You did not just see that. That was not queenly at all. Do not tell my mother."

Declan shook his head. "What's gotten into you?"

"Castle fever. I haven't been stuck inside this long in forever."

Declan cocked his head. "Ah. The real reason for this trip is revealed. It's selfish."

"No. I'm a political savant. This is a triple win situation. We all get something we want."

Declan looked at Ryan, "Did I say I wanted to practice my powers?"

Ryan raised his hand. "How am I getting something I want?"

I narrowed my eyes at him. "Ryan Hale, I've heard you rave about your mother's berry pies since you were in the lower guard. So, stop pretending you aren't aching to see her."

"Fine. I could eat."

I laughed.

Ryan shook his head. "I need to go grab a few guards."

"Guards? Why?"

"Because a crown princess doesn't travel unescorted. Unless she's planning to try to escape."

Both men stared me down. "I'm not trying to escape. Really," I sighed. "Fine. Get the guards."

As Ryan sauntered off to request more guards and horses, I turned to Declan. "This will be fun, don't you think?"

Declan bit his lip and shook his head. "Did you really think this through? Do you really think the people of Terra want to see the invader knight?"

"Invader?"

"Foreigner, then?"

My blood boiled. "Who called you that?"

He snorted. "It gets whispered nearly every day. Surprised you haven't heard it since you came back."

I raised a brow. "Well, it seems I have some work to do on the nobles then. But, let me assure you, the people of Evaness don't feel the same."

"What?" Declan's blue eyes flickered to mine, confused.

I smiled at him. "You'll see."

Just then a page approached with a message for me. I stepped away from Declan to read the letter, and then bent and whispered instructions to the boy. He scampered off with a grin. And I couldn't keep a wide smile off my face.

"Good news?" Declan asked.

"We'll see."

Ryan arrived shortly after that and we set off on a winding trail to the northwest. We let the guard spread out around us, so that we had some semblance of privacy.

"Quinn's pouting that you didn't invite him," Ryan gave me a sideways grin.

I rolled my eyes. "Please, he's probably already snuck down there. Besides, he got 'alone time' with me last night."

Ryan belted out a laugh and Declan shook his head.

I turned to look at Declan as we cantered along. "Have you thought of any possibilities regarding that request I told you about?" I didn't want to use Willard's name in front of the guards. Just in case.

Declan shook his head. "Duke Aiden's about to arrive. Your mother's having me research Abbas and his father's holdings before his arrival. She wants to make certain Sultan Raj isn't hiding anything."

I grimaced. "I hope you find something."

"No, you don't."

I sighed. "I don't want her to go."

Ryan clucked at his horse and then turned to join the conversation. "She'll have to leave at some point, Bloss. There isn't a crown here for her. And it's not like princesses abound, she's one of what—three eligible in the next decade? There will be a lot of suitors visiting. Hell, she might even start a war."

The war comment prodded at me and I blurted out without thinking. "I would rather have trusted you all to take care of her."

Declan stopped his horse. Ryan pulled his horse up beside mine and grabs my reigns. "What's that mean?"

I stared at Ryan's deep brown eyes and worded my statement very carefully. "It means my mother went to an awful lot of trouble to ensure she had two female heirs."

"Why?"

The geas wouldn't let me answer.

Luckily, Declan stepped in. He wrangled his horse clumsily until it was next to mine and Ryan's. He waved the guards near us on and waited until they were out of earshot.

Declan grabbed my hand. "She thought she'd need the spare." His eyes searched mine. I couldn't respond, couldn't confirm or deny. I simply squeezed his fingers as tight as I could. It was the best I could do to let him know he was on the right track.

"Is this the riddle, Bloss?" Declan whispered.

I squeezed his hand again.

"Can you squeeze my hand once for yes, twice for no?"

As soon as he asked that, the geas locked my limbs. I couldn't move. Shite.

"What's wrong with her?" Ryan reached over and pulled me off my horse, onto his lap. He pulled my stiff limbs into his warm, hard chest and rubbed my back, then gently tried to uncurl my frozen fingers.

Declan held the reigns to my mount, keeping her steady. He looked at me and then met Ryan's worried gaze. "I think she's under a spell. And I don't think she can say what kind."

*T*he rest of the ride was somber as Ryan and Declan fell back and held a whispered conversation. They refused to let me be part of it.

"You just lock up. You'll end up falling off your horse," Declan shushed me and sent me up to the front.

Ryan made several guards ride near me and make small talk. I'm certain it was as uncomfortable for them as it was for me.

I cursed myself for saying anything. My mother had given my husbands an out with the dragon hunting cover story. If something happened to me, nothing had to happen to them. But what if I died publicly? And dragons couldn't be blamed? Or what if the people waited a decade for me to return from dragon hunting, but grew impatient? What if they rebelled? A million other negative scenarios flooded my head. The last thing in the world I wanted was for my knights to have to follow me into death.

Maybe I should just divorce my husbands, renounce the crown publicly, and then hand them all over to Avia. But Connor's smile flashed through my mind. Ryan's dark eyes as he said dirty things. Declan's thoughtful gaze. And Quinn, on his knees, gripping my ankles, begging me not to go. The last image startled me. It wasn't what I'd expected.

Are you in my head?

No one answered.

I shook my myself out of my reverie and smiled at one of the younger guards. Shite. I was getting paranoid. Sard that. Today was supposed to be about Declan. Not me or my problems.

"Who wants to race to the first farmhouse?" I called out. I spurred my mare to a gallop before anyone else could respond.

By the time we reached the farmhouse, all serious and somber thoughts were gone. At least from my mind. The guards, Ryan, and Declan seemed to have scolding thoughts on their minds.

I laughed as I dismounted on my own.

"Let's go talk to Terri, the local burgmaster."

Ryan stomped next to me, still in a bit of a pout. His horse had lost, by a lot. Of course, it had a lot of extra weight to carry. "You know Terri?"

I grinned. "Spent a whole summer in his corn field."

"That better not be a metaphor," Declan added wryly as he joined us.

"It's not." I scrambled ahead to shake Terri's age spotted hand. He didn't recognize me, of course. I'd been a tall blonde woman when I'd helped him. Not the petite princess his filmy eyes looked at now. He was a bit startled when he heard my plan, but quickly agreed.

We waited in the village square as everyone from town gathered with baskets and curious faces. Terri looked proud when he announced that Ryan and his wife would be joining them for the day. He forgot to mention Declan. I wasn't sure if it was on purpose or not. Terri was on in years.

The village reaction was mixed. Some people came up to greet us, others stood back and whispered behind their hands.

"It's because I'm here," Declan muttered to me.

"Bull. It's because half the women in the village are secretly wondering if they can smother me in order to get their hands on you."

He chuckled. "And what would they do if they caught me?"

I shrugged. "All the wrong stuff. They wouldn't know they need to hold you down and spank you before they rode you hard."

He laughed and held out his elbow to escort me up the road, but his eyes were alight. Perhaps even on fire. "Is that what you would do?"

I tilted my head close so I could whisper up at him. "If you're a good boy and control your magic today, that's what I *will* do."

Declan's eyes dilated as he looked down at me. "Challenge accepted."

My heart swelled. Nerdy sweet little Declan was stepping up and teasing me back. I didn't want to jinx the possibilities by thinking about more. I'd just bask in this … whatever it was. I winked and patted his hand. I gestured up the rocky hill we'd followed the villagers to and he looked at the hundreds of thorny blackberries lining the hill. "Have at it, love. I want you to reduce the thorns and multiply the berries. One berry at a time."

He groaned.

Ryan, who'd been visiting with locals and friends he'd grown up with, bounded over. "Are we ready to start?"

"Declan's thrilled," I said. "Want a first row seat with me?"

Ryan shook his head. "Sorry, promised I'd help my mother—" he hurried off.

"Aren't you going to introduce—"

But Ryan was gone.

I bit back my disappointment. Of course, he wasn't going to introduce you, idiot, I told myself. No expectations. I left him. Still, it hurt.

Declan helped me climb a bit of ridge and we selected a bush. I sat beside it, facing him. I tried to wash away all thoughts of Ryan and focus on my sweet, blond scholar, who was already shivering in the brisk fall air. "Alright, have at it."

"That's it? You would have made an excellent tutor."

"Try to send a small burst. To reduce a single branch of thorns and produce berries there instead."

Declan shook his head but held out his hand. A yellow glow built around his fingertips. And then it zinged toward the bush.

BAM!

The bush exploded in berry juice, splattering both of us with purple liquid.

I wiped my eyes. "Well, that's one way to do it." I tried to clean my face with my skirt, but the stain was everywhere.

"Sard!" Declan shook the gooey mess off his hands. "We need to change."

"Why bother? You might just do it again."

He stared daggers at me.

I simply pointed to the next bush. "Try again, sir."

"Can you really control your power that precisely?" he challenged.

I stood. I straightened my sleeves, making sure my wrists were covered. I grabbed his hand. I met his eyes, trying not to get lost in their blue depths. I took a deep breath to center myself. Then I sent a tiny pulse of peace through his fingertips, up his arm, and across his chest. I spiraled peace down his torso like a snake. And when it reached his dick, I made the power pulse. Again. And again. Driving home the point.

Declan's eyes widened. His breath caught. His back arched a bit like he was in pain. He gave an involuntary little moan. "Wha—what?" Declan looked down in alarm. "You can do that?"

"It's just concentration."

"It's not. You made me—" He shut his mouth and widened his eyes for emphasis.

It took me a second. I glanced down at his trousers. There might have been a damp patch underneath the berry juice. "Declan, did you …?" I grinned. "I've never had that effect before." I mentally filed that away. It might come in handy the next time I saw Quinn.

Declan groaned. "Now, we really have to go clean up."

"No."

"But people will see—"

"They'll see your purple-stained pants. Move to the next bush. Try again. Tiny pulses. Like ants."

"But—"

"Do it, Declan. Or I'll pulse you with peace again until you scream my name and make everyone turn and stare."

He went to the next bush. And a third. And a fourth. But on his fifth bush, he turned every thorn to berries. After he realized what he'd done, he turned to me in shock.

"I … I did it."

I squealed. But we were on a steep ridge full of rocks. So, I couldn't hug or jump or do much more than wildly clap my hands.

After Declan changed bushes six and seven, I let out a loud farm-girl whistle. Nearly every head on the hill turned toward me. "Can everyone step back from your bushes please? Two feet ought to do! And then our amazing Knight, Declan Hale, will transform all the thorns into more berries!"

I got a lot of strange and questioning looks, but the title of crown princess came in handy for eclectic requests.

Declan just stared at me, aghast. "I've done three bushes. Three! And now you want to ask me to do this in front of everyone!"

"Declan, you already know how to do it on a huge scale. It's easy. Just let your power rip."

He did. For a moment, the bright yellow pulse made it feel like a midsummer afternoon. And when the pulse faded, the bushes were so loaded with berries that the branches sagged to the ground.

A laugh and a cheer went up through the crowd.

I used my booming voice once more. "Let's declare this Declan Day! A half-holiday!"

A cheer went up around us.

"To the genius of Evaness! Who can trade thorns for berries and turn weeds to wheat!" I shouted.

The little group around us all shouted, "The genius of Evaness!"

Declan turned an adorable shade of pink. I think the tips of his ears might even have turned full red. Or it could have been the berry juice. "I … it was nothing."

"I'm having beer and food delivered to the town square. Meet us down there!" I screeched to the people.

A roar went up. And it was smiles and hugs all around.

"I really didn't do anything … like you said, the big part is easy."

I stood on my tiptoes and bopped his nose. "No getting out of it. The palace is throwing these people a party. And they deserve a little rest. So shut your trap." I turned back to the crowd. "Declan deserves a party. Am I right?"

"Right!"

"Three cheers for Declan!"

The crowd clapped and wolf-whistled. Two men came and grabbed Declan, despite his sticky state. They lifted his protesting form onto their shoulders and awkwardly ran him to the base of the hill.

Ryan strolled over to me, from where he'd been picking berries with his mother.

"You brought us to my hometown to make him a hero?" Ryan shook his head.

I just smiled at him. "You're already a hometown hero and you know it. Besides, I can see it in your face. You like seeing him happy."

Ryan shrugged, watching the villagers pass Declan around.

"Fine, don't admit it. But you do."

"You know he gets motion sick, right?" Ryan asked.

"Nope. No idea."

"Can't ride a pegasus to save his life. Nearly died on that horse on the way here. Part of why we hung back so much. When he first took the ship over from Sedara, he—"

"Well, he'd better hold it in now. I don't want Declan Day ruined."

Ryan laughed and trotted off after the crowd. "I'd better go get him down."

I got to work.

After a quick rinse at the burgmasters, where Ryan kindly brought Declan and I some clothes from his family, I went out to the square to coordinate the celebration.

As planned, the page from this morning and a group of kitchen servants arrived in a wagon weighed down by kegs of beer, wine, suckling pig, and wheels of cheese. The smell of fresh bread also wafted toward me. "Wonderful. Would you all please set it up in the clearing right there? Picnic style," I gestured to a field of clover that was dulled from the chill of fall. "Once you're done with set up, you're welcome to stay and celebrate, of course."

A few of them raised their eyebrows, but they all got to work. And not a single one left after set up was done.

Four hours and quite a few kegs later, Ryan and I sat on the ground and watched the villagers dance around a bonfire. One old man played a fiddle, and many clapped their hands. The children giggled and wove in and out of the adults, playing crack the whip.

Declan plopped down beside us. "Thish is great."

"Yesh it ish," I couldn't help but tease him. "I don't think I've ever seen you drunk before."

"I don't think I've ever been drunk before," he responded.

"About time then," I patted his arm.

He grabbed my hand. "Thank you Bloshie. You're good at spreading Peach. Piss. Peash. I can' talk."

"That would be the alcohol." I tried not to laugh.

He pointed at the smiling people. "You did thish. Made them happy."

I turned so our knees touched and waited while his eyes struggled to focus on mine. "No, this is Declan Day. You did this. You do this. Every day. I know it can be hard to see, when you're up there in the castle running the numbers. Calculating the boring-ass stuff you do. But, Dec, you help these people when times are hard. You keep their children's bellies full. When they've lost hope, they look to you. Do you know how many people I've seen cry … tears of joy … because you saved them? Your power is amazing. But the way you use it ... thank you. Thank you for being selfless." My eyes smiled in gratitude, and I stroked his cheek.

He smiled and leaned into my hand. And for a second, he looked completely lost in bliss.

Then his eyes popped open. "I think I'm gonna be shick."

And he was.

CHAPTER SIXTEEN

*D*eclan lay with his head on the floor. His legs were tucked under him and his butt stuck in the air like a toddler. Next to him was a chamber pot. Ryan had already emptied it two times.

We were in Ryan's old home. A farmhouse, down the road from the town square. Ryan's parents had given us the master bedroom, insistent we use it to care for Declan. Then they'd gone back to the celebration.

I ran a wet washcloth over Declan's forehead one last time. But, when he emitted a snore, I gave up the task and stood.

I sighed. "Well, I didn't quite expect that." I shook my head at Declan and turned to Ryan. "If you want to go back out with your family, visit with your mother and fathers some more, I'm fine here. I can keep an eye on him." I gestured at my silly, snoring husband.

Ryan didn't respond, and I looked up. When I did, I saw a bit of hesitancy in his eyes.

"Um …" he glanced toward the door. Then back to me.

He didn't want to leave me. But he didn't want to take me. Sard.

My tongue tripped over itself. "You don't need to feel obligated to stay with me. This is your town. Your friends. I promise, I didn't bring us here to make things awkward for you. And you don't have to lead me around or anything. I'm fine. I'll just stay here. Perfect excuse, right?" I didn't know what to do with myself. I put the rag in a basin. I grabbed a blanket out of a chest and unfolded it. I laid it over Declan's back.

Ryan didn't speak.

So my mouth continued to ramble. "Poor Dec. I just wanted … he was so hurt this morning. Did you know people at court call him the invader knight? I just wanted him to know—never mind. Please tell your mother thank you for the dress. And your dad or brother or whoever's clothes Dec has on. We'll wash and return them. I'm pretty sure ours are ruined."

"Bloss …"

I rubbed Declan's back again, feeling nervous and jittery. Why was I feeling nervous? What was wrong with me? I was acting like a school girl. A stupid one. Ryan was going to leave and have fun with his family and friends. And that was fine.

He was going without me. It was what I deserved. Which made me think … I hadn't told him yet. I suddenly realized why my hands felt clammy and my throat kept constricting.

"Before you go … this morning, Wyle sent a page to me with a message. He let me know that the spell regarding … your release … has been undone. I have the note," my hands fumbled with my dress. It took me a second. "Oh, right. Not my dress. Here. I'll get it, so you can see it." My heart thundered in my chest as I stood back up and ruffled through my ruined dress to find that slip of parchment. It was soaked, but luckily still readable.

"What release?"

"The um … the spell where you can only find physical release with … me." I stared at the floorboards, cheeks burning.

I'm a sarding idiot, I thought. I could talk dirty to all of them. I could tease them endlessly. Why the hell was this making me so uncomfortable?

Ryan reached out and grabbed my hand. "Really?"

I nodded. "Yes." I made myself take a deep breath and look at his eyes. I handed him the slip.

He stared down at the words for a long time. When he looked up, his face was stone. I didn't know what that meant. Shouldn't he be happy?

For the last two weeks, there'd been lots of innuendo and naughty exchanges. But he'd never made a move to kiss me. Touch me, yes. All the time. But that was just his pent-up frustration, right? It wasn't me. Tonight, he'd prove that. Tonight, he was free. My stomach lurched at the thought and I closed my eyes.

"No. Look at me."

I opened my eyes and peered up at Ryan's face, once again trying to read him. But his face had grown harsh, determined. The angled planes were even more obvious in the candlelight, the rough cut of his jaw lined in a day's stubble. His thick lips were closed, and I couldn't tell if his expression was angry or not. My nerves doubled. Did he take it as an insult? A rejection of him? "I thought it was the fair thing to do. I don't want you to feel obligated—"

Ryan reached for me, grabbed me at the waist and pulled me flush against his body. His lips skimmed my ear. My pulse turned to thunder.

He stopped. He let go and pushed me roughly back.

"Obligated to what?"

"You don't have to be with me. I won't make you. You should be free to love whomever you want."

"And you?"

I turned to him, hesitantly. I forced myself to meet his eyes. "I'd never have agreed to the marriage contract if I didn't want you." My eyes flickered down to the floor. Shite! I was coming across as skittish. As if I were still the young girl that ran away from him all those years ago. Why did he have this effect on me?

Ryan dipped his hand under my chin and raised my face. He waited until I looked into his eyes. His deep brown, burning eyes.

"I can't do anything with you while you're wearing my mother's dress. You smell like her."

My mouth dropped open. That was the absolute last thing I expected him to say.

"Take it off."

I stared into his eyes and slowly realized Ryan had slipped into his dominant persona. He hadn't headed out the door to find the first girl he could. He'd stayed. The desire I saw in his eyes squashed my insecurities. My nerves melted into elation. My body throbbed as I got to say the words I'd teased him with for a fortnight. Words that now made my lady bits pulse with desire.

"Yes … sir."

I reached up to undo the string that tied the bodice of the dress closed. I untied it and pulled it over my head. I grabbed the ruffled, white one-piece gown underneath and slowly edged it upward, giving him time to trace the lines of my body with his eyes. I tossed it aside, and it landed half on Declan's face. He didn't notice.

"Turn around."

I turned, slowly. In a full circle. When I returned to face him, Ryan's eyes locked on my mound. It made my heart patter faster and faster in my chest. I wanted so badly to run to him. To rip his clothes off and expose him as well.

But Ryan radiated dominance. He wanted me, I could feel it. I could see his desire bulging. But he was going to make me work to get it.

Since we were playing this game, I decided I should up the ante. Perhaps I could make him as desperate as I felt. As delirious with desire as I was.

"The girls in the bawd houses … they turn a bit different-ly," I whispered.

Ryan's eyes jerked up to mine. "Show me," he growled.

I grabbed a wooden chair from the corner and dragged it over to him. I sat down on it, facing him. I waited until his gazed drifted to my face before giving him as naughty a smile as I could manage. Then I slowly spread my legs as wide as they could go. I could feel my nether lips part; I was so wet, I was certain he could see the gloss coating them.

Ryan licked his lips. His breathing grew ragged.

Seeing him, sensing he was close, that soon he might just grab me and slam me into the wall and give us both what we wanted, I pushed further.

Slowly I dragged my right leg skyward, until it was straight up in the air. I pointed my toes. I let him watch me in an open split for a moment, wishing he'd step forward and just take me right there in the chair. I shook with lust.

I swung my right leg over to the left side of the chair until my foot made contact with the floor. I stood and twisted to face the chair. I bent forward over the chair back to give him a good view of my ass—

Smack!

Ryan spanked me. Not too hard. But not gently, either. I sucked in a breath.

Sard! The spank nearly made me come undone. I panted, roughly, waiting for him to grab me, or to hear his pants hit the floor.

Neither happened.

"Get on your knees. And stay there. Wait for me."

I sunk to my knees next to the chair. My entire body was strung so tight, I felt I might snap. I felt like one more word from him would make me shatter into a thousand pieces in an endless, mindless orgasm. But he was going to make me wait. Dominant asshole.

My nipples puckered in the cold. In anticipation. I heard the door to the bedroom open behind me. It swung shut. I heard footsteps fade. Then I couldn't hear anymore.

I waited.

I waited.

I waited until pinpricks grew in my legs and I had no choice but to move them. I waited until the goosebumps turned into shivers. I waited until I realized ... Ryan wasn't coming back.

That's when I curled into a ball and cried.

✿

a hand on the nape of my neck pulled me out of my tear-induced stupor.

I turned, wiping my wet face on my arm.

Come here, Dove.

Quinn pulled me onto his lap. He stroked my back gently. Stroked my arms.

What are you doing here?

I heard you crying.

But—how?

Hopped on a pegasus.

I nodded and snuggled further into his chest. He rocked me back and forth.

He left me. I know I deserve it. But he left—

I'm here, Dove. I'm not going to leave you. Quinn chafed warmth back into my hands. He gave me gentle, chaste kisses all along my forehead and cheeks. *Shh. Shh. It's alright.*

Is this what it felt like? I'm a monster. I swear, I didn't—

Dove, you didn't leave us naked in the middle of the room.

But, Connor—

Will come around. Hush.

He rocked me. Then stopped. *Look, Dove.*

He pointed toward the bed. From under it, out hopped a bunny. Then a deer seemed to stand from behind the bed. Birds fluttered down from the flower-patterned canopy.

What? How?

The animals came closer. The bunny snuggled his head under my hand. I swear, I could feel him—the soft feathery texture of his grey fur on my fingertips.

I turned to Quinn. *You're making me hallucinate again?*

Hallucinate. I would call it more 'an enchanted state.' Sounds better.

I rolled my eyes.

What? I thought princesses loved woodland creatures. No? Would you prefer—the creatures disappeared. Instead, they were replaced by flaming salamanders running up and down the walls.

You shite! I gave a broken laugh and leaned into Quinn. I pressed my nose against him.

Too much? he asked.

No. You're perfect. And then I closed the tiny gap between us. And I kissed him. In real life. I ignored the fact that I'd been naked for another man, that tear tracks still streaked my face, that my eyes were probably puffy and swollen. All I thought about was how much I was falling for Quinn.

The kiss was sweet and pure. And it seemed to wash away the insecurities I'd just felt.

I pressed my tongue toward his lips and he parted them. I leaned further into him, pressing my body against his, taking his black hair in my hands. One of my hands slid along his pointed elf ear and he shuddered.

Like that?

Love it.

I stroked the edge of his ear again as our tongues danced and his fingers wandered down my spine to grab my ass. He pulled me even tighter against him.

Just then, the bedroom door swung open and Ryan entered with a carafe of wine and two glasses in his hands. "I hope you're ready for—what the hell?"

Quinn and I broke apart. I tried to climb out of his lap, but he wouldn't let me. He held onto my hips. He let me turn enough that I could see Ryan, who had stopped in the doorway and was glaring down at us.

Quinn stood, dragging me behind him. I tried to wipe the tears off my face, but I was sure it was still blotchy.

I wasn't sure what Quinn thought at Ryan, but Ryan exploded.

"What the sard are you talking about? This was my night. We'd agreed. I just went out for a second to get some goddamned wine so I didn't shoot my load in two seconds!"

Quinn must have said something then.

"—I wouldn't do that!" Ryan leaned around Quinn, making eye contact with me. "I didn't leave you here to teach you a lesson, Blossie," he whispered gently. "The burgmaster wanted a word, and then one of my fathers, and my uncle—"

My face flushed. Shite. I was so stupid. What an idiot. Of course. His family rarely saw him. And it was a party out there. Of course. "I'm sorry," I whispered. "I thought—"

"I know." Ryan set the wine and glasses down on the dresser with the basin and rag. "Come here." He held his arms out for me.

I walked around Quinn toward Ryan. The tears started up without my permission. "I would have deserved it, if you had left," I said, as he wrapped me up in his arms.

"No, you wouldn't have," Ryan grunted. "You didn't leave out of spite or anger. You left because of whatever stupid spell is on you." He crushed me into a hug.

"I did," I muttered into his neck. "I really did."

Ryan latched onto the back of my thighs and lifted my legs so that they surrounded his waist. He hugged me closer, kissing the top of my head. "Little Dearling. I'm not gonna hurt you. Okay? I won't ever hurt you."

My tears turned to sobs. I couldn't help it. I ugly-cried as he held me.

When I opened my eyes to wipe them for what must have been the fifth time, I saw two little raccoons perched on the ground on their hind legs, staring at me. As soon as they realized I was looking, one of them started doing somersaults. The other held out its hands, like it wanted to hug me.

I choked. "Dammit Quinn!"

"What's he doing now?" Ryan growled, hugging me tighter.

"Making me laugh."

One of the raccoons ran to Ryan's foot and started pulling on his pant leg, as if he were trying to drag the half-giant away.

I swiped my arm across my face one last time. "Alright. I'm done crying. Okay?"

The raccoon who'd been somersaulting stopped and ran back to me, chattering happily.

I tapped Ryan on the shoulder. "You can put me down now."

"What if I don't want to?"

I rubbed his shoulder, sliding his shirt aside, the sculpted muscle gliding beneath my palm. "I need a drink." I did. My throat was scratchy.

Ryan sighed. "Fine. But don't judge me for the hard on."

"I won't if you don't look at my ruined face."

"Deal."

He let me slide down slowly. His erection was incredibly evident. Almost intimidating. Half-giant meant half-giant everywhere.

"You like crying?" I hoped not. That was a little too much kink for me.

"No. I haven't had a naked woman pressed up against me in six years, Bloss."

"Got it," I nodded.

Quinn handed me a glass of wine, which I drained as if it were whiskey. "Oh, I needed that."

"Now, that, I liked," Ryan said as I handed the glass back to Quinn. "A princess who can drink like a sailor."

"And curse like one too," I gave a wink, but my eyelashes were still crusted together from the tears, so I don't think it looked sassy as I'd intended.

Quinn handed me a refilled glass. Then he handed one to Ryan. He picked up the carafe and held it in his own hand.

"Now what?" I asked.

Now we drink. And see if we can convince you to take us both on at once.

Quinn must have muttered the same in Ryan's head, because Ryan lifted his glass with a, "Hell, yes!" He downed it in one.

I smiled and shook my head but downed the second glass of wine at their urging. A minute later, the alcohol hit. "So, question. Four years together. No other women. You guys ever help each other out?" I looked from one to the other. The idea was kind of hot.

"She's officially drunk," Ryan grinned.

I looked at Quinn's grey eyes. "Come on. You didn't ever send them dirty images like you sent me?"

I don't kiss and tell, Dove, he winked.

"Bullshite! You told them everything you'd done to me."

Ah, well. Now, everyone benefits from that.

Across the room, a wavering voice said, "Everyone would benefit knowing they can come from just your magic, Peace."

I turned. Declan was peering at us with bleary eyes. "Are you naked, wife?" he asked, squinting.

"Yes."

"Sard it. Get over here so I can see."

I laughed and walked over. When I bent to check on him, Ryan groaned.

"That ass!"

"Get over here and spank it, why don't you?" I winked back at him.

At that, they all moaned.

I rolled my eyes and leaned forward to feel Declan's fore-head. "Are you feeling okay? Need anything?"

"Yes. Come closer," Declan breathed.

I leaned down. And that's when Declan's arms scooped me up. His hands wrapped around my back and he rolled me so I was flat on the floor. He mounted me and pinned me down. Then he slid down my body until he laid spread out across my lower body, his head resting on one of my thighs. He locked his arms around one of my legs, his legs around the other. "Now, don't move," he ordered.

"What are you doing?" I asked.

"I'm a human chase titty ... a human chassity ... you know what I mean—belt."

Declan swallowed, and made a huge effort to speak slowly and clearly. His eyes bugged out as he said, "No way I'm gonna let these sarding beardsplitters in there when I can't. Ughh ... my stomach did not like that move."

"Declan!" Shock and awe rocked me to the core. Sweet Declan had gone insane. And dirty. Was he into the group thing? I didn't even know if I was into the group thing.

"Sard off, Dec!" Ryan came over and gave him a tap with his foot.

"No," Declan snuggled in stronger. "She can get you off with her power like she did me. That's it. Then, we're getting married. And we're doing it all together. Fair and square."

"Married?" My heart dropped. He couldn't mean that. I mean, yes, everyone else thought we were married. But he couldn't actually want to marry me. No. It was drunk talk. Nothing more. "He's crazy."

I left my inner monologue to find two very intense pairs of eyes staring down at me. One set chocolate, the other grey.

"What does he mean, you made him come with your power?" Ryan asked.

"I didn't mean to. I was just demonstrating control today—"

"It was awesome. Best orgasm I've had in years," Declan yawned. "Give it to them, Bloss. So I can go back to sleep."

Yes, give it to me, Dove, Quinn's eyes bore into mine.

I bit my lip. Seeing the two of them looming over me, desperate and hard, it took my breath away. But if I couldn't touch them, at least I deserved a sarding show out of this. "Strip," I ordered.

Two seconds later, a pile of clothes landed on Declan's face.

"I know what you're doing," he muttered, through the cotton. "Not letting go. And if you get cum on me, I'm killing you. Tomorrow," he yawned again.

Ryan stood on one side of me, a muscled warrior who was so tall and stacked he had to duck and turn sideways to fit through most doors. His body was ripple after ripple of muscle lit by candlelight.

Quinn stood on my other side. He was fair-skinned and compared to Ryan, he looked slender. But he still had defined shoulders and pecs. A tattoo of a ship ran across his abs. And the contrast of his black happy trail against his white stomach left me aching.

Both men proudly stroked their erections. Ryan's was thick, like him. The thought of him spreading me open had me quivering in fear and excited anticipation. Quinn's was long, and the head of his dick had a huge mushroom tip. The kind the women at the whorehouse always gushed about, saying it could rub some spot inside them and make them come apart at the seams.

Sard.

I grew slick against Declan. I wiggled, trying to get free.

"No," he murmured, pressing a soft kiss against my hip. "Help them, Bloss."

I reached out my hands.

"What do we do?" Ryan asked.

"Keep stroking." I breathed, breasts heaving with desire.

I tried to push my power at them. But I couldn't. I tried again. It was there, tingling beneath the surface of my skin. But it wouldn't release. It was trapped. I looked up at them. Their eyes were fixed on me. If they watched, they'd see the price of my power. Sard. The geas wouldn't let that happen.

"Close your eyes," I ordered.

I grabbed their shirts from Declan's face, and pulled them over my wrists, hoping the fabric would hide enough. I'd have to be exact, only use a bit of power.

Declan was facing away from me, so as long as he didn't move, that wouldn't be an issue.

I stared up at Ryan and Quinn, their faces contorted as they both stroked their lengths. And I let a tendril of peace unfurl from each hand. A green arrow of light shot toward each of the men. I hit them each on the head of their dicks. I focused, making the power swirl down their shafts, constricting and releasing, and constricting again. I reached their balls, ran my power smoothly like a snake across the surface and to the skin behind their sacs. Then I sent that little pulse of peace up into them from that sensitive spot, right to that little gland that made men roar.

Ryan bellowed as I watched as a fountain of cum erupted from him.

Quinn came shortly after, his spray jetting out, his eyes flying open and finding mine.

I released the tendrils of peace, sure to keep my throbbing wrists hidden. I ignored the pain there, because the throbbing between my thighs was so intense.

"Please, Declan," I begged, grinding my hips up toward him so that there was no doubt what I was begging him for.

Declan reached between my thighs, stroking softly.

I groaned in frustration. "Declan, you put your mouth on me right now!"

He complied. His tongue flicked over my opening, stroking from top to bottom.

"Yes, again!" I ordered. As his tongue slid down, I arched up. The pleasure warmed my entire body. By the third stroke of his tongue, I was nearly mindless. My legs were thrashing.

A set of lips closed around my nipple.

My eyes flew open to see Quinn, suckling my right breast.

Ryan knelt on my other side. He slid my arm over, to give himself more room.

"WHAT THE SARD!"

Everyone stopped. And my orgasm, my beautiful orgasm, popped like a bubble. It disappeared into thin air as Declan and Quinn stopped what they were doing and turned their heads to stare at Ryan.

Ryan lifted my bleeding wrist. His eyes turned on me accusingly. "What is this, Bloss?"

Declan sat up. He grabbed my wrist and blinked a few times. "Her arm is full of scars."

Quinn uncovered my other hand, and the matching wound.

I held my breath. I was caught, like a deer.

The men exchanged glances.

Finally, Declan's eyes settled on mine. "Humans and half-humans have to pay a price for their magic, since humans aren't naturally magical creatures. Bloss, is the price of peace magic … your blood?"

I couldn't answer, only widen my eyes.

"It is, isn't it?" Declan continued, not at all discouraged by my lack of response.

"What the sarding hell does that mean?" Ryan asked.

Declan stroked my wrist gently and said, "It means … if she uses too much power, she dies."

CHAPTER SEVENTEEN

"Sard that!" Ryan grabbed me and pulled me away from the others, into his lap. "Don't you dare use that sarding magic ever again, Bloss." He cradled me and used his magic to pulse gently over each of the wounds in my skin, closing them. He gritted his teeth and swallowed his rage after.

Quinn stared at me, tears forming in his eyes, until I felt compelled to reach out and take his hand in mine.

I tried to send a little hopping bunny through my thoughts, but he shook his head and kissed my knuckles.

Declan bent his leg and leaned on it, contemplative. "That's why you've always worn long sleeves. Huh. I just thought you were cold."

I bit my lip and shook my head. I still wasn't sure how much of the geas was active. I decided to test it. "Padded sleeves." So, it was loosened. I could say a little.

Ryan turned my head toward him. "But when I was still a guard ... we'd have combat practice ... your mother would always make you come down and stop us."

I nodded.

"Bitch," he tucked me further into him, my face nestled against his rippling pecs.

"That's why you left," Declan mused. "Before we married."

I nodded.

Both Quinn and Ryan looked to him for an explanation.

"If the Queen dies, her knights go with her."

Ryan squeezed me even harder.

Quinn sent me a mental image of a red ribbon flying through the air, surrounding the two of us until we were pressed together. The ribbon wrapped around us tighter and tighter, sealing us together until we were unable to move.

"I didn't want that for any of you," I muttered. "You all deserve a queen that actually has a chance."

Quinn snorted.

I turned and looked at him. "All it will take is one war. If it gets bad enough, I can't help it."

Ryan looked down at me, "In the weapons room?"

I shook my head. The geas let me say, "No control. It was instinct."

"Then we'll just make sure there are no wars," Declan declared.

I laughed, somewhat bitterly. "The seven kingdoms of Kenmare haven't been able to go without war for more than a decade. There are centuries of history betting against you."

"Well, maybe all those other rulers didn't have the same motivation we have," Ryan growled.

"And what's that?"

His hand slipped down and stroked my inner thigh. "We've been waiting years to get between these legs. No way I'm letting some war mongering assholes mess that up."

Ryan's declaration broke the tension. And we all laughed.

*

*W*e returned to the palace in the dead of night. For once, I didn't check on Avia. Instead, I went to my old room, and all three men followed. They slumped onto my bed surrounding me, each one slinging an arm across my body. Declan ended up at my feet, grumbling, but I promised him we'd rotate the following day.

I woke up with a crick in my neck, to find Connor staring down at all of us, his lips curled in disgust.

"Orgies, Bloss? I suppose enough time in a whorehouse—"

I sat up in bed, rubbing my eyes before glaring at Connor.

He deserved to be told off, but I didn't bother to defend myself. It would only make things worse. And a queen who can't hold her tongue isn't much of a queen.

Declan popped up at my feet. "Did you know Bloss bleeds —" the geas cut him off. He ran a hand through his blond hair. He opened his mouth several more times, but anything he wanted to say must have been prohibited. My mother had set up the spell so the geas applied to anyone who knew about my power. Now Declan, Quinn, and Ryan were bound.

"Frustrating, isn't it?" I told him.

"What's going on, Declan?" Connor ignored me.

Quinn sat up. He focused on Connor, but frowned. Eventually, he turned to me.

I can't tell him anything.

Thank my mother's geas. Can't reveal my weakness to the world. Of course, it's only a matter of time before someone finds out ...

Declan clapped his hands and said, "Alright, let's get a move on." He pointed at Connor, "You need to spend the day with Bloss checking Lady Agatha's livestock issue. We have planning to do. Prince Abbas coming to court Avia is only increasing the tension with Sedara. Macedon has also submitted a request to have their princes visit. And I need to unravel that with Quinn and Ryan," Declan turned brisk and business-like, even bossy.

"What?" I gaped.

"What?" Connor gaped. "Foreign diplomacy is my arena. You go check on Lady Agatha's cows!"

"We don't think this is diplomacy. We believe these are the first moves of war. Macedon and Cheryn have been itching to take on Sedara since the end of the last Fire War. Ryan needs strategic help getting Evaness set up to defend itself. I don't trust either of these visits are purely about finding a wife. I'll need to move our supplies around to support Ryan. Quinn will need to piece together what his associates can find out. Once we've determined a plan, then you and your official policies will be decided. But, get the hell out so we can do our jobs!" Declan stood from the bed and stretched, as if he had not just commanded every eye in the room.

I stared at him, open-mouthed. I hardly noticed when he offered me a hand to help me down from the bed. My stomach was in knots, but my core was on fire. Declan being all scholar-in-charge was … I had trouble controlling my breathing.

Declan noticed and smiled, pulling me closer.

I leaned up to whisper in his ear, "Are you still drunk? Or what the hell was that?"

He leaned back down, his hands falling on my hips. "I'm a switch, sweetheart. But that? That was me hurrying you the hell up in your seduction of Connor. So we can wed and I can …" his fingers circled my hips suggestively.

"What about all that talk of war?" I nibbled his ear, on the side away from Connor.

"That's me being overly cautious. I did get up a few hours ago, to hurl my guts out again. The ambassador had been hinting at an interest in courting Avia. But an official request from Macedon arrived yesterday."

I pulled back so I could look in his eyes. "Do you really think—"

"We're not gonna let it come to that, Bloss. Now, go do your job and seduce your fourth husband."

"If I do, can we play tutor and student sometime? Because I like bossy you."

I get to watch, Quinn chimed in. *And maybe be the angry monarch who walks in and decides he wants in on the—*

Declan grinned. "Get out of here, before I decide fairness is overrated."

"Fairness is overrated," Ryan grumbled as he poured water in a basin and then splashed his face.

"What the sard are you talking about?" Connor grumbled.

No one answered him. I went to the bell pull and asked the responding maid to summon my handmaiden so I could get dressed.

I turned to Connor. "Want to go to the kitchens and have them pack us a lunch? And ask Jace to get us a pegasus?"

"Gargoyle," Ryan interjected. "They're safer."

Connor glared at all of us, cursed, and turned on his heel and stomped out the door.

❦

We landed in one of Willard Ward's fields and spent the day speaking to the farmhands. For once, I didn't stumble all over myself. Connor looked an ass a few times, using uppity words. But eventually, he learned to tone it down.

It was a brilliant afternoon as we walked through the harvested fields of hay, brisk and warm all at once.

I smiled at the sky. "It's been quite a while since I've had the sun on my face in the afternoon."

Connor grunted and squinted beside me. "Do you smell that?"

"What?" I tried to subtly check my breath. We'd eaten with the local burgmaster, and the luncheon meal had been fish.

"Not you," he sniffed the air again. Then he bent down and put his nose to the earth.

"This field is full of cow patties—" I grimaced.

Connor rolled his eyes. "I'm not such a palace bumpkin as to think that! Get down here."

I rolled my eyes and got down on my knees next to him. I inhaled the dirt. "Nothing."

Connor held up a finger. "Wait," he sniffed, and crawled. And sniffed again.

I held in my laughter, but only just.

"Here. Come smell here."

I stood and walked over to him and then bent down to the earth again. I sniffed. There was a hint of something ... "Is that sulfur?"

Connor snapped his fingers. "Yes! That's what it is." He stood and brushed off his pants, then helped me stand. "Perhaps they have hot springs running under this area. Or sulfate salts in the ground." Connor began to walk and look at the ground.

"What does that have to do—"

"Declan will have to verify, of course, but if the cows are desperate due to lack of rain and they're drinking water with sulfates ... that could be a big part of the problem. Why didn't Declan just make more rain for them?"

I sighed. "Something to do with the fact that I believe the opposite of rain is earth. He was worried he'd cause a giant sinkhole. Though he did work on control yesterday. I wonder if I could come back with him and he could try just a small area. One bit at a time."

"So, you admit that me coming out here was useless. Why the ploy? And don't lie to me Bloss. I can feel your emotions. I can tell when you're lying," Connor's eyes blazed.

I took a step backward. "I … um…" the truth spilled out without my meaning to say it. "They want me to seduce you."

"What?"

"Declan wants me to seduce you. He wants to get married. All of us." I shook my head. "They won't listen when I tell them I can't be queen. They're determined …" my heart swelled at the thought of my three sweet, idiot husbands. There. I even thought of them as my husbands. Gah!

They had argued with me long into the night that they could prevent war and stop my power from eviscerating us all. They were so naive.

I glanced back up at Connor, who was staring at me in shock. I shrugged. "They want me to seduce you, but I don't know how. How do you seduce someone you've just always loved?" My voice broke a little, though I tried to hide it.

"How do you know we were ever in love?" Connor's voice rang out bitterly. It felt like it echoed through the empty field.

"What do you mean?"

"Well, your mother's spelled every other damn thing in our lives. How do you know that wasn't a spell, too?"

My mouth dropped. My heart dried up and shriveled. It felt like a peach stone hanging in my chest. Dead. I'd thought leaving Connor at eighteen had been hard. This was worse.

I stood still as a statue and watched Connor tromp away from me, across the field. I didn't call out to him because I had no answer for him. Because I honestly had no idea. Was everything we'd shared just an illusion?

CHAPTER EIGHTEEN

*T*he trip back was made in painfully awkward silence. I carried water and earth samples, so we could have Wyle test them and let us know what was hurting the cattle. My arm held Connor's waist as lightly as possible. I swallowed tears the entire flight.

I was so grateful to see Quinn when we landed. Immediately, I went over to him and grabbed his hand.

I'm not the emotion-reader in the group, but he doesn't look happy, Dove.

I clutched at Quinn's hand. *He thinks Mother spelled us to be in love.*

Quinn raised an eyebrow as he turned to escort me into the main hall. *Well, that puts a damper on things.*

Just a bit, yeah.

I came out here to tell you that the Sedarian ambassador has burst into your mother's chamber.

I took off at a run.

Ass! Mother's too ill for that, I thought.

Quinn and Connor followed, so I assumed Quinn filled Connor in, but I didn't bother to ask as I hurried, in an unqueenly fashion down the great hall. I ducked around a corner and shooed a few guards out of the way so I could enter the secret passages. I hurtled up to Mother's hallway and exited, panting.

"—with aar enemies! Thaar haave been blatant attacks! Blatant! And you've taarned a blind eye! Did yaar think it would go unnoticed?"

I stopped, wiped my forehead, and tried to catch my breath. Then I turned the doorknob and stomped like raging giant into the room.

I glared down at Meeker, who had been waving his fist at my bedridden mother. "What the hell are you doing, you gnashdab! Why are you in the Queen's chambers when there are plenty of knights you can jabber on—"

"Those knights of yaars are all locked up. Planning a waar, it's whispered."

I snorted. "Couldn't be the ball that's coming in two days time with the arrival of Abbas, could it? Couldn't be that my own husbands—whom I haven't seen for four years in a quest to keep your wretched hide safe—might also be planning something special for us on that night? You are aware, you ole' windbag, that we never did have a wedding ball of our own?"

Meeker stopped. He froze, torn between his anger and a bit of doubt. But anger won out. The old man pointed a finger at me. "Yaar hosting our enemy."

"Enemy? There's been one confirmed instance of aggression this past year, I believe," I stared Meeker down, grateful for all the tutoring sessions with Declan.

"One confirmed, but you and I both know thaar's been many more than that. Thaar an enemy."

Connor and Quinn strode up behind me at that point. And Connor did what Connor does best. He read Meeker's emotions and played the old man like a fiddle.

"You're right, Meeker. We are bringing Abbas here. But they say to keep your friends close, and your enemies closer. What an opportunity to get one of the princes, on his own, away from his brothers, ripe for … questioning," Connor raised an eyebrow.

A slow, devious smile spread across Meeker's face. "Ahh. Now I see." He strolled toward us.

Connor clapped an arm across Meeker's shoulders. "Come, have a drink with me, and we can discuss everything we aim to find out during this 'visit.'"

Meeker rubbed his hands together like a play-actor portraying a villain onstage. He nearly forgot to bow to my mother on his way out.

"Apologies, Yaar Majesty," Meeker's hair flipped forward when he bowed.

I turned to my mother, who maintained pretense until Meeker was out of the room. But she collapsed onto her pillows as soon as he was gone.

"Are you alright?" I rushed to her, ignoring my fathers' protests.

I grabbed her hand and held it, in a way I hadn't since I was eight.

Mother coughed. Peter dabbed at her mouth with a handkerchief. He folded it over, but I could see it was speckled with blood.

She took a drink of water from a cup Gorg held out. And then she inclined her head to me. "You two offset each other well."

I pinched my lips together. "He doesn't think so."

She shook her head. "You always have. You always will. It's meant to be."

"He thinks you spelled him to love me—"

Her hacking cough cut me off. Blood didn't just drip from her lips that time. It sprayed out. I was forced backward. I reached for a handkerchief, but Gorg waved me off. "Go, little one. Let us take care of her."

My heartstrings were already stretched tight from the confrontation with Connor earlier. Seeing how frail my mother was just reminded me the end was near. And my chest grew as taught as a violin. It felt as if one more thing, one more tiny minuscule thing, would be all it would take for me to snap and break.

Quinn took my arm and led me away. He could tell my mind was elsewhere, because soon, the woodland creatures popped out of the walls to play.

We passed several doors with woodpeckers chewing the wood and spraying bits onto the floor. And at the end of mother's hall, a guard stood on duty. Another woodpecker hammered steadily at his helmet. That finally drew a smile.

I pulled Quinn around to face me and gave him a gentle kiss on the lips. *Thank you.*

He smiled. *Will you come with me to see Wyle? I need to pick up some things—*

Oh! Perfect. I need to drop off the samples we got today. Oh, wait— I patted my wrists. I'd had a little coin pouch with the samples in it.

Shite! I must've lost it when I ran, I thought.

You need this? Quinn held up a pouch and smiled. *We followed you. Connor figured you'd lose it. Apparently, it was a habit growing up?*

My cheeks reddened. *I always forgot my assignments. I'd set them down somewhere and forget. Connor always found and brought them for me.* The memory took on a bitter tinge. Now that I wondered if the sweet gesture might not have been his at all.

When we reached Wyle's room, our exchanges only took a few minutes. He said he'd have some test results back to me in a few days. And he handed Quinn a new set of Flight and Invisibility potions and a closed crate.

Stocking up for the prince's visit, Quinn winked at me.

I followed Wyle to his work bench.

"How are you doing on breaking all those spells mother set?"

He sighed. "It's on the list, Princess. But I did have to finish these orders from Quinn and your fathers placed a few more about chains and rings and whatnot. Everyone's in a tizzy over this visit. I'll get them finished soon."

It was the best I could hope for. I nodded. "Thank you."

And then I asked, in a low voice, "Wyle, what can undo a geas?"

"Well, now, there's no human magic that can undo it, that's certain. I won't be able to help you. You have one you need to undo?"

I smiled and shook my head. "Just curious. In case I ever need to set one. If magic can't undo it, what can?"

Wyle smacked my back. "Oh, come on, Princess. You know that. We went over it the first year I tutored you. Only the natural magics can undo a strong mage's spell like a geas. Elves and djinn have natural magics of their own. But for humans like you or I … you'd need love. But only the truest kind of love. Born of trust."

My throat constricted. Connor would never trust me. The other men might like me. But love me? Could they possibly come to love me … before the war between Cheryn and Sedara—the war brewing overhead like a thunderstorm—rained down hellfire?

I was doomed.

If I couldn't break the geas, I couldn't tell them. My power might not only kill me. It might kill others, too.

☙

Quinn took me back to my room, and I curled up in the middle of the bed, three of my husbands wrapped around me. It had been delicious the night prior. But, that night, three men and all their body heat became unbearable.

In the middle of the night, I gently extracted myself. Once I was free and cooled down, I was wide awake. I decided I should go bother Squawk and see if she was excited for her suitor's arrival. I tugged on Declan. He was the lightest of my knights. He was also a bit prone to sleep-walking, as I'd discovered the night prior.

I tugged until Declan slipped off my bed and fell the the floor with an *oof*. He didn't wake. I almost laughed. But I tugged him to his feet. His eyes cracked open.

"Declan?"

His response was utter gibberish. Perfect.

I tugged my sleeping husband behind me and we went into the hall.

My slippered feet slid across the marble floor.

I was nearly to Avia's door, when I saw a shadow. I froze. Fear smacked me in the ribs. There shouldn't be a shadow there. The hall was a dead-end. I slid into an alcove, behind the statue of a satyr. I shoved a murmuring Declan behind me.

Click. Click. Click.

It sounded like claws scratching against the marble.

I craned my neck to peer around a goat ear.

It took everything in me not to scream.

Skittering down the hall, toward Avia's new room, was a monster.

It was twelve feet tall, with the head, torso, and arms of a man but the body of a scorpion. He was a sickly yellow color and his eyes were black. Soulless. He smelled like burnt oil.

I shook Declan. But he didn't wake. He just backed away and mumbled. He didn't respond when I slapped him.

Sard. Sard, I thought.

I called out to Quinn. He didn't answer. Of all the nights for him to be dead asleep. I yelled at him mentally again. *Quinn!* He still didn't respond.

The scorpion man neared Avia's door. Thoughts flew out of my head.

Rage settled over me like a cloak. And I moved on instinct. My only thought was to stop this monster before it got to my sister.

I stepped out from my hiding spot. I lifted my arms and sent a blast of peace toward the scorpion-man.

The blast was so strong my wrists slit. My leg ripped open along an old scar. It burned like fire. But I bit down on my tongue and ignored it.

The scorpion man turned. He saw me and roared. He charged.

I tried to duck, but with my wounded leg I wasn't fast enough.

He slammed me into the statue.

My vision went red. Flickered black. And I couldn't help it. My mind screamed, *Quinn!*

I sent another blast of peace into the monster's torso, my hands searching for his heart. I just needed one direct hit.

He landed one instead.

The side of my face smashed into the wall. My thoughts … started … to scatter.

No guards came running. Quinn wasn't here. Avia hadn't fled her room. She was still in there. Whoever had sent this monster was going to try to get her. I had to stop them.

It was up to me. There was no one but me.

My hands shook as I reached up again. My fingertips touched the monster's rib cage. But before I could send another pulse of peace, he lifted me overhead to throw me.

I shoved my hands down in the general direction of his head. I grabbed fistfuls of his hair. I screamed as I shot out every bit of magic I had.

The skin on my arms shredded like potato peels. My stomach burned.

The monster set me down. He blinked several times and shook his head like he was dizzy.

I stumbled back. The cut in my leg was too deep. I couldn't run away.

I watched the monster closely.

I saw the exact moment that my peace magic lost its hold.

His eyes hardened. The scorpion tail arched behind him.

I scrambled backward. But I slipped in my own blood.

The scorpion man roared as he sent his tail barreling toward me.

I could see the poison glinting on the tip. The hooked barb pressed against the bodice of my gown.

And suddenly, it was gone.

I glanced up, confused.

A golden arrow pierced the monster's torso. As I watched, a second split his throat.

The scorpion man started to tip forward. I dragged myself sideways. But not fast enough.

The monster's body came crashing down on my leg. Lightning bolts of pain shot up through my spine. I fell back against the marble floor.

Two arms grabbed me roughly under the armpits and yanked me free of the monster's weight.

That's when the monster disintegrated, leaving nothing but a pile of ash in his place.

Of course he did, after crushing my leg.

"Piece of turd-walloping nastiness," I cursed through my teeth. My head spun as I was pulled into a sitting position.

I locked eyes with Quinn.

Behind him Declan burbled and walked into wall, still asleep.

Quinn's voice in my head smacked me down.

You're a sarding idiot.

Me? I couldn't even get out an indignant, 'I'm a monster killer.'

I collapsed.

❦

I woke healed and in bed late the next morning. Quinn was with me, stroking my hair. My entire body felt good. Great even.

What happened?

His grey eyes stared down at me. *Ryan healed you. He's currently working out his rage on in the practice arena.*

I mean, what happened with that monster? You saw it, right? You shot it with arrows?

Quinn sighed. An audible sigh. *Dove, you should really talk to us before you go wandering around at night.*

In my own home?

Ryan believes you about the threat to your sister.

He does?

Yes. And with that and all these issues between Cheryn and Sedara ... we need to be prepared. The fact that Macedon wants to send an entourage, too ... it makes Ryan nervous. He decided he's going to up the drills for his guards. To keep them on high alert.

What's that got to do with that creature?

That thing was one of Wyle's creations. I picked up a couple bottled mixes with my other potions last night. It was a spelled creature—a security protocol meant to test the guards, who failed, by the way. And are now facing your very pissed knight.

Wait. That scorpion-man was a spell? But it fought me.

Sentient spell. Wyle's been secretly developing them for your mother for the past two years.

I covered my forehead. *I feel so stupid.*

You should. I'm rather mad you waited so long last night before you woke me up. We told you not to use your powers.

First off, I tried. You were dead asleep. And I thought that thing was going to kill Avia!

Yes, well, Avia's another issue. Your sister wasn't in her room.

I bolted upright. "WHAT?"

Yes. Seems she and Mateo were sharing a late night snack in the kitchens. Supervised, thank goodness. But—

My anger and embarrassment were suddenly redirected at Avia. *I don't want her marrying this prince. But I don't want her messing up the relations with Cheryn or Macedon either. And she knows that there's someone else out there plotting against her. Sarding teenager!*

Quinn grinned at my angry expression, *Much like you were, running off, doing what you wanted—*

Not the same. She's being sarding stupid!

Speaking of sarding ... you and I are alone. In your bed. Without Declan here to be a beaver dam. Quinn leaned toward me and Avia flew out of my thoughts. All I saw were Quinn's grinning grey eyes, his black hair tumbling over his forehead, those lips. The lips that had tempted me the very first time I'd seen him.

His lips latched onto mine. And it was as if I were caught in a cyclone. He was so intense. So persistent. His hands were everywhere. And then mine were too. The kiss grew and whirled around us, making me dizzy. I fell backward onto the sheets. Quinn caught himself on his hands and stayed suspended over me. His lips dipped down. And the kiss continued.

His hand snuck under my chemise and slowly he began to pull it up. I had nothing on underneath. When the only thing that had separated my naked skin from his was gathered above my waist, Quinn pulled away from our kiss and made his way down my body.

Is this really happening? I was breathing hard.

Yes, Dove. Oh, hell yes, he replied. And then his mouth was on my core. And I couldn't think straight anymore. My thoughts turned into tingles. Hot wet tingles that radiated out to my thighs. I whimpered and ground myself into him. And then, he was gone.

What the—

Another mouth replaced his. Big and insistent. A tongue nearly twice the size of Quinn's pierced me briefly and then licked my pussy lips. Hot breath coated my entire mound and my need intensified. I looked down to see Ryan's head buried at my center. His long, strong tongue lapped at me from bottom to top. He used two fingers to part my opening, so he could wrap those lips around my clit. He devoured me, and I moaned, coaxing him to keep going.

Quinn's mouth landed on my nipple and sucked it in deeply. He pulled twice with his lips before releasing.

I arched off the bed, grabbing onto Ryan's thick arm at my hip with one hand. I reached my other hand out and latched onto Quinn's hair.

"Yes! Please," I pleaded. Quinn put my other nipple between his teeth.

Ryan unsealed his mouth from my mound and slid a thick finger inside me. "Are you a naughty little princess, Bloss? Tell me," he murmured.

I was moving, nearly incoherent with pleasure as I responded. "Yes. Yes. I'm a naughty little princess."

"I'm gonna make you wear your crown and nothing else when I rut you," Ryan said before bringing his teeth to drag over my hip bone. He started curling his fingers faster inside of me.

It was silk and fire and every sensation at once rocketing through my body.

Quinn pulled his mouth off my breast and came up for a kiss, swallowing my moans. He put his hands over my breasts, squeezing my nipple between his pointer and middle fingers. An amazing hot pulse of pleasure shot up my spine. My skull went hollow.

"You're amazing," I ripped my mouth away from Quinn and yelled out as I started to reach that peak.

But Ryan's hand was yanked away. Then Quinn was thrown across the bed, landing flat on his back next to me, his dick tenting his pants skyward.

Declan leaned over me.

"What the hell? I said not until we're married."

Quinn responded silently.

Declan just snorted in reply. He snapped at Ryan. "You said you'd stop him."

Ryan shrugged. "Look at her. Who could say no if they walked in and saw her spread-eagled, naked, moaning?"

Declan groaned but shook his head. "Let's go, Bloss."

He led me toward the dressing room, where he summoned a maid. Declan insisted on staying with me as my hair was done. When I was ready for the day, he grabbed my arm and pulled me down the hall.

"Why are you so mad?"

"Because, we're a team. We're about to be a family. And we need to damn well act like one. Which means being considerate outranks being horny."

I nodded. "You're right."

But then, the strangest sensation came over me. A very naughty thought rose in my chest like a bubble. The perfect revenge against Quinn and all of his hallucinations dawned on me. "But I'm not certain Quinn can help himself."

"Well, he'll have to!"

"You know, Declan, what might be fun ... is if we tease Quinn a little."

Declan cocked his head. "What do you mean?"

I pushed Declan into an alcove. "Don't you think he deserves a bit of his own medicine? Shouldn't we show him just how thoughtless he's being?"

"What do you mean?"

"Quick. Picture me naked. Picture yourself running your hands all over me. Picture cupping my breasts. Squeezing them. Suck my nipple into your mouth!"

"What—"

"Just picture it!" I covered Declan's eyes with my hand. Then I continued, "You unbuckle your belt. Drop your pants. Turn me to face the wall. Stare down at my naked ass. Do you like it, Declan? You like my ass." I closed my eyes so I could better imagine it. "You kiss my neck and rub your hand along my mound. And then you line yourself up—"

What the sarding hell are you doing? Quinn burst into the alcove where Declan and I stood, fully clothed.

I opened my eyes and grinned. "Quinn-bear. Do you remember all those times you embarrassed me? When I promised you I'd get revenge?"

Quinn's gaze roamed over a fully clothed Declan and me. His eyes narrowed.

Bitch.

I grinned.

Watching him stomp off was the highlight of my morning.

CHAPTER NINETEEN

The next few days were a blur of preparation for Abbas' visit.

First, I sat through lecture after lecture on Cheryn. The sultan, Raj, and his first-born son were both near immortal. The sultan was over a thousand years old and had wished himself an endless supply of wealth. So, despite Cheryn's northern location, full of mountains and few resources, the palace itself was grand, and the royal family lived in luxury. Abbas was half-djinn; he had superior speed, could smell fear, and supposedly half-djinn could grant three wishes in their long lives.

"Has he already granted any?" I'd asked.

"No one knows," Declan responded.

After we'd gone over the schedule, and Cheryn's traditional greetings, and some basic arrangements for the suitor's ball held a few days after Abbas settled in, I was finally free to do what I wanted to do.

I cornered Avia in her chambers when she was being fitted for dresses; I reamed her for scandalously consorting late at night with an ambassador's son.

"Well, I like him!"

"That's wonderful, but you can't like him until we've formally rejected Abbas' suit and the one coming from Macedon. So until then—"

"You got Connor in your contingent of knights, why can't I—"

"You can. You most likely will," I growled. "If you'll just wait long enough. Sedara and Cheryn are chomping at the bit to get at one another. By the time you're of age, this crown and whatever knights you choose—"

Avia covered my lips with her hand. "I didn't mean it." Her eyes were glossy.

I sighed and pulled her in for a hug. "I know. But that's the reality. You probably can choose him. If you wish. But you have to be smart, Squawk. You can't make enemies of two countries before you take the throne."

"I said I took it back. I don't want him or the throne."

I huffed. "Let's move on from this, shall we? I love the golden gown. It's perfect."

Avia grumbled and stared at herself in the looking glass. "I wish I didn't have to wear it for a stranger."

"I know."

"He probably has a snaggle tooth and horrid breath."

"That's true."

Avia pulled a pin out of her dress and threw it at me. "You're not supposed to agree! You're supposed to reassure me."

I shrugged. "Sorry. Connor's the one who's good at that."

She sighed. "You're right. How are the two of you?"

"Same."

"I'm sorry."

"Me too."

We were sharing a sisterly moment, that Ryan was studiously trying to ignore, when Declan barged in. "Did you hear?"

Everyone turned to face him. He shut the door and looked around surreptitiously. "Wyle tested the water and the land samples you brought back. Neither are contaminated with sulfur or sulfate salts. That's not what's killing the cattle. It's dragon's breath."

The air was sucked out of the room.

Everyone became a statue.

"The beast ..." I whispered. "The one I heard they're sending after Avia ..."

This isn't happening. This can't be happening, I told myself.

What's happening?

I didn't bother to respond to Quinn as I made my way to the bed and sat. Memories swirled through my head. Memories of shadows cast by huge wings. Of air so hot it hurt to walk outside. I gulped. Lewart, my birth father, ran through my thoughts. The hazel eyes I'd inherited had been his.

Sard. Sard. Sard.

Avia came to clutch at my hand. "It's not going to happen, Bloss. It's not going to happen to you."

"What's not going to happen?"

Avia's mouth struggled with the geas. I'm not sure how she did it, but she managed to say, "Knight Lewart."

Ryan and Declan exchanged a glance.

"Your father?" Declan looked at me.

I nodded.

"He passed during the last Fire War," Ryan stated.

Again, I nodded.

"He and his team were cut down—"

I started to shake my head but the geas froze me.

Luckily Declan saw. "They weren't cut down?" He turned to Ryan. "Tell me everything you know about what happened. She can't talk again. Must be related to her magic."

"Knight Lewart was the dragon-charmer. That's what they called him. He could tame the wild beasts. It's why everyone believed it when Queen Gela said Bloss had gone dragon-hunting. She's his birth daughter. Everyone assumed she could charm the beasts as well."

There was a long, pregnant pause.

Declan turned to stare me in the eyes. "Did you inherit your father's power, Bloss?"

I couldn't move. Couldn't blink. Couldn't breathe. Beside me, it seemed Avia's body was locked just as tight.

Declan turned back to Ryan. "Tell me how he died."

"He and his contingent were after one of the last dragons. In the mountains that border Cheryn. They'd traced a black flame creature there. But they were attacked. Some group, thought to be from Gitmore, cut them down. Hacked them to pieces with swords."

Declan bit his lip. "And the dragon?"

Ryan shrugged. "No one knows."

Declan turned and stared from me to Avia, and back again. "Avia knows," he told Ryan. "Avia and the Queen."

Ryan nodded. "Makes sense."

Declan started to pace, glancing over at me every few seconds. "Bloss injures herself when she uses her power. Her skin slices open."

Ryan started. "Yes. Like a sword. I thought she'd injured herself in the weapons roo—"

Declan spoke over him, tension mounting in his voice. "Bloss says she can't control it when she's threatened."

Ryan inhaled sharply. "Are you thinking…"

"What happens when the threat is overwhelming? When the threat is something like a dragon? What if no one was cut down? What if they met the dragon … and Knight Lewart—"

Ryan scooped me into his arms. "She'd never do something like that."

"Not on purpose. No. But this geas, this spell preventing her from speaking, is there for a reason."

Ryan stroked my hair and held me closer. "I don't want to believe it."

"I don't either. We can never let it get out."

What? What can't you let out? Quinn walked in at that moment.

Declan turned to him. "Shut the door."

Once it was shut, Declan's mouth became a thin line as he said, "Our princess's power doesn't only draw on her own blood. It can draw on those around her when she's under duress. To the point of death." He stared into my eyes. "If anyone ever found out, they'd know how to make our Bloss self-destruct."

Ryan cursed. "And right now, there's a sarding dragon somewhere on Lady Agatha's land."

All eyes turned to stare at me, as though I was a bomb, ready to burst.

I was. I wouldn't be able to help it. I felt the truth of it in my bones. My magic swelled at the very thought of the monster.

All it would take would be one little spark.

From the mouth of a dragon.

CHAPTER TWENTY

*R*yan's response surprised me more than anyone's. He immediately swept me down to the library. He started pulling books out and flinging them at Avia, Quinn, and Declan, who'd trailed after us.

"We need to research. I don't know sarding what—but dragons, magical locks to lock Bloss's shitefire power— Quinn, why haven't your people figured out who's sending this beast yet? Sard!" He cursed and threw a book across the room. It knocked over a candelabra which, luckily, wasn't lit.

He stomped back over and grabbed me roughly, then pulled me down to sit on his lap. He buried his face in my hair. I rubbed his neck, absently, still in shock.

Just then, Connor walked in.

"What's going on?"

ANN DENTON

Declan filled him in. Well, filled him in to the extent that
he could, given the geas. He was able to get out more than
I would have: he spoke about the dragon, my theory it was
after Avia, and the suspicion that Knight Lewart's death
wasn't from an attack.

"Well then who the hell killed him?"

"What if no one did?"

"What?"

Declan opened and closed his mouth several times. "Acci-
dents happen," was all he managed.

Connor snorted in disbelief. "Men don't get sliced to
ribbons by accident." His eyes found mine. I could read
the pain in his gaze. My father's death was nearly as
painful for Connor as it was for me.

Lewart had been Connor's mentor growing up, the one
who'd taught him how to work the courtiers, to soothe
them and manipulate them all at once. My father had
always tried to ensure he used every possible option
before he used his peace power.

My mother had thought that was the reason he'd died. He
hadn't used his power enough to gain control over it.
Thus, my endless tests, the constant pushing, the padded
sleeves on my dresses … she didn't want the same fate for
me. But no matter how much I'd practiced, my dresses
were always stained with blood. Forcing peace onto
others always had its price.

I buried my head in my hands. I'd run from the palace to escape this very fate. To find a legendary wizard, one who may have existed only in whispered longing by those with hopeless cases. A man who could make wishes reality. I'd searched for four years through every town, village, and hamlet in Evaness for a man who could change the price of my power.

I should have tried harder. I should never have gotten bogged down in jobs or work or let myself be distracted. I should have gone to Gitmore in disguise. Some of the best wizards in all the seven kingdoms were in Gitmore. Enemy territory. But no one would have recognized me. Why hadn't I done that?

I hated myself. I should have done more. My thoughts rallied against me, smacking me down one by one: Now a sarding dragon is coming. I'm going to have to face it. And after … Avia isn't even prepared. She isn't ready to handle the aftermath. And my knights. My four beautiful knights.

The thought of what could happen to them …

I pulled my hair, trying to release the tension that strained underneath my skin. The guilt and fear inside me roared and writhed, like they were beasts themselves.

I should never have come back, the thought pushed its way to the front of my mind.

My eyes flickered from face to face: Ryan's was grim, his beautiful eyelashes hiding his expression as he stared at the floor; Connor was confused, his mop head of curls so adorably mussed on his head; Declan was muttering to himself, a trait I now found endearing; Quinn was staring right at me with those endlessly gorgeous grey eyes. My gut wrenched, like a catapult had launched a flaming stone into my stomach.

My mind was clear though. It said: I have to leave them. I shouldn't have come. If I'd just hunted down the creature myself, just sent a letter instead of running back to Quinn, they wouldn't be here arguing with me. They wouldn't be in danger…

My eyes welled up, but I forced the tears down.

Sarding hell. I knew I was cursed. I never should have dragged them back into it. And now, to see any one of them hurt, it would kill me. Gah! I was stupid. Selfish.

I took a breath and tried to focus myself. Panic only led to bad choices.

Calm down, I scolded myself. There's still time. They aren't dead yet. You still have time to leave. You still can run. You still can try to save them. So that dragons won't snatch them out of thin air as they did Lady Bane and her husbands.

That memory twisted my stomach and I had to grab onto Ryan's shoulder to stay upright.

No, no, no.

Quinn must have told everyone what I was thinking, because Connor turned to me and said, "Bloss, calm down. We've had Wyle add as many precautions to the castle as possible. There's a fire shield above us. You'll be fine. Dragons won't get to you. Or Avia."

He didn't know about my power. So, he couldn't understand why my hands wouldn't stop shaking. Or why my throat went dry.

I can't face the dragon in the castle. I'll hurt people. So many people. I need to get away—my thoughts were logical, even if my body was in a panic. The years of strategy practice under pressure kicked in.

I stood, pushing off Ryan's arms. I paced nearby as the inkling of a plan took shape in my mind. "I should get a spelled disguise from Wyle. I should look like Avia and go back to Lady Agatha's lands. I'll draw it to me." I looked around the room.

Every head but Connor's shook, vehemently.

"No," they chorused.

They're wrong, I thought. This would work. At least well enough to give them time to prepare. And protect Avia.

"It has to be. I can't be near anyone. Ryan, your men can clear everyone off the land. In that cave, I heard those men say the beast would be drawn to Avia. It will be drawn to me if I look like her. And then I'll tame it. Like my father." I spoke with confidence, using every ounce of court-practiced fakery I had. I'd never tamed a beast in my life. We'd thought dragons were gone. Since I was eight years old, everyone had believed them killed off.

"NO!" Ryan roared.

I took a step back. His anger was ferocious.

"Absolutely not, Bloss," Declan dismissed me and opened a book.

If you run, I'm going after you. I'm going with you. I won't leave you, Quinn threatened.

You will sarding not. I am still your ruler.

"This isn't up for discussion, this is the plan," I said aloud.

Declan slammed his book shut. "You think you can order us around?"

"I'm the crown princess."

"You're our wife," Ryan roared.

"No. I'm not. That's why I ran. Because if a queen dies, her knights do too—" Tears filled my eyes. It didn't matter that I wanted to be their wife. Needs always came before wants. And a queen has an endless list of needs to attend to. Another of my mother's heartwarming sayings. Love … wasn't an option.

I turned to Avia. "When I'm—spread the dragon hunting story. That I've gone to the mountains again. And when you're of age … please consider them—"

Avia covered her ears and started screaming. "I won't! I won't!"

"What the hell has everyone so worked up?" Connor asked.

"Bloss is trying to commit suicide," Declan said dryly.

"What? She's a beast tamer, a peace maker, just like her father. She'll be fine—"

"Her power—" Ryan growled

"Is uncontrollable," Declan got out.

"What?" Connor was incredulous.

Quinn grabbed Connor's arm and stared at him. A minute later, Connor turned to me as his face paled.

His mouth was a thin line. "That's not sarding possible. She would have told me." He stomped toward me and grabbed my arm roughly. He pushed up my sleeve, exposing the cross-hatched scars on my arms. The fresh bandages. The proof that my power had a deadly price.

He looked up at me; the fury in his eyes was as hot as dragon fire. "What the ever-loving hell? You hid this from me, Bloss?"

"She can't talk about it, churl," Avia had uncovered her ears. She came up and pried his arm off mine. "Nobody can."

"What?"

I ignored Connor's anger. I stared at Quinn. *How'd you get around the geas to tell him?*

Sometimes, I can string together enough mental images to get a point across. Quinn showed me. Quick images of dragons and knights and blood.

273

"Why are you sarding ignoring me? When did everyone figure this out?" Connor whirled and raged at the room at large.

"Ten minutes ago. And no one is ignoring you," Declan sighed. "This is why we need to do things as a group, Quinn." Declan gestured at Connor who was heaving breaths, as if he wanted to throw things just as Ryan had. "You see this? Who here wants to be in his place?"

Connor punched Declan. "I don't know what the sard you're talking about."

Ryan grabbed Connor by the collar. "Watch it. Right now, he's the only one on your side, you pretentious ass."

"What side? Why are there sarding sides?" Connor bellowed.

Quinn took over again.

Connor's eyes darted between him and me. "Marry her? Are you joking? Why the hell would you marry a woman who abandoned us and—"

Ryan clapped his hand over Connor's mouth. "You don't want to finish that sentence. You don't want me to hit you."

Connor jerked away and walked toward the door. "You've all been sarding spelled! You know that? Every step of the way. That's all this is."

"You think we've been spelled to love Bloss?" Declan asked.

"Of course, we have."

I know I haven't been, Quinn stared steadily at Connor. But his words rushed over me, filling me with both elation and terror.

He can't love me. They can't love me, my mind said.

No. You can't. You shouldn't. Don't make this harder—

Quinn just glared at me.

Declan shook his head. Pity came over his features as he regarded Connor. "You can tell yourself you were spelled if you want. But haven't you researched spells? They don't have the capacity for more than a single emotion. If you were under a love spell, you'd never be able to hate her this much."

Connor's mouth gaped open.

Mine would have done the same, if I hadn't started kicking myself. I'd studied spells with Wyle. I'd made love spells. Not good ones. But I should have remembered. My stomach sank. Connor's hatred was real. But a tiny piece of me, a piece tinged with regret and longing, rejoiced. Because it meant my memories were true. And my love for him was true. I loved him. Just as now, I loved all of them.

One look at Connor told me it didn't matter. No amount of logic was going to erase his anger at me ... or Declan.

Hurt and disappointment skipped across my stomach like stones. I tried to ignore it, but defensive words popped out before I could reign them in. "For the record, I've asked Wyle to remove all spells from all of you. Except for those that keep you physically safe." As soon as I said that, I wanted to kick myself. Those words didn't matter. Wouldn't matter to Connor, who was determined to hate me. But my stupid mouth continued, "He's also supposed to be working on the distance spell, which he's loosened, so that no one has to be within ten feet of me anymore."

"No!" Declan and Ryan protested. Quinn shook his head and slipped toward the door.

"Where are you going?"

To make sure Wyle does not follow your order on that one. No sarding way we're letting you go again, Bloss. You're stuck with us. For life and death. Quinn slammed the door closed behind him.

"You idiot!" I screamed at the door, rushing after Quinn.

Ryan grabbed my arm and held me back. He pulled me against his chest. "Bloss, we're your knights. We're bound to protect you. Even from yourself."

Tears streaked down my face, racing the pain radiating up from my heart. "You can't."

"We can."

I shook my head but didn't speak. Further argument was pointless. We were at an impasse.

And they were wrong.

I looked over. Connor was arguing with Declan over the complexity of love spells. Avia had pulled the bell pull and was pacing, waiting for a servant to arrive. I could feel the tension threading through the room, tying everyone up in knots.

Declan and Connor's voices rose another decibel.

"Ask the sarding queen if you don't believe me. Bloss left so you wouldn't bleed out like a stuck pig, you yellow-bellied cringeling!"

"What did you call me?"

"You're scared!"

Connor grabbed Declan's shirt. "I'm not—"

"You're scared she'll do it again. But guess sarding what? She won't. Because none of the rest of us will let her."

He was wrong.

I'd leave them behind. Even though the thought left my insides as dark and lifeless as a shadow.

I'd figure out how to get away from them and seek out that dragon.

Connor pushed Declan away. Declan just snarled, "Find your bawbles and your spine. Because we've got a sarding dragon to face, a shite-show between Cheryn and Sedara coming down the pipe, and a godforsaken suitor—"

A page rushed into the room, interrupting Declan.

"The party from Cheryn. They're here! They arrived early!"

CHAPTER TWENTY-ONE

"Shite," I blew out a breath. I turned to everyone in the room. "Get changed. Quickly. Formal greeting wear. Ryan, full armor for you and your men."

"Won't that look aggressive?"

"We don't know who sent that sarding dragon. Could be Macedon. Gitmore. Cheryn. Could even be Sedara; they could be angry we're considering Cheryn as allies. So, we are all on guard. At all times. And if you aren't going to let me go back to Lady Agatha's province, then we need soldiers sent there and we need to move the cattle and people away from there without arousing suspicion. Declan, I'll let you handle the latter. Quinn, find out who sent this beast. And I want two people protecting Avia at all times."

Avia opened her mouth in protest but I raised my hand. "You didn't want the crown princess job. So, you're listening to me until you're forced to take it."

She glared at me. But everyone broke ranks and went their separate ways to get ready and execute orders. Declan trailed after me as Connor stomped off, muttering to himself.

As I was stuffed into a blue brocade dress with a train that took two servant girls to manage it, I ran through the possible suspects in my head.

Whoever had set out to attack Avia had done so before I returned. Abbas' visit had been scheduled before then. So, if our northeastern neighbors, the royal family of Macedon, had been feeling slighted since their princess was overlooked, that was a possibility. Was a slight enough for an attack?

I was doubtful.

But Cheryn and Sedara had been fighting, or at least swiping at one another, for nearly a year. What if Sedara was more than just annoyed by my mother's choice to entertain Cheryn's princes as suitors for Avia?

I dug my fingers into my palms. Too many countries hated us right now. Those theories didn't even count our long-time enemy, Gitmore. We'd stripped them of weapons at the end of the last Fire War. They'd been pretty bitter since.

Sarding hell. Of all the times for a stupid suitor visit. We'd be up to our eyeballs in formal events and bullshite public outings when we needed to hole up and strategize.

I bit my lip as a maidservant twisted and plaited my hair and placed a tall filigreed golden and pearl crown on my head. The front of the crown had a headdress that dipped down onto my forehead, where diamonds dangled. Beautiful. Intimidating. Heavy as hell. I looked at my reflection, practicing my face for greeting the smarmy ass who'd come to inspect our kingdom and see if he found it beneficial to ally with us.

I couldn't think about him coming here to judge Avia. That just made my cheeks grow red hot as I thought about yanking off my crown and smashing his crooked teeth out with it.

My personal butler appeared at that moment. "The party from Cheryn has arrived and is awaiting you in the throne room, Your Highness."

"It's just the one prince?"

"Yes. Abbas. The eldest, Your Highness. The others are ill at the moment."

I nodded in acknowledgment. "Wonderful. Will my mother be greeting the party from Cheryn as well?"

He shook his head. "No, Your Highness. Her Majesty is not feeling … well, at the moment."

I fought the bile that rose in my throat. My first formal appearance with a foreign royal, alone. I might rather face the dragon. At least then, I'd know what was coming.

I took a deep breath. Declan came forward and claimed my arm, having just thrown an embroidered doublet over his shirt and tossed on an ornamental sword. I looked at the pair of us in the mirror for a second. We were opposites, with my long brown locks and his blond hair. My coloring was olive-toned, whereas Declan had a hint of pink to his skin. In our formal wear, standing straight and solemn, we looked like different people. We didn't look like a scholar and an unruly princess. Our reflection showed a queen and her knight.

I hope this intimidates the shite out of Abbas, I thought.

"Come on, Peace."

I squeezed Declan's arm one last time, shutting down all the jingling nerves inside. I would do this. I could do this.

Time to play pretend.

The herald announced all four of my knights first, and they preceded me into the throne room. When I was announced, I slowly made my way across the hall and up the steps to my throne, the largest of the five on the dais. I turned, waiting for the servant girls to hastily fix my train and trail it over the stairs. And then I sat. Everyone relaxed from their bows.

I met Abbas' gaze for the first time. He wasn't incredibly tall, maybe five foot ten. But his face was well-made, sharply defined. He had a smooth dark brow, brown skin and eyes, and his hair was jet black. He had a beard, which to me only emphasized his age difference from my sister all the more. Dressed scandalously for our court, he wore only loose pants, tied with a draw-string. He wore no shirt, leaving his sculpted abs on display. His muscled biceps were laced with tattoos and he had rings on nearly every finger. Wonderful. Avia was a teenage girl. Warning her away from him would be like warning bees away from flowers. Bears away from fish. Dragons away from sheep.

Salamanders away from fire, Quinn contributed, helpfully.

Shut it. This is terrible.

Abbas' eyes met mine and I gave a jolt. Somehow, his dark gaze shot right through me. He was a sarding predator. And for a millisecond, he let me see it. My stomach dropped. His grin widened. And he didn't have crooked teeth. His smile was perfect. Perfectly feral. He'd eat poor Avia alive.

Stop it! Djinn can smell fear, remember?

Shite. I widened my fake smile and focused on the bunny rabbits Quinn conjured hopping between the nobles' feet.

I could feel Abbas' gaze on me though, studying, judging. I wondered what he saw.

Avia was announced. And the weight of his gaze lifted, like a physical force, from off my shoulders. He turned to see Avia.

My younger sister paraded in, her crown a small tiara of silver leaves and diamonds. She was dressed in a deep gold, and her hair had been put into ringlets. She looked every bit the innocent treasure. My heart swelled with pride and misery. My eyes swept the room.

Abbas' gaze was riveted to Avia as she came up the aisle toward the dais. Unfortunately, so was Mateo's. I spotted the ambassador's son staring longingly at my sister.

Dammit.

Luckily, mother had trained Avia well enough that she gave no one in the crowd more than a passing glance. She joined us on the dais.

The herald started spouting formalities as we all smiled at the crowd.

Quinn, keep your eye on Meeker, the Sedarian ambassador. And on Mateo.

On it. I have people in the crowd as well, already positioned near Meeker. I'll put someone on Mateo.

Who do you have on Abbas?

A couple invisibles in his rooms. No sign of those stolen elven chains yet, though they report he has a glowing blue ring in his room. That might be a djinn thing though? I think I saw that on another half-djinni down at the tavern in the capital ... I also have a couple other servants ready to use disguise spells and replace his servants on my word.

Good. Think you could get a hair bead on him?

No. But the way he looked at you, I bet you could.

I suppressed a shudder. *I don't know if my hands are quick enough for that.*

We'll let Connor get a read on his moods, and then we'll talk.

Once the official announcements were over, I had to invent an activity to keep us entertained until it was time for a welcoming feast. Since Abbas was not supposed to arrive until nightfall, the kitchens weren't ready for the feast yet. So, instead, I turned to the nobles gathered in the throne room and said, "We will retire to the yellow salon for entertainment. Our first game shall be jingling. Be warned, any of you who enter the yellow salon, you will be made to participate." My eyes twinkled.

I was using a tactic my father Lewart often had. It was a dual-purpose exercise. It was team-building for those with nothing to hide and it helped me sort out courtiers with too high an opinion of themselves or those desperate for approval. It would let me take the measure of Abbas and see if he was as aloof as reports painted him. Or if he was willing to engage with my sister and strangers and adapt to new circumstances.

The crowd broke, and people milled about.

Abbas headed straight for the dais.

He bent over Avia, giving her a rakish grin. Dammit. His smile was far too alluring. She'd never last a second. I wouldn't have, at her age.

I blew out a breath, glad his gaze wasn't directed at me.

But, suddenly, it was.

Abbas stared at me over Avia's head. His black gaze trapped me for a moment, before Declan took my arm and tugged me away.

"May I escort you, Princess Avia?" Abbas spoke for the first time. His voice was smooth, musical.

Avia giggled.

Shite. Shite. Do we have to let him escort her, Quinn? He's not even decent!

I watched Avia and Abbas walk down the steps. I had to wait for the room to clear before my two maids removed the ridiculous train from my dress so that I could walk unhampered. The crown, unfortunately, stayed. I felt like hurrying after Avia, propriety be damned, and wedging myself in between the two of them, like a little old lady chaperone.

When I arrived at the yellow salon, Lady Agatha had already begun the game. I nodded toward her.

The game of jingling was simple. One person was it. And they received a string of bells to place over their neck. Everyone else was blindfolded and attempted to catch the jingler. Whoever won got to wear the bells next.

Blindfolds were passed to my knights and myself. We all took them once Quinn reassured us he had several invisibles in the room near us keeping watch.

Right before I slid the strip of cloth over my eyes, I saw Abbas approach Lady Agatha and take the bells.

Shite. I should have picked a different game, I thought.

Have your men watch Avia.

I'll head that way myself. Quinn gave my hand a squeeze and headed off.

I stood at the side of the room, listening to the jitters and giggles as bells rang and people ran into one another. I definitely heard two people nearby not stop at running into one another but begin locking lips.

I started to rethink my decision. But then I reminded myself, Abbas had the bells on himself. He couldn't possibly kiss my sister without drawing a crowd to him.

A man's hand caught mine. Instead of the apology and laugh I expected, the stranger remained silent. Lips touched my fingers.

"Ryan?" I breathed. He'd done that once before, in the practice yard.

But Ryan didn't answer.

Isn't he beside me? Where did he go? My mind worried.

Fear trickled down my spine as someone planted kisses on each of my fingertips.

"Who are you?" I whispered. But dread pooled in my limbs.

When one of my fingers was sucked into a warm mouth and caressed by a hot tongue, I whipped my blindfold off my head.

Abbas released my finger from his lips and smiled his wide, feral smile. He let the bells on his chest chime. "Why … Princess Bloss … you found me."

CHAPTER TWENTY-TWO

"*T*hat smarmy psychopath!" I raged, stomping around my room that night.

All four of my husbands had gathered to strategize, and it had been my first opportunity to fill them in on Abbas' little prank. Other than Quinn, of course, who'd heard about it endlessly all afternoon in his head.

"He's trying to goad you," Declan shook his head.

"But why?" Ryan asked.

I stopped and pointed wildly at Ryan. "Yes. That! Why? Why antagonize me if he's here for an alliance?"

"Maybe he doesn't want the alliance," Connor crossed his arms. "He did seem pretty self-satisfied all afternoon. I got a couple hints of intrigue from him. He was very interested in Quinn's mental communication abilities."

"What about Avia?"

Connor shook his head. "Polite disinterest was the best I got. Boredom even, when they sat together at dinner tonight. But … when he looked at you—"

"Yes?"

Every eye in the room focused on Connor, who ran a hand through his unruly brown curls and then cupped his chin. His eyes flickered from Ryan to Quinn and then Declan before he answered. "It was hard to describe. There was a hint of desire. But the overriding emotion was excitement. Or maybe … elation?"

"What the hell does that mean?" Ryan got angry. He stomped over and grabbed me, dragging me back to the chair to sit on his lap. His arms locked possessively around me for a moment.

I was starting to recognize his need to hold me when he got upset.

Connor eyed the pair of us for a moment before he said, "I'm not sure."

Declan pinched the bridge of his nose. "I think he's trying to get a read on the five of us. Trying to be divisive."

"Again. Why?" I leaned my head back against Ryan and let him stroke my arms.

Quinn turned and looked me in the eye. *If it was me, I'd use it as a distraction technique. For whatever it was I really wanted.*

"Well, if he doesn't want Avia and he doesn't want me, what the sarding hell does he want?"

The silence that followed my question was deafening.

We didn't know.

*T*he day after Abbas' arrival and finger-sucking ploy, was hectic.

I had a morning breakfast with all the ambassadors. Connor accompanied me and did his best to smooth things over with Meeker, the Sedarian ambassador, who still had a bee in his bonnet over Abbas' visit. He was doing an excellent job until...

"Haven't haard a single thing about his plans!" Meeker scolded as he shoved a buttered croissant into his mouth. He kept talking even as he spat bits of crumb. "He's such a smug bastaard though. Waatching me, knowing he's gaat elven chain. Good luuck with him activating thaam though! Ha."

I tried not to hide my ignorance of the subject. Other than understanding elven chains controlled the person who wore them, I knew very little about how they worked. The elves on the Isles of Peth typically guarded their secrets well. Only the country of Sedara had ever gained their confidence. "Well, thank goodness for that. Then what they stole has little value."

"I didn't say thaat—"

"So do they have the ability to activate the chain?" I took a sip of my juice. "Or did they steal something they couldn't use?"

"I, they—" Meeker suddenly stopped talking and glared at me, realizing Abbas could activate that chain.

Hell and sard. Not what I wanted to hear, I thought.

"Do you think Abbas is too old for my sister?" I asked, staring over at the pair of them, who'd shown up across the hall and were serving themselves breakfast. I pretended I hadn't noticed Meeker's slip.

"Entirely," Meeker eyed me.

"I'm inclined to agree. What kind of country has a suitor visit before the girl is even of age? It's rather manipulative, isn't it? To influence an innocent young girl that way?"

Next to me, Connor squeezed my hand twice as Meeker went stiff again. And all Connor's hard work went to nothing.

I stared at Meeker as though I didn't know what I'd said. But, Sedara had sent Declan over when I was only fourteen. My mother had declared him her ward and sent him to class alongside me. She'd never given him the lavish reception of a suitor, hadn't told me about it until I was eighteen. I was certain Meeker considered my mother's actions a slap in the face.

I considered her sensible, recognizing what a snake-in-the-grass Abbas was. Declan had been my age and hadn't had nearly the same seductive powers when we were younger. But throw a young girl a ball, as we were about to do in a few days … lots of princesses could get swept away in the romance of it all. I wouldn't let Avia be one of them.

I wasn't quite sure why my mother had allowed Abbas to have the full suitor treatment. I thought perhaps her illness had made her leave the details to her butler, Jorad, who ran everything in the castle according to a long book full of protocols. If she was well, I very much doubted she would have approved how Abbas kept his hand low on my sister's back. So low it could easily slip—

"Should I go break up the happy couple?" I asked, as I saw Avia start. She didn't squeal, but I was pretty certain our honored guest had just taken privileges.

I stomped toward them, flames in my eyes, just as a young serving girl carrying a white daisy approached us and stopped to speak with Connor.

"Your Highness. Avia," I greeted them both and allowed them a moment to get the annoying curtsy and bow out of the way.

Abbas looked amused, his eyes dancing as he studied me. He knew exactly what had brought me stomping over.

"My, Princess Bloss, you look quite excited this morning. And the Sedarian ambassador, sadly, looks a bit put out. Why might that be?"

I turned so I could see Meeker out of the corner of my eye. He was red in the face, ready to burst with rage. I only hoped the new rage I'd given him outweighed the old, and that he'd forget he'd essentially confirmed that the elven chain stolen by Cheryn was an active threat.

"Meeker was just warning me about you. He seems to think that you're dangerous."

"Does he?" Abbas laughed.

"Well, it was rather confusing. He thought you dangerous but an idiot. A dangerous idiot."

"And why is that?"

"He thinks you have elven chains but aren't smart enough to activate them," I gave a playful shrug, watching Abbas carefully.

His courtier's smile didn't drop. Not an inch. His expression didn't tighten. But his abdomen did, ever so slightly. And then his fingers flexed.

He did have the chains. And he didn't like Meeker's insult. Insults riled him.

"What did you tell Ambassador Meeker?"

"I told him that if Cheryn had any ill intentions toward us, they wouldn't have sent their least powerful prince as the representative suitor."

Abbas' eyes narrowed.

I batted my eyelashes up at him. "If you'll excuse me, I'd like to steal my sister away." I linked arms with Avia and hurriedly left the chamber.

"Are you mad, Bloss?" she asked, as I opened a seam to a spelled passageway and pulled her inside.

"No. But they certainly are," I responded as I lifted my skirts and began to lead the way back to my chamber.

"Why would you do that?"

"Angry men make mistakes," I replied. "I need to know who our true enemies are—who sent this beast after you and what the hell Abbas wants."

Quinn, get shadows on Meeker and Abbas. Now.

Yes, Dove. And may I say, beautiful performance?

I grinned as I led my sister around a dark bend in the tunnel.

We emerged in my chambers and Avia was shaking her head like our governess had. "This sounds like a terrible idea."

"Avia, you've watched Ryan and the others fight, right? Have you ever participated in a sparring match?"

She shuddered and ran her hands over her arms. "No! That's sounds awful. Why would I want to do that?"

"Because … someone has it out for Evaness. I'm forcing the fight. If you'd sparred, you'd know: it's far less painful to give a hit than to get one."

❧

*T*hat afternoon, Quinn and Declan joined me in my room to discuss Abbas.

Meeker had been ranting to his staff about my churlish and immature ways all morning. But ranting meant little.

Abbas hadn't said a word to anyone. Quinn's people had followed him around, and only seen him go on a nature walk through the palace orchards, where he'd been accosted by a rabbit, nearly tripping over it.

"Wyle says that elven chains need a ring to activate them. And a magical spell. Not impossible. But Abbas is the djinni who only received speed as his power. I doubt he inherited enough power himself to activate it. He could have a witch or mage in his entourage who could, though," Declan said.

He has a glowing ring in his rooms, Quinn said. *But he hasn't put it on. That could be a power source. No one in his entourage has done any active spell work though.*

"Would his brothers be able to activate it?" I asked.

"Probably," Declan sighed. "If they'd come."

I kicked my legs up on the side of my chair and played with my hair. "Conspiracy theory. Most husband groups are not like mine, cobbled together. Most are families of brothers. Or groups of male friends who seek a wife. Would you, in a normal situation—not ours—have let your brother go to meet your future wife without you?"

"No," Declan shook his head vehemently.

No sarding way.

"Well, then, further conspiracy. What if his brothers are here somehow?"

"The spell at the gates removes all disguise spells," Declan gave me a look that said I was an idiot.

I glared at him. "I said it was a conspiracy theory."

"The brothers have been ill since their mother passed away four months ago."

I sighed. "Fine."

It's not a terrible theory, Dove. The rest of them are shape shifters. It's just ... highly unlikely.

"I just ... something in my gut just feels wrong. Abbas shouldn't be here alone. He should have rescheduled. He didn't. Why not? Why did his brothers let him come? Unless they're desperate for this alliance? Unless there's something here they really want or need. Something they can't wait for..."

I trailed off. Evaness was a prosperous and fertile country. We had fertile fields.

If Abbas was desperate enough to come here without his brothers, why the hell was he insulting me? I yanked a hank of hair, frustrated. I was going in circles. I was getting nowhere.

"Dammit!" I cursed, just as my door swung open.

"Dammit!" Connor's voice reverberated off my walls. He stomped in carrying an armload of white daisies. "Stop sarding trying to buy my forgiveness with pranks! You think sending every cute serving girl under the age of six with a flower is going to convince me you're not a liar? That we aren't spelled?"

I watched Connor dump the daisies all over my bed. "I didn't—"

Next to me, Declan and Quinn burst into laughter.

Connor and I turned to face them.

I put my hands on my hips. "I'm guessing you two have something to do with this?"

Declan shook his head between guffaws. "Nope. Not me. But I think Quinn's getting desperate."

Quinn nodded. And then he started moving his hips suggestively, pumping the air.

I smacked my hand over my forehead. But I couldn't stop my smile. "I'm sorry, Connor."

He stared at all of us a moment, before he turned and stomped out.

I rounded on Quinn. "You pissed him off."

No, Dove. He was holding in a laugh that entire time.

"Oh." I stared out the open door with longing.

"I'm gonna go follow him," Declan grinned.

"Why?"

Declan paused at the door. "Oh. I forget. You weren't here. Well, a few years ago, I was curious. Connor's power doesn't have a color when he uses it. And I was wondering about the price. I mean, why should he lose his emotions? If he was just seeing other people's emotions, you'd expect him to then be kind of obtuse after. To go emotion-blind or something. But we think he actually drinks in emotion a little. Sips it. So, he drinks in others' emotions and loses his own."

I bit my lip. That made so much sense. And I'd been gone when they figured it out. I'd missed a huge piece of Connor's life.

Before guilt could flood me, Declan added, "So, I'm just gonna follow Connor around for a bit, thinking all kinds of dirty thoughts about you. Let him drink that in."

Quinn gave Declan a huge smile and a nod.

Dec turned to me and winked. "Trust me, we'll get him turned around."

A girl could only hope.

CHAPTER TWENTY-THREE

T he next day was an exercise in caution as I
waited to see what Sedara and Cheryn
might do.

Ryan had to work with his guards and begin the process
of clearing Willard's province out. Connor got the
unhappy task of breaking the news of herd and population relocation to Willard and his mother—though the
official stance was water poisoning in the area. Declan
stayed at my side, as he could tote his books and ledgers
anywhere. And Quinn disappeared off to do whatever he
did. Hopefully ferret out the dragon and its keeper.

Since it was a crisp fall day, but decent enough weather,
some acrobats had been arranged to perform on the front
lawn at luncheon. And then Avia and Abbas were to take a
turn around the garden.

Unfortunately, my sister ended up with a stomachache
after eating and had to beg off.

Sarding hell.

I had to figure out who could entertain the foreign prince for two hours.

I sat on the grass in my mint green gown, a small gold circlet in my hair. I worried Quinn's bead beneath my fingers as I scanned the crowd of nobles on the lawn, looking for a suitable victim.

A hand interrupted my view. A strong, wide, dark-skinned hand, with a scar running along one thumb. I looked up to see Abbas smiling down at me. Today, he was dressed in traditional Evaness clothing, so his sculpted pecs were not on display. But his tight breeches left little to the imagination.

Abbas' dark eyes bore into mine. "Since your sister has sadly been forced to leave us, I wondered if you'd care to join me and show me these magnificent grounds, Your Highness."

I raised my brows. Not the reaction I'd expected after I'd insulted his magical prowess. Men typically didn't like to be labeled 'smallest' at anything. "Actually, I have—"

"You have plans more important than the pending alliance between our countries?" His tone was soft but lethal.

There it was. That hint of a threat I'd been looking for.

"We do have a lovely group of poinsettias to the east," I pasted on a smile and let him help me to my feet.

Behind me, Declan struggled to roll his parchment and close all his books.

Abbas tucked my hand over his arm and began to walk to the gravel path. But the distance spell tugged at me and I planted my feet.

"We need to wait for my knight."

Declan hurriedly gathered his supplies in a bag and slung it over his shoulder.

"You're perfectly safe with me, Your Highness," Abbas joked lightly, but his eyes sparked with anger.

I grinned. "I might be. But you are a young, attractive, highly-eligible prince. Did you ever consider you might not be safe with me?"

Abbas' studied my face as his grin grew. "You're not the shy flower you were growing up."

"We've met?"

He laughed. "I'm heartbroken you don't remember. It was before the last Fire War. So you might have been six."

"If I was, then you would have been utterly disgusting, sorry. Boy germs and all that."

"All that indeed."

I gestured right and we went down a path lined with ever-greens that smelled of juniper and pine.

We walked in silence a moment, appreciating the peaceful crunch of gravel underfoot. The chatter from the rest of the nobles faded to bird-like twitters.

A bluebird alighted on a nearby branch, quite close to Abbas. He stopped, stared at it, then waved his hand to shoo it away.

"Don't like birds, Prince Abbas?" I laughed as the bird flew skyward but then dived back down toward Abbas' face, clearly dive-bombing him in retribution. Abbas' long hair was nearly his downfall as the bird got a piece and yanked. "Ah! They don't like you. I'll have to tell Quinn. My knight's under the impression that woodland creatures and nobility are fond of each other."

"Little asswipe," Abbas muttered under his breath.

"Oh, don't let a silly bird ruin our enchanted outing."

"Enchanted?" he grinned. "I knew you were taken with me, but enchanted is a strong word."

"Particularly for you," I winked.

His smile dropped a little. "May I ask where you heard such awful rumors about me?"

I almost felt bad. But the persona I adopted was intended to push him. To find that secret moment when I pushed too far and the courtier faded and truth remained. Nice wasn't an option. Not when I was hunting those who might hurt Avia. Or Evaness.

I waved my hand back and forth casually in response to Abbas' question. "Oh, you know how servants talk. Your youngest brother is supposedly the most impressive. But sadly, he couldn't come to visit."

"You certainly know how to cut a man's ego."

"Is yours large enough to cut?" I pushed harder.

Behind us, Declan's blush was hilarious. The innuendo was too much for my sweet knight.

Abbas grabbed my hand and tucked it gently back into his. He clearly had no issues with innuendo. "I'll let you stroke *my ego* anytime you want, Princess."

"I'd have to use my pinkie then."

His dark eyes glittered as he leaned down toward my ear and whispered, "I love it when you take out your little claws. One day, I'm going jam you so hard that I wipe that smug look right off your face. You'll be screaming my name."

"What a lovely double entendre," I pulled away and turned to Declan. "Can I take that as a direct threat against my person and have him locked up?"

Abbas didn't look worried in the least. He still held my hand, still had that smug grin slicing across his chiseled jaw. Perhaps he was only playing. Perhaps he wasn't truly a threat. But those who didn't have magic had to find their strength in other arenas. Was Abbas a good liar? A skilled manipulator? I didn't know.

I looked back at Declan, since he didn't answer right away. "Should we detour to the dungeon? Or not?"

Declan glared at me for making him this uncomfortable in front of a stranger. "Most people would only hear the sexual implications, *wife*. Unfortunately, I don't think it's quite enough," Declan said.

"Damn. I'll have to goad you into real threats."

Abbas grinned. "I look forward to it. I thought you were giving me a tour of the grounds."

"I am."

"You haven't pointed out a single plant."

I put my hand to my mouth in mock horror. "Oh dear. I'm sorry. To your left are trees. And some bushes. And beneath all of those is a marvelous little plant called grass."

"You're an illuminating tour guide."

I decided to push again. Without sugar-coating. "Why did you come without your brothers? If you all seek Avia's hand, why not all come at once?"

Abbas looked down at me. With the afternoon sun behind him, I couldn't read his expression. "The country of Evaness is well connected. You have access to trade with Lored. You have a working treaty with Sedara that gives you access to the elven weapons created on the Isles of Peth. You even get along with your neighbor, Rasle, to the west. How is that?"

He hadn't answered my question. I noted that fact but didn't press. I had a feeling that the answer was not a happy one.

"My father, Knight Lewart, embraced negotiation. Lots of it. Eventually, Queen Gela agreed."

"Negotiation. I've heard of this concept. I believe my father calls it losing."

His sarcasm wrung an unwilling laugh out of me.

He looked pleased with himself, allowing his free hand to come and stroke my hand, where it was tucked into the crook of his arm.

Declan cleared his throat behind us, but Abbas didn't seem to notice. Or else, didn't seem to care. I was too interested in what Abbas might say to yank my hand away. A tiny concession to this prince, a tiny hand stroke to let him think he had me enthralled, was worth it to get him to open up regarding his intentions.

"What do you see as valuable enough to consider an alliance with me, Bloss?"

I noted Abbas' informal use of my given name and it took everything within me not to stiffen. "Your brother's magic. Your wishes. Your people have a wide range of gifts. The djinn are quite lucky."

"Ah, yes. But, with magic comes arrogance. What happens to those who are not as gifted? Or not gifted at all?"

"We all do the best we can with what we are given." I patted his hand and gave him a pitying look.

"I don't speak of myself."

"Don't you?"

"Imagine being born with a certain gift and then one day you found, it was gone? What if gifts could be wished away?" Abbas' tone was smooth, smiling, rich as chocolate. But his words were sharp enough to cut me to the bone.

I stopped and turned to face him. I studied his eyes, his perfectly pleasant expression. He gave me nothing, no clue as to his true intentions.

Shite. I wish Connor was here. Or Quinn had put a bead in Abbas' hair, I thought.

Did the Prince of Cheryn just threaten me? Or offer to solve the problem of my power?

CHAPTER TWENTY-FOUR

*O*nce I escaped the uncomfortable tension of Abbas' company, I went to check on Avia. I made Declan call Quinn and pull the next room over trick for the distance spell. I wanted to tend to my sister.

Avia turned toward me from where she lay nestled under the covers. She looked rather green. And her hair clung to her face.

"Oh no," I shooed away her handmaid and grabbed the wet rag the woman had been using. I placed it on Avia's forehead, dragging my fingers along her warm cheek.

"Squawk, what happened?"

"Something I ate, I think."

"Think you'll be better for the ball tomorrow night?"

"I'd better be," her lips drew into a thin, determined line. "It's nearly my seventeenth birthday and I was going to pretend it was my celebration."

I chuckled. "Goose, it *is* your celebration."

She shook her head. "No. It's for Abbas. All this fanfare is because he's part djinn."

"Or because he's seeking to marry you?"

Avia rolled her eyes. "If one of the non-magical princes of Rasle came here, would we show them this much care?"

I shrugged. "I've never lived through a true foreign suitor visit. Mother just chose for me."

"Bullshite!" Avia said, then clutched her stomach. "Ugh. Don't get me upset."

"I'm not trying to get you upset," I leaned my elbows on the bed and propped up my head. "It's true."

"You didn't need a ball. And mother didn't choose for you. Not really. You had a crush on Ryan the moment you saw him," Avia countered. "You loved Connor your entire life."

"But Declan and I used to get into debates during our classes. We were always arguing. We never got along."

"First of all, that's because you're both always so arrogantly certain you're right. You through instinct, he through endless research. He's a perfect match for you. Besides, don't you remember the cakes incident?"

"You mean fiasco?"

"He multiplied chocolate cakes for you. By the hundreds."

I rolled my eyes. "He just didn't have good control over his power. He didn't know how to go small."

"Bloss, he was sarding in love with you. Everyone else saw it. You were too blinded by the other two to notice. And too immature to even manage a thank you at the time, remember?"

My face heated up and a little part of my chest constricted. "He was not."

I would have known. Wouldn't I? I thought back. But my memory was hazy.

"He always stared after you when you'd walk down the hall. Always."

"Stop. Now you're making things up."

Avia held up two fingers. "Swear it." She paused and bit her lip. "Confession, I may have noticed because I may or may not have had a childhood crush on Declan."

My jaw dropped. "What?" And, despite myself, despite knowing that Declan was grown, that it was a childhood crush, that my sister would never do anything to hurt me, that Declan foolishly was thinking about marrying me ... I felt jealousy rise up inside of me. Some part of me claimed Declan as mine.

Shite. She's right, I reeled from the revelation.

Some part of me claimed all of them.

"What about Quinn?"

"Please. He's a walking orgasm."

That's true.

This is a private conversation. Get out.

All right. But only after you admit it's true.

You may be slightly attractive.

I'll take it.

Shitehead.

Sard me. I'm in love with them. All of them. I couldn't deny the truth of that thought.

Tears filled my eyes. "We need a new topic." Because even if I wanted to claim them, I couldn't.

"Don't Bloss," Avia reached out and grabbed my hand.

"Don't what?"

"Don't run again. You'll kill them."

"No. I'll kill them if I stay. War is brewing."

She squeezed my hand hard. "Forget that. You love them. Admit it."

"Of course, I love them! That's why I need to sarding get out of here."

Avia sighed and leaned back against her pillows. "You need to solve the problem with them, if you love them."

"Not necessarily," I said. "Abbas said something interesting today … something about taking away gifts."

Avia sat straight up in bed then, even though it made her wince. "There's something off about him."

"You don't think he's handsome?"

"I'm not blind. But I'm also not an idiot."

"Why do you think he's here?"

"I'm not sure. But it's not for me, I can tell you that. He couldn't be more disinterested if he tried."

I stared at her. "That can't be. He definitely spoke about alliances with me."

"I definitely think he wants to ally with you. Emphasis on the lie part."

"Do you mean lay or lie?" I laughed.

"Probably both," she winked.

We giggled at her joke, letting the light-hearted moment break up our serious conversation, until Avia held her stomach and I helped her lie back down.

"I'm never eating cold pheasant again," Avia swore.

"Yes, I'll hold you to that until tomorrow," I grinned. My sister's appetite would never allow such a thing.

We smiled at one another for a moment. But soon my thoughts grew pensive again. I confessed to Avia, "Abbas might be able to help me."

Avia grabbed my hands and squeezed them. The look on her face was grave. "I already told you, don't trust him, Blossie. Something's off with him."

"But he's part djinn. Djinn have the power to grant wishes," I pulled away and crossed my arms.

"Wishes always go wrong," Avia shook her head. "You wish to end a war, you get a dictator. You wish for safety, you end up in locked safely in a prison cell. Even if he has the best of intentions, which I doubt, we can't trust him. Besides, don't half-djinn only get to grant a few wishes anyway?"

"Three. In their semi-immortal lifespans, they only get three." I leaned my head back against the chair and stared at the ceiling. "Shite, Avia. I just don't want a dragon to …" I couldn't say it.

"I know. It won't. We'll come up with a plan. It won't."

That night I slept curled up next to my little sister.

In the morning, Avia was better. And I thought the ray of sunshine peeking through the window signaled a good day.

But then Ryan entered with news that a large black shape had been spotted flying over the Cerulean Forest during the night. The forest where Cerena's cottage was located. That was only a few hours away from the palace.

My need to run intensified.

I had a dancing refresher course with Connor the morning of the ball. It didn't matter that a dragon had been spotted. My mother had ordered the refresher. So, I was not allowed to skip it.

"Calm down and focus," Connor admonished, after I'd stepped on his toes a third time.

"I shouldn't be here. I should be out there. I should be chasing that thing," I gripped his shoulder harder than needed. As if that would somehow convince him to let me go with Ryan and his team, who'd set out to investigate at first light. I'd barely had time to kiss Ryan goodbye before he'd been out the door, heading to a gargoyle to mount up and search the forest and the skies for signs of the beast.

"If you'd just help me convince Wyle to break the distance spell—"

Connor reached up to loosen my grip. He stopped our waltz, no doubt annoying the piano player who'd started and stopped eight times over the course of this lesson already.

Connor gazed steadily at me. "Bloss, Ryan is on this. Quinn's people are looking into it. I've spread rumors that we've been doing nightly air patrols. That should douse the mass panic. You need to trust us."

I wrung my hands, mimicking the feeling in my gut. I was a twisted, gnarled mess inside. "I ... I'm not used to doing that," I confessed, staring at the black and white pattern on the marble floor.

"I'm aware. If you were, you never would have run in the first place."

I glanced up. "I am sorry."

He shook his head. "I'm just ... so angry at you." He dropped his grip on me and took a few steps away. He looked at the piano player. "Can we have the room for a few minutes? I'll fetch you when we're ready."

The piano man slunk off in a hurry.

Connor turned back toward me. Without an audience, the anger on his face was blinding. He didn't bother to contain it. It hit me like a blast of heat, the kind that comes from stepping out of the shade into the midday midsummer sun. I withered.

"You didn't trust me enough to tell me. You didn't trust me enough to take care of you, to protect you—"

"I couldn't—"

He shook his head. "You could have found a way. Look at now. How'd you get the other knights to figure it out?"

"I ... but I'm different now. Back then, I was so scared of stepping out of line."

"You ran away! How much more stepping out of line does it get?"

"I was trying to save everyone."

"By leaving me? Leaving your other knights? Leaving your mother without an heir? Leaving Evaness without a god-damned queen?" Connor snapped. "You're so much smarter and better than the rest of us that you didn't need our help?"

I took a step back. His fury smacked at me. Punched me. Hit me like a plank. My chest felt bruised, beaten. It was hard to take a breath. Because he was right. He was completely and utterly right. I'd been arrogant.

Connor didn't let up. He had four years of pent up anger, of hurt and loss and self-doubt swirling inside him that needed to pour out. And pour it did. "You think your mother didn't search for a cure? Are you that stupid? To think that Queen Gela didn't use every resource she had to help you? She's always thought of you. Always! She never told me exactly what was wrong, Bloss. But she did take me aside after you left. Told me something wasn't right with you. I thought she meant not right in the head —which still sarding applies—"

"You're right." I sank to the floor and hugged my knees. My head felt hollow. Everything I'd done, and all the reasons I'd had, took on a new light. "You're right."

"Of course, I'm sarding right! I know I'm right."

"I'm sorry." I dipped my head onto my knees. I clearly pictured each person I'd left behind. And how their life had been made that much harder. Trying to take on my responsibilities, to cover for me, to act as though everything was fine; I'd hurt a lot of people.

Connor came up and loomed over me. "I don't give a damn that you're sorry. I don't *believe* that you're sorry. If you were, you wouldn't be thinking about leaving. You're exactly the same as you used to be. You haven't grown up at all. You're a scared little girl who wants to run away and leave everyone behind to pick up the pieces behind you."

I curled up further, tucking my head and hiding from the truths he hurled at me. It hurt, realizing how wrong I was. It physically cut me. Made me feel ill. I had hurt so many people. So, so many people.

Quinn appeared at the door.

What's going on?

Connor didn't respond. He just stomped out, leaving me behind in a broken heap. The irony of it wasn't lost on me.

Quinn knelt beside me. *Are you okay, Dove?*

I didn't answer. I just stared off into space, feeling as jagged and broken as glass.

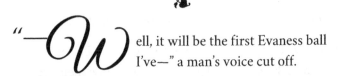

"—ell, it will be the first Evaness ball I've—" a man's voice cut off.

I glanced up. I was still curled up on the dance floor; Quinn was beside me, rubbing my spine. I'd been staring silently at nothing for over an hour.

Avia and Mateo had come into the room, hands linked.

As soon as Avia spotted me, she dropped Mateo's hand and rushed forward.

"Bloss, what's wrong?"

I shook my head and laughed. I had to fight to keep the laugh from turning into a cry. My voice croaked as I answered, "Connor just pointed out what an ass I am."

"Should I punch him for you?" Avia stroked my arm.

"No. I feel like I should let everyone line up and take shots at me."

"If we all did that, there'd be nothing of you left."

"I might be alright with that," I sighed, rubbing my face.

"Quinn, can you and Mateo give us a minute?" Avia asked.

Quinn stood, stretching. He nodded at Mateo and they moved a few feet away.

"So … tell me."

"He just said what you said last night, essentially. Don't run."

"See. I'm right."

I sighed. "You're right. I can't run. But … at this point, I don't know what I can do to convince any of them to trust me on that front."

Avia smiled with a glint in her eye. "I might have an idea." She turned to Mateo. "M, can you please show Quinn that demonstration of the wild orangutan your brother ran into in Lored?"

Mateo instantly turned red. "Um … I, that's not really something I—"

"It's for a very good cause," Avia cut him off and turned to Quinn. "And you, sir. Don't you dare listen or I'll put cinnamon into every dish you eat from now on! I know you hate it. That's right. The chef told me your weakness."

Quinn put a hand on his chest in an exaggeration of innocence.

Avia just shook a warning finger at him. Then she turned to Mateo. "Alright. Go ahead."

And that's when the Macedonian ambassador's son stooped, swung his hands over his head, and started screeching.

I turned to Avia in fascination. "You have him wrapped around your finger."

She winked. "I'll help you do the same." She leaned in. "Now, here's the plan."

My eyes widened as she whispered. And I couldn't help that my heart thumped faster from nerves. "Are you sure it's a good idea?"

"It's the best way to prove you're serious."

"But what if they won't—"

Avia rolled her eyes. "Ask Quinn."

I turned to look at Quinn, who was completely ignoring Mateo as the other man bounded around the room, hooting and hollering. Quinn's eyes were firmly fixed on mine and a small smile stretched across his lips.

Were you listening?

Of course, I was listening, Dove. I'm a spy.

Well? Will it work? Do you think—

Yes. Quinn's grin stretched wider. *It'll work.*

I turned to Avia and gave her a slow nod. "Alright. You have full reign."

Avia hugged me and squealed. "Oh! This ball just got a hundred times more exciting!" She sprang to her feet and grabbed Mateo. "Come on!"

"Where are we going?" he asked as she ran out the door.

My sister didn't respond. She simply tugged him behind her and disappeared down the hall.

Quinn came forward and captured my lips in a soft kiss.

Come, Dove. Let's get my princess ready for the ball.

CHAPTER TWENTY-FIVE

I'd never seen the ballroom look more beautiful. The room was lined in archways and marble pillars. The pillars had been decorated with climbing vines with pink leaves that glowed slightly. I was certain Wyle had been put to work. The parquet wood floors had an intricate rose pattern that almost looked woven. They gleamed under the candle chandeliers.

An orchestra sat on a high balcony, overlooking the dance floor. To one side were thrones on a raised dais, over-looking the splendor of it all. Normally, my mother and fathers would look down from those thrones. But my mother's condition didn't allow it this time. The thrones remained empty.

Instead of focusing on that, I allowed my gaze to continue around the room, where tables were piled high with food sculpted into different towering shapes.

Along one wall at the end of the dance floor was a mirror. And that's when I saw the full effect of my gown for the first time.

Mother had commissioned me a silver dress. It was lined with the most delicate lace, lace that was actually soft to the touch. The neckline scooped low, and the waistline high, allowing my skirt to flare out naturally. Diamonds were sewn into the lace lining my collar and the sash that snugged the dress to my waist. A wild crown full of shells and jewels adorned my head. My silver sleeves were thin and covered in lace. I couldn't help but turn and admire how the silver shimmered in the candlelight. Silver was a color typically reserved for brides.

It was almost as if mother had known. My cheeks flushed at that thought.

It had been a long time since I'd been this anxious. I'd had to deal with nerves day in and day out when I'd been on the run. I'd learned just to ride the adrenaline. But tonight, I was nervous. Quite nervous.

Even as the crowd bowed at my entrance, my attention wasn't on them.

My eyes searched for my knights, who'd already been announced. Who'd entered the ballroom before I had, due to Avia's prodding and threats.

I stared down the stairwell at the four men who'd captured my heart.

Ryan wore a metal breastplate, the sign of my house engraved in the middle. A burning rose. Declan wore all blue. His light blue shirt and vest offset his eyes. Someone had thrown Connor into hunter green. Even though his eyes were blue, it had always been my favorite color on him, because his eyes were a shade of blue that could transform based on what he wore. His curls were still a beautiful mess. No one could ever tame his curls. And Quinn wore black. Even at a ball. Even at our own cele-bration, he was dressed to fade into the shadows. But his eyes, his eyes were alight with happiness.

I looked from man to man, making eye contact with each of them. My heart filled. It filled with so many emotions it felt like my body was a dam about to burst. Heavy guilt. Potent fear. Lust. Gallons of lust. Drops of trust sprinkled like oil among the other emotions. And sweet, new, blooming love, floating atop all the others. I felt sure every emotion inside me would spill out onto the dance floor and sweep every person there away in a riot of feeling.

I loved Ryan's dominance and confidence. And I loved that tiny caring streak he liked to keep hidden. The streak that made him agree to help Declan. I loved Declan for his dedication, his intelligence, and his dry wit. I'd always loved Connor. His beautiful, beautiful soul, and how he went out of his way to help everyone feel good about themselves, feel confident and listened to and important. My eyes met Quinn's. I was pretty sure he'd been reading every thought I had since I walked through the door. I projected thoughts directly at him.

I love you Quinn. Your jokes and your silliness. I love so much that you've trusted me ... been there for me, and that you forgave me. From the second I arrived, you forgave me. You let me know forgiveness was possible. If you hadn't ... I might have given up.

His eyes sparkled with tears.

I smiled at him as the herald trumpeted and announced my name.

And then, breaking protocol, Avia appeared beside me, a cleric at her side. As the potential bride for the match with Abbas, she was supposed to be the last to enter. And she was supposed to enter alone. She'd forgone her moment ... for this.

Avia clapped once, breaking up the scattered murmurs that had started upon her arrival.

My eyes scanned the crowd. Abbas stared at my sister with interest. Mateo stared with open adoration. Meeker, the Sedarian ambassador, crossed his arms. Lady Agatha frowned. The expressions for this break in protocol ran the gamut.

"Good evening," Avia said to the crowd, not the least bit cowed by the mixed reactions. "We are so grateful to celebrate a potential alliance with Cheryn tonight. And to welcome the prince of that great nation. But you will have to excuse me. And indulge me a little. I'm a romantic at heart. And my sister and her husbands never got to have a formal ceremony. Never had the chance to have their own wedding ball. And so tonight, we'd like you all to bear witness, as the future Queen of Evaness renews her vows to the knights who so bravely protected our kingdom as she traveled far and wide to protect us."

Murmuring started up in the crowd. But I didn't notice. My eyes were firmly fixed on the four men at the foot of the stairs, begging them silently to say yes. Tears filled my eyes. And I swiped at them, because I needed to see. I needed to see Ryan's mouth curve into a smile. I needed to see Declan shyly bite his lip and grin. I needed to see Connor stare right at me, straight into my soul, and evaluate me. I tried not to waver under his stare, but it was hard. The tears kept coming and I wiped them once they spilled onto my cheeks so that I could maintain eye contact. I needed him to know I meant this. That I acknowledged what he'd said. That I agreed with him. And that I wouldn't run again. Finally, Connor gave a slow nod.

The cleric stepped to the head of the stairwell. "If the gentlemen will come join the princess …"

My knights came up the stairs and arranged themselves facing me.

"Please, repeat after me. I renew my vow to honor and trust you, to keep and hold you, to work with you for the betterment of Evaness. I bond myself to you. In mind. In body. In spirit. For all the days of my life."

I spoke the words with a smile as a tear traced a path down my cheek. Because never in my entire life had I felt so exposed, so raw, so scared … and yet so uplifted. So relieved. So light. Like the burdens and fears I'd been carrying had melted away. I felt like I was floating midair. Like I'd drank a bottle of Flight. It was more intense than any magic potion I'd ever consumed. My love for them encompassed me, filled me from head to toe. It was powerful, swirling inside me, making me dizzy and light-headed. And happy. So happy.

Ryan was the first to step forward and kiss me. He wiped away my tears and said, "I love you too, Little Dearling." And then his lips planted a chaste kiss on mine.

Declan was next, taking my hand and kissing it before cupping my cheek and kissing me softly. He didn't speak. But his shining eyes spoke for him, unshed tears glistening in the candlelight.

When he stepped back, Connor stepped forward. And my trembling ramped up anew.

"I'm scared, too," Connor whispered in my ear. "But thank you. For choosing not to run away again. Thank you, for choosing us." And then his lips lightly touched mine, sending electricity down my spine.

Quinn came last, a smirk plastered across his features. *I knew you couldn't resist me for long.*

I gave a broken laugh.

And then he grabbed me, dipped me, and gave me a kiss that made the crowd holler.

CHAPTER TWENTY-SIX

*W*e danced. I danced with each of my husbands, laughingly stumbling through court dances that I hadn't done in years and my feet failed to remember. I didn't know if the nobles noticed, or if they wrote off my clumsiness to the happy tears that continually seemed to streak down my face. Frankly, I didn't care.

Avia danced with Abbas, looking very self-satisfied whenever I caught her eye. She did mouth, "Told you," a time or two at me.

I couldn't even roll my eyes at her. I was too happy.

I was filled to the brim, overflowing even, with joy that was light and frothy and airy. The world had never looked more beautiful. My husbands had never looked more delicious. I leaned in more than once, propositioning them. Declan nearly caved, but Connor intercepted us before we could sneak off the dance floor. He swept me off for a new dance.

"Something's wrong with that boy who's been hanging around Avia," Connor told me. My eyes swept the room.

Mateo stood off to one side, a flagon in his hand and a scowl on his face.

"He's furious. With you."

"How can you tell? What if he's furious with Abbas? She's dancing with him."

Connor shook his head. "I just can. I'm not sure how."

I sighed. "Well, I did tell her to focus on Abbas and leave Mateo alone for now. We can't have her ruin a potential alliance."

"How likely do you think alliance is?" Connor whispered when he pulled me close, so that no one around could hear.

"Depends on what Quinn's people find. Have you heard anything?"

Connor didn't answer, but Quinn did.

Some of his servants went out tonight. To a local tavern. Have some people there buying them rounds.

Got it. Hopefully they find something.

I'll let you know if they do.

Connor spun me, and I was about to lean in and propose a long session of nakedness when Abbas cut in.

He bowed, as if he weren't being a complete ass.

I smiled stiffly.

"May I, Your Highness? I have not had the opportunity to congratulate you," the silk-tongued rat bastard said, pulling me smoothly away from my husband.

Connor just smiled and made his way off the dance floor.

I turned to face Abbas and curtsied. "Thank you, for your congratulations."

He studied my face. "You are very attached to your knights."

The observation made me wary. "They are excellent men. I'm honored to be their wife."

He tilted his head, allowing his raven black hair to sweep his shoulder. He wore a loose white shirt and fitted breeches tonight. But he'd long ago tossed his vest and jacket aside. He was hardly decent for a ball. His tattoos were clearly visible through the thin material of his shirt, which gaped open scandalously at his chest, allowing the sculpted middle of his pecs to peek through. His beard was oiled and sleek and looked soft.

"You're certainly going all out in your attempt to seduce my sister," I raised a brow as he led me through a slow spin. I gestured at his shirt.

"Are you certain it's your sister I'm trying to seduce?" Abbas whispered as he pulled me back in.

My eyes jerked up sharply and I struggled to keep my face neutral as I studied his. "You're here to court my sister. You'd ruin a potential alliance?"

"If I were to join your knights, it would simply be a different means of alliance." He was utterly calm as he spoke, utterly confident. His eyes stayed on mine, measuring my reactions. His dark, enchanting eyes didn't waver.

My heart thumped at this turn. Out of all the possible motives for Abbas' visit, I'd never imagined this.

Quinn, get Connor and get over here. I want to know his intentions and thoughts.

I watched my knights exchange a look and then each latch on to a female courtier and step back onto the dance floor. My tone when I looked back up at Abbas was calm and measured. "You come for my sister, and yet you proposition me. Does that not make your intentions duplicitous?"

"Ah. You mistake my father's intentions for my own."

"You'd defy your father?"

He shrugged a shoulder and the corner of his mouth quirked up. "He desires an alliance with Evaness. I ... desire you."

Shock rolled through like an oceanic fog. It clouded my thoughts. "This … is unexpected."

Suddenly a squirrel appeared on top of Abbas' head. It held a pair of nut in its hands and swung down from Abbas' hair to shove the nuts into his mouth.

I couldn't swallow my laugh quickly enough.

Abbas' eyes tightened.

"I'm sorry. So sorry. Quinn is making me see things."

"The mind-speaker?"

"Yes. He can make me see things sometimes."

Abbas grew intrigued. "And what did he show you just now?"

I took a deep breath. But truth was easier than inventing a lie on the spot. "A squirrel. Shoving its nuts in your mouth."

Abbas' chest shook in quiet laughter. "He doesn't like my proposition. Luckily, he has no say."

Two squirrels appeared then. One on either of Abbas' shoulders.

I closed my eyes. There was no way I could not react to whatever Quinn might do next. I followed Abbas' by feel through the next few steps of the dance. "Your Highness —" I started.

"No," Abbas cut me off and my eyes flew open. "You aren't to respond yet. Think about it. My country is full of magic. An alliance with us could only increase the amount of magic here. My powers would be at your disposal. And I hear you might have need of a little magical assistance …" his eyes grew calculating.

I sucked in a breath.

Does he know about the dragons? Or is he talking about my power? I wondered.

Quinn what is he thinking?

The sarder is deliberately clouding his thoughts. He keeps picturing squirrels, erasing any other thoughts that might start to form. He knows I'm listening.

Shite.

My gasp had let Abbas know he had the upper hand. There was nothing I could do to take that back. So instead of bluffing, I asked, "Why would you propose this? What is it you want?"

"You're not reason enough?" Abbas' lips quirked.

"I'm not that naive."

"Let's say I have a vested interest in an alliance with you. Consider my proposal."

"Without an honest answer, I won't."

"It was an honest answer. Just not a specific one."

"You expect me to trust you—"

But before I could finish my sentence, Abbas kissed my hand and strode away, leaving me in the middle of the dance floor, mid-song, as women in a rainbow blur of dresses whirled by.

CHAPTER TWENTY-SEVEN

*C*onnor gently left his dance partner, so he could accompany me off the dance floor.

The rest of my knights followed suit.

We officially retired for the evening, allowing everyone one last opportunity to bow before they began to truly enjoy themselves without the supervision of their monarch.

Our group made its way out into the hall and down a long corridor. We didn't speak until we reached the Royal Wing.

As soon as we'd passed through the guarded doors, I whirled on Connor. I grabbed his elbow. "What was he feeling? Did you get any glimpses?"

"There was a tinge of desperation I think might have been real. But, like Quinn's been telling me about his thoughts … Abbas is a master, Bloss. He was great at masking. He brought in an overload of emotions so quickly. It was like he was shuffling cards."

His servants at the tavern seem sloppy drunk, and all they know is that Abbas and his father had words before the prince's departure. They seem too mixed up to give my people a real rundown on what those words are, Quinn reported.

I bit my lip. "Why would he want to break from his father?"

"The djinni who's been ruling Cheryn for centuries? Maybe because he's evil. Crazy. Crazy evil. Who cares?" Ryan scooped me up. "Let's figure that out tomorrow. You're our sarding wife now, Bloss. Declan can't block this cock anymore." He nuzzled my hair. "I'm gonna pound you so hard, they'll hear it in the ballroom. Maybe even in town."

Declan stole me out of Ryan's arms. "Wait. There's only one fair way to do this. We're all gonna want to go first. So …" Declan backed up against my door. He turned the handle with one hand and threw open the door. His other hand reached into his pocket. He pulled out a pair of dice and balanced them on his palm in front of him.

My eyes narrowed. "You're going to gamble for me?"

"Hell yeah!" Ryan scooped the dice out of Declan's hands.

"Hell no!" Connor and I both shouted.

I started and stared at Connor. "Why did you say no?"

A blush spread across his face. "Well … because you should get to choose. Right?"

I laughed. "I was gonna say you can't gamble. But you can bid for me. I'll auction myself off. Whoever bids the most outrageous sex act wins!"

I pulled off my crown and skipped through the door. I turned around to look at the four of them. They were still in the hallway. Frozen. Gaping.

"Well … come on!"

They all tried to barrel through the door at once. They got stuck. And lots of pinching and prodding and elbowing ensued until Ryan broke through first.

"Yes!"

I shook my head. "You haven't won anything … yet." I leaned against the end of my bed. I plucked at my dress, dragging the silver skirt up, up, up to my thighs. Up a little further, until my most intimate spot was bared to them.

"Who's going to bid first?" I asked.

Four pairs of eyes snapped from my swollen, wet cunt up to my face.

"You … didn't wear underthings," Declan's voice was pained.

"Nope. The entire time I danced with each of you, I was ripe for the plucking."

"I bid … I'll spank you and then give you four orgasms with my fingers," Ryan sputtered.

My nipples tightened at that.

I saw Ryan's shaft start to grow in his pants. And my eyes were drawn there. His hand snuck down and he stroked himself over his pants. My breath caught.

I'll make you come apart on my mouth so many times you pass out, Quinn said.

I turned to him. His grey eyes were magnetic, drawing me toward him. It was all I could do to stay in my spot. The other men shimmered and disappeared from my sight. Only Quinn and I were in the room.

Come to me, love. Let me kiss your lips. I'll—

"What did he say?" Declan urged.

The other men shimmered back into view as Quinn's illusion vanished.

I wagged a finger at him.

You're a naughty little cheater.

He shrugged, not at all remorseful.

Can you make sure everyone hears you at once?

It'll be a little bit like shouting but … Quinn repeated his bid. The guys and I flinched. Quinn's internal shout was like a gong in my head.

I apologized to everyone. "Sorry. I thought it would be fairer if you knew exactly what Quinn bid." I didn't share about the cheating because I wasn't ready for the game to devolve into fighting.

"You can spank me and ride me and deny me orgasms until you've come as many times as you want," Declan promised.

I stared at my blond-haired knight. He would be the only one to make that kind of offer. To let me take my pleasure from his body, rather than to give pleasure to me. I wavered. What would be better? Control or a complete lack of it? As I stared at Declan, he sank to his knees. My pussy pulsed at the sight and my breathing came hard. Some part of me loved the idea that he'd be at my mercy.

All eyes turned expectantly to Connor.

He stared at me for a long moment, as his blue eyes swirled with emotion. He cleared his throat and then said, "I'll make love to you Bloss. Love."

My heart melted. It felt like sunshine burst through my chest, like rays were shooting out my limbs.

"No fair!" Declan cried, standing up and stepping between us. "I call emotional foul. That was not a sex act."

I laughed. "Always a stickler for the rules, Dec."

"Well?" He crossed his arms. "Who's it going to be?"

My eyes flickered across each one of them. The energy in the room crackled like lightning.

"Bloss Boss," Connor whispered.

Declan stepped back and clamped a hand over Connor's mouth.

"You will choose me, Little Dearling," Ryan commanded.

I clenched my thighs together upon hearing that.

Then Quinn held out a hand. *Come on, Dove. You know you and I go together like peas and carrots.*

Shock buzzed over my skin. The heat dropped from my core. Instead, my body turned ice-cold. I dropped my skirt. "Where did you hear that?"

What?

"Say it again. So everyone can hear."

A strange glint came into Quinn's eyes as he projected the thought to everyone in the room. *You know you and I go together like peas and carrots.*

Connor turned toward me, looking hurt. "I thought … I mean I hated that saying, but I thought that was our saying."

"It was," I scanned Quinn coldly. "It was how I ended every letter I wrote to you for the past four years."

The entire room grew silent. Everyone turned to Quinn.

"What does that mean, Quinn?" Declan asked. "You took the letters?"

Quinn blew out a breath. *Sard. I discovered the letters and alerted the queen. I was ordered to take the letters. Part of the assignment to find Bloss. Take them, scan them for hints of her whereabouts.*

"Those were my letters. Why didn't you give them to me after you searched them?" Connor took an angry step toward Quinn.

I put a hand on Connor's shoulder, holding him back. Anger frothed in my belly. But I recognized my mother's hand in all this. She'd always been so controlling.

Quinn ran a hand through his hair. *First, I was told not to let you become any more miserable than you already were. That first year, the three of us basically took on your position. Secondly, I reread them a lot. I hadn't met Bloss. It was the only way I got to know her.* He turned back to look at me, regret coloring his features. *I wasn't trying to hurt anyone.*

"Sard! I want to sarding hate you. But Queen Gela," Connor shook his head. He knew exactly what mother was like.

"You had letters and it still took you four years to find her?" Ryan was incredulous.

At first, my instructions were to find and monitor her. But, once Cheryn stole those magical chains, Queen Gela wanted me to get you home, immediately. It still took a few months to track your exact location down.

"She knows war is coming," I breathed.

I believe so. And she's never told anyone else this. But she's the one who invited Cheryn's princes here to court Avia.

Sard. A war. A real war looming. Mother had already picked sides. And she hadn't even told me.

"Any other sarding secrets we need to know about now that we're married?" I asked. My anger and irritation at my mother and Quinn infused my tone. It was harsh.

Declan slowly raised his hand in the air. "Ryan and I … we have kinda … helped each other out on occasion."

It took me a minute to process what he was saying. The change in topic was so abrupt. "What? Do you mean … sexually?"

"Um…" Declan shrugged.

Ryan cuffed him over the head. "You weren't supposed to tell anyone!"

"She said any secrets! We're married now. That qualifies—"

I laughed. My anger dissipated, and I walked forward to kiss Declan on the cheek. "Thank you."

I turned to Ryan, who was still muttering under his breath.

"Ryan, are you embarrassed?" I teased, looking up at my blushing giant. "Don't be. One day, I'll probably ask you to punish Declan for telling your secret. So I can watch."

Ryan turned his hot gaze to mine. "Really?"

Heat fluttered down my spine. "Really."

Sard. I hate to interrupt this just as it's getting hot again. But one of your fathers is in the hall.

I strode quickly to the door. My knights had left it open.

My father, Peter, hovered a few feet past the door frame. His face was drawn and grey.

My heart immediately imploded. "What is it, dad?" I asked.

"Blossie. It's your mother."

CHAPTER TWENTY-EIGHT

*W*e entered the queen's chambers in a rush, crowding through the door. But as soon as we were in, we stopped.

She was gone.

I could feel it. Her presence, which normally filled a room, was nowhere to be found. She'd had an energy in life that could throttle you, make you feel small, or make you glow with pride.

My fathers surrounded her; one of them held each of her hands, Peter walked up to touch her knee. Johan's face was red and blotchy from tears. Gorg was more stoic.

I stepped forward so that I could see my mother's face. It was relaxed in a way it never been in life.

It felt like someone had taken a broken bottle to my ribs, as though glass was cutting through me, all the way down to my bones.

My mind couldn't think, couldn't form words. Inside me, there was just a tiny yelp. The cry of an abandoned child, one now forced to face the terrors of the world alone. I collapsed to my knees.

Someone put their arms around me. I didn't look to see who, because the tears came then. Long and loud and hard.

I cried until I felt like I was floating. Like reality was gone and I was no longer tethered to the world. An image popped up in my brain. Of Quinn and I floating through the sky, twined together by red ribbon. The ribbon slowly extended and pulled Ryan into my line of sight and bound him against Quinn and myself. The ribbon pulled Declan in and added him to the knot. The sentient ribbon reached out one more time, unfurling its long arm, searching through the sky for—

"Connor," I breathed.

"Yeah?" A broken whisper sounded in my ear.

I opened my eyes in shock, wiping my face quickly with the palms of my hands, clearing my vision. Conner was on the ground, cradling me. He'd wrapped me in his arms and pulled me onto his lap. His brown curls were mussed. And his eyes were red and swollen, tears still leaked down his face.

I reached up and grabbed his face in my hands. I wrapped my arms around his neck and pulled him into a tight hug.

The awful feeling in my chest eased. Still, I clutched at him. Connor had hardly touched me since my return. I'd known I'd missed him. But being in his arms made me realize how much more I needed him—needed, not simply missed him. He'd been my rock. My entire youth, he'd been my rock. During my travels, he been my rock without knowing it. I'd lived to write those letters to him. To feel connected and not adrift. I burrowed deeper, resting my cheek on his shoulder, burying my face in his neck.

Connor didn't protest, he just began to stroke my back.

When my limbs were numb, I finally struggled to stand. Connor helped me to my feet. Then he held my hand.

I stared down at his hand clutching mine. It was a struggle not to collapse in tears again. But my body was empty.

Quinn held out a cup of water. I took it gratefully with my free hand and downed the contents.

When I was finished, I noticed that my husbands had formed a protective semi-circle around me. For the first time, I saw Avia. Gorg, her birth father, held and rocked her at the foot of the bed.

There were long moments of staring. Long moments of nothingness.

Eventually, I cleared my throat. There was work to do. And, as mother always said, 'Royalty must set aside emotion and do the work. And there is always work to be done.' The eyes in the room turned to look at me.

"We have an official proclamation to make. The funeral arrangements were already planned. Unless you'd like to make any changes ..." I added, looking toward my three fathers. Inside I was pleading, hoping they'd want to change the awful, archaic ritual of cliff jumping after their queen. But I didn't allow my face to show those hopes. The choice was theirs.

"No changes," Peter responded.

Avia burst into a new round of tears.

I mentally asked Quinn to comfort her.

Once he'd scooped up my little sister I turn to my fathers and gave them a nod. "Then the funeral will be at dawn." The water would be at its coldest. Hopefully, that meant it would take them more quickly. Less painfully. I bit back the trembling of my lip.

Sard it all. I'm changing that law, come hell or high water, I thought.

Ryan put an arm on my shoulder. I was about to shrug him off because I couldn't stand a comforting touch, not when I was barely holding it together. But he turned me toward him, and his voice was steady. "I will have my men prepare the ship and have the archers ready."

"Do you think you could, the arrow—" I asked.

He nodded. "I'd be honored."

Ryan turned to Connor. "You should alert the heralds in each town. Provide the script."

Next to me, Connor nodded. He untangled our fingers and lifted my hand to his lips. He kissed my hand, his face twisted with sadness. "I'll be right back, Bloss Boss."

He'd used my pet name. My heart gave a feeble jump. But it was so weighed down with pain. I'd lost my mother, was about to lose my fathers. War loomed. And there was a dragon somewhere in my country. Despite my best efforts, a whimper escaped.

He kissed my hand again. "Promise. Right back."

I let him go. I swallowed the lump in my throat and watched Ryan and Connor walk out. Then I turned to Declan. "I'd like the list I'm sure you have drawn up, of all the possible contingencies upon mother's … passing. I'd like to go over it."

Declan nodded.

I turned and meet each of my fathers' eyes. I gave them each a small nod. I couldn't do anything further. I'd collapse. I'd fall to the floor and never be able to get up again. I left Quinn with Avia.

Declan and I walked out the door.

When we turned the corner, mother's butler, Jorad, saw me. He bowed. "Your Majesty."

I straightened my spine, though the words were like a lance through my middle.

I'm Queen. Queen, I thought. The word strangled me like a noose.

*he funeral was held at dawn, when orange stripes of light peeled away the darkness from the sky. But dawn's rays didn't touch me. I was still as dark as midnight inside.

My knights were all in full armor and they stood behind me on the cliffs. Quinn still held Avia as she cried.

My mother's body floated away with the tide, poinsettias surrounding her and stuffed underneath her limp hands. As if flowers could make death more beautiful, or this ritual less grim.

Ryan used a bow to shoot a flaming arrow at my mother's funeral ship. It caught, and I watched the flames slowly spread across her form.

I clasped hands with each of my fathers before they each took a running jump over the sixty-foot cliff edge. They started after a burning boat, on a futile quest, in a desperate attempt to mesh their souls with my mother's.

Tears streaked my face. I watched them as the crowd behind me lessened, as the sun jaunted through the sky.

I couldn't turn away. I watched them turn into pinpricks in the water. One of their heads bobbed under the waves.

I choked. I felt like puking. My body revolted against the stupid tradition that was killing them. But I couldn't stop it. They'd chosen it. So, I sent a pulse of peace magic after each of them, hoping that I could give them a moment's respite before the end, hoping that as the water filled their lungs that their bodies will forget to fight and just quickly and gently fade into eternity.

After the green pulse faded from my hands, Ryan took me in his arms. He patched the ragged wounds on my arms with his soft healing magic. And I leaned into his strength. Until he handed me roughly to Declan.

"Sorry, Bloss. I need to go punch something," Ryan strode off.

I turned with Declan, emotionally exhausted and ready to head up to the castle to hide in my chambers.

But we ran into Willard and Lady Agatha, who'd stayed the entire morning. I wasn't exactly surprised by Lady Agatha, as she considered herself one of mother's closest companions and would want to publicly reinforce that impression. But I would have thought Willard would be overseeing the migration of their herds to more southern territories. Or helping his tenants find temporary housing.

Instead, Willard came up to me, fury making his jowls shake. "You didn't hunt dragons during your travels. Not at all. And now, suddenly you're back. And a dragon's entered our lands? What are the chances of that? Hmm? You're a liar."

My stomach dropped.

Sard. How does he know about the dragon? I wondered.

"I didn't lie to you, Willard. I took a mage's oath. How could I lie?"

"I don't know, but you got around the magic somehow."

I refrained from rolling my eyes because his fury was real. His fear was real. And it was well-founded.

"I am just as concerned about the issues on your lands as you are." I refrained from saying the word dragon, as we were still in a public place. "Your herds and people are important to me. Which is why I am shocked you are not moving them to safety when they are being poisoned in their current location."

Willard squinted at me. "It's nearly winter. And your solution was to tell me to basically clear out my entire province! That's not a solution at all."

"Ryan's sending men to deal with the issue."

"Issue," Lady Agatha interjected, pulling her embroidered handkerchief down from her large nose. "You can't even say it, can you? Dragon?"

"Is your goal to cause mass panic? To cause a riot? Or is your goal to save as many of your people and as many of your cattle—hence, your profits—as you possibly can?" I sneered. I had always hated Lady Agatha. Only now I was finally in a position to show it.

"You care for your province. Or it won't be yours much longer," my eyes flashed.

Willard's face flushed. Lady Agatha's mouth dropped open.

But I was done with them. I had played mother's court games all my life. But I was done with court games. I preferred the straight, loud-mouthed barmaid form of communication.

I prefer it when you shout too, Dove, Quinn interjected. *I'd love to hear you shout my name. Think you can do that later?*

As always, my knight made me smile, even as I strode away from two of the most frustratingly stupid members of my court.

I want Willard followed, I told Quinn. *I don't trust him. My gut tells me this show of anger isn't new. And see if you can find out how he knew about the sarding dragon!*

It's done, Quinn agreed, before opening up the carriage door for me.

Declan helped me cram my long black funeral dress into the carriage and then my knights climbed in behind me.

We rode back to the castle in silence, me trying to watch the sky and avoid thinking about my mother or fathers, Declan staring at a ledger he'd found in my mother's chamber, and Quinn silently communicating with his network of spies.

When we reached the castle, Connor came down to help us out of the carriage.

I'd refused to let him go to the funeral as it would be awash with emotion and he'd end up drained. Instead, I'd had him take an Invisibilty potion and go with one of Quinn's people down to the guest wing. He'd been snooping around Abbas' servants all morning, attempting to unearth the prince's true motives.

When we reached the royal wing of the palace, I grabbed Connor's hand. Once we were inside my room, I shut the door. "Well?" I asked.

"One of the footmen did mention that Abbas and his father had some sort of disagreement. But that could have been over anything. The sultan isn't known for his good temper. Overall, the mood of the servants seemed frazzled. They were packing up some trinkets to ship back to Cheryn. It seems the prince has a fondness for souvenirs."

I couldn't hide my disappointment. "You didn't feel any stress or secrets on any of them?"

"Not in the rooms I was in. We didn't get to his personal chamber though. I didn't get to see his personal butler."

I scrubbed at my face. It was sore from all the tears over the past few days. My cheeks were raw to the touch. "Well, if we can't find out what he wants through spying, we're going to have to try something else."

"Yeah?" Connor asked. "What?"

"More magic."

CHAPTER TWENTY-NINE

*C*onnor, Declan, Quinn, and I made our way across the castle via the spelled passageways. I was done with crowds, at least for a few hours. My coronation was at sunset. But I was drained. I needed to recharge before I had to fake smile through a ceremony I wished was still a distant hazy future event. Not the bleak thing I knew it would be.

We had just darted from one secret passage across the hall to another (our goal of Wyle's tower was all the way across the castle) when Quinn made us stop.

Willard's meeting with some traders from Sedara. I need to hear this.

We all waited in the dark, leaning against the stone walls of the tunnel as Quinn had a silent debate with his minions.

Declan got bored enough that he divided the darkness to create a little bit of light where we stood. He and Connor and I began mimicking some of Quinn's more comical facial reactions.

Connor had just scrunched his nose like Quinn when the latter sent a curse reverberating through all our heads.

Shite!

"What? What is it?" I pushed off the wall. What would have my spy master so concerned?

Quinn looked at each of us in turn. His storm-cloud eyes settled on me last. And I didn't like the fear swirling in their depths.

Willard's meeting with our lovely Sedarian ambassador, Meeker. They went for a ride in the woods. One of my invisibles trailed them, though they set up spelled boundaries. My guy is good though and used his bottle of Flight. Their boundaries didn't extend overhead.

"And?"

And they were talking about trading an Evaness port in exchange for elf-made ice cannons. The kind that might be used to kill a dragon.

"Willard's land doesn't have a port." I said. "It's grazing land."

Yes, well they also discussed the possibility that Evaness ... needs a new monarch.

The words were a punch to the gut, the kind that goes all the way through the spine. It stole my breath. I stumbled backward into Declan, who put his arms around me.

"Sard. Sard. Sarding hell." I muttered.

"We aren't going to let that happen, Bloss Boss," Connor tried to soothe me.

"We have a treaty with Sedara," I bit out angrily.

"Countries will use you and toss you aside at their first convenience," Declan said wryly. "A lesson I learned when I was first sent here."

"If Sedara's going to help Willard try and unseat me ... they're looking for war."

"This smells rotten. Think about it. Would Sedara be this angry over a suitor visit?" Declan asked.

"Meeker was furious. It took me ages to calm him down," Connor responded.

"Would Willard bring in a dragon to kill your sister, but change his plans when you returned?"

I sucked in a breath. "He did ask me if I actually hunted dragons. When we had the mage spell."

Everyone exchanged dark glances.

But then Declan squinted. "All of this gives Abbas a wonderful place to negotiate from. I wonder how much his hand helped stir that pot?" He turned to face me. "How much more likely are you to consider his proposal if you think Sedara is against you? If you think your own people are turning against you? It seems rather suspicious to me."

I'm sending someone to check Meeker's chambers, Quinn told me. *We'll see if the real Meeker is in the woods or not.*

"You think one of Abbas' people is posing as Meeker?" I asked.

It's possible.

Anything is possible, I retorted.

The possibilities crowded my mind, each one clamoring for attention. I put my hands to my head, trying to stop the noise. My first day as queen, and plots already circled me like sharks.

Is this how Mother felt? I wondered.

Perhaps this was why she'd wanted to control every last detail of every person around her. Was it because so many uncontrollable forces raged against her at every turn? Was that what holding the crown meant? She'd never said as much in her lessons, but I suspected it was true. Holding the crown was simply holding a target, waiting for the next person to toss their knife at your chest.

Connor stroked my arm.

Quinn sent a pair of turtle doves cooing and circling through the corridor. One of them landed and pooped on Connor's shoulder.

"That's not nice," I eyed Quinn.

Just getting him back for cheating at sex games yesterday.

You're a silly asshole. I rolled my eyes. But Quinn quelled the panic that had been rising in my chest.

I took a deep breath. "Let's go. We'll deal with Willard later, when Ryan's back. Right now, let's go see Wyle and see what he might be able to do for us. Let's work on the Abbas problem first. I want to know why he's here and what he really wants. Then we'll tackle Willard. He's not nearly as bright."

I didn't say aloud that Meeker concerned me as I strode back down the passage. That the power of Sedara backing an idiot like Willard concerned me. Their navy made them the strongest kingdom of the seven. And if they were determined to replace me with a puppet king … a shiver ran down my spine. I'd prefer if Abbas had sent a fake Meeker to meet with Willard. I hoped that was the case. I'd rather one enemy than two.

I pushed myself to walk faster. I'd see what Wyle had in his bag of tricks to force the truth from Abbas.

Then I'll wallop that shite-eating little Lord Willard. And his mother, too.

I had no doubt Lady Agatha was aware of every move her pudgy-little-roll of a son made.

I wrung my hands as I tried to weigh whether or not I could handle an alliance with Abbas. He was smooth, but not forthcoming. He made my skin prickle. In sensuality but also in fear.

Quinn butted into my head. *There's something wrong about Abbas. I don't trust him,* he yelled at all of us.

"New rule. Unless it's an emergency or naughty bidding, you're gonna have to tell us each individually," I held a hand over my ringing ear.

"Abbas does have djinn powers though, if we're considering alliances," Declan countered. "His brothers can conjure. Not in the castle, obviously, with our preventative spells. But that could be useful."

I stopped in my tracks. "Wait. Isn't one of his brothers … can't one of them shape shift?"

Connor waved a hand. "Anyone with a good spelled disguise can do that. We don't need him for that."

"Unless he can turn into a dragon," I responded. No hedge-witch spell would be strong enough to transform a human into one of the most powerful magical creatures known to man. Even Wyle had never managed it, and I knew for a fact mother had made him try during the last Fire War. But djinn were a different story. Full djinn could easily transform. A half-djinn—I didn't know the limits for half-djinn.

We all stopped and stared at one another.

"Why didn't all the brothers come on this suitor visit again?" I asked.

Connor bit his lip. "Their official response was that two were ill and the other two susceptible to catching the illness. Magic fever. Quite dangerous to half-djinn. Their magical and their human sides war against one another. And it's contagious. The recovery is slow, I've heard."

"Why was Abbas able to make it?" I asked.

"He typically stays at their military outpost instead of in the palace."

I stopped walking. "Shite."

"Do you think the illness is a lie? You think one of the brothers has been the dragon prowling around?" Connor asked.

"What did your ambassadors in Cheryn say?"

Connor shook his head. "No one's seen the princes. They've been in quarantine for over a month. But you really think … a dragon?"

I bit my lip. "I don't sarding know. But now I really want to do a mage spell with Abbas so he *has* to tell me the truth."

I ran my hand along the seam that opened the spelled passageway and pushed open the door. We came out at the stairs at the base of Wyle's tower.

I nearly ran into Abbas, who was walking toward a nearby door that opened to the winter garden and poinsettas outside. His shirt was half-buttoned, per his usual half-dressed state, and his hair was slicked back. He seemed slightly out of breath. And slightly startled to see me at first. Of course, his surprise quickly transformed into something else.

"Your Majesty," Abbas crooned. "How wonderful to see you."

He smelled of smoke. Probably from attending the funeral. There had been bonfires lit on the cliff to keep attendees warm.

Abbas' eyes twinkled down at me.

I stiffened and straightened my mourning gown.

He can't read thoughts, can he? I asked as dragons and Abbas collided in my mind's eye.

Not according to my sources.

"Prince Abbas. Thank you for your attendance this morning."

"Yes, of course. Your mother was one of the few monarchs my father held any esteem for, so I was more than happy to attend and represent Cheryn."

I studied his face. "It is sad. But she was ill. And I believe she made her peace with it."

"I'm glad you were able to make it home to say goodbye. I'm certain that you also gave her a great deal of peace," Abbas stroked my forearm.

I glanced up at him, trying to read his expression. Was he sincere? "I heard your own brothers are ill. I'm so sorry. It's hard to see a loved one—"

Abbas's eyes flashed and his smile widened. "Yes, quite hard."

He's lying. I can't tell about what, but Connor says he can feel the lie.

I reached out and rubbed Abbas' hand with my own. "If there's anything I can do …"

"Well, you can marry me," Abbas winked.

My cheeks flushed. "I don't think that will help your brothers."

He raised an eyebrow at me. He leaned forward and whispered, "Perhaps it would."

I shivered. His breath had raised the hairs on my neck. My body wanted to lean toward him. But my mind was torn.

Is this a lie? Are his brothers really ill? Is that related to his desire to marry me? Or is it all a trick, a ploy? My brain rambled.

Sultan Raj loved mind games. I felt certain his son did, too. I stepped back. "Enjoy the gardens, Your Highness."

"Won't you join me?"

"I've a meeting to attend." My mind flickered over Willard's betrayal. The sooner I found out how Wyle's spells could help me untangle Abbas' truths and lies, the sooner I could strip Willard and his family of their titles.

Abbas stroked the inside of my wrist. "The crown is heavy isn't it? I can lighten your burden, if you wish. As an engagement gift."

What double speak. Does he mean take my crown? Or help me? I was mentally exhausted by trying to figure him out.

What's he thinking?

He's shuffling his thoughts again, Quinn ground out. *Been shuffling this entire time.*

I ground my lips into a tight smile. "That's unnecessary."

"I'm happy to do it."

"It's unnecessary because we aren't engaged."

Abbas' let go of my hand and stroked his beard. He gave me an evaluating glance. "Oh, we will be."

I reminded myself to breathe through my nose instead of letting out an angry huff. I had to appear calm and unaffected, though his arrogance rankled me.

Damn him. Abbas was so tempting, his eyes so delicious and full of naughty promises that I was flustered in spite of my brain screaming 'caution.'

I turned on my heel and stomped up the many twisting stairs to Wyle's tower.

Connor, Quinn, and Declan trailed behind me, recognizing my mood as explosive.

I smacked open the door to Wyle's chamber. No knock. No pretense. I just shoved it open so hard it banged against the stone wall.

"Wyle!" I called.

I took one step into the room and stopped.

In the middle of the stone floor was a deep red puddle. Shards of bone and skin protruded from it. Blood spatter coated the walls, the worktables. Everything.

"What the hell?" Declan asked as he came up behind me.

"What happened to him?" Connor asked. "Blow himself up in one of his experiments?"

"I hope so," I whispered.

I grabbed a yardstick and stuck it into the gooey puddle in the floor. The stick caught on something and I dragged up Wyle's goggles. "It's him."

I stuck the stick in once more and stirred, hoping to find a beaker or some kind of evidence that Wyle had done this to himself.

What I found was a chain. I dragged the chain out of the puddle with my stick. I bent and wiped the chain on my dress. It was gold and interwoven with a blue material that glowed slightly.

"Does that look like elven chain?" I asked Declan.

He squatted next to me. "I'm not sure. Why?"

"Elven chain controls the wearer, doesn't it?" I asked, using the stick to pick up the dripping, broken necklace.

"Yes."

Connor piped up. "Cheryn supposedly stole elven chain from Sedara several months ago. One of those pirate attacks."

"So this could mean Abbas ..."

Connor shrugged. "It could. Though Sedara always has access to this type of chain. So, it could mean them too."

I held up the chain and stared as it dripped blood onto the floor. "If this is elven chain, then Wyle's death wasn't an accident. If it is, someone controlled him and I think it means my mother's security spell activated."

What's that?

"She had spells created that ensured anyone who betrayed royal secrets ... would explode."

Everyone turned to stare at the puddle that used to be the castle mage.

"What secret did he give up?" Connor asked.

I looked grimly at each of my husbands. "I don't know."

CHAPTER THIRTY

e left Wyle's tower a somber group.

Ryan joined us at the base of the stairs. He saw the trail of blood my skirt left on the stairs behind me.

"Not mine," I reassured him. "Quinn, fill him in while we walk through the spelled passages back to my chamber."

I fell back as we walked, thinking. Planning. I'd hoped to use Wyle to help solve my problems. But clearly someone had anticipated that move. Or used Wyle for their own devices. There would be no easy path ahead for me. No one would just bow down, roll over, and confess everything I wanted to hear.

Unless …

I grabbed Connor when we were halfway through the secret passages snaking along the castle walls. I handed him the elven chain. "Can you get that cleaned up? And then maybe test it? See if it makes the wearer do whatever you want."

Connor gave a little grin. "We can test it right now. Hey Quinn, come back!"

Quinn stopped walking. He'd been ahead with Ryan. But he returned to us.

Connor said, "Your Queen commands you to kneel."

Quinn raised an eyebrow at me.

I sighed. "Just briefly, if you don't mind."

Quinn knelt.

Connor grabbed the bloody chain, ready to slip it over Quinn's neck.

Declan grabbed the chain and yanked it back. "No! Don't!"

We all turned to look at him.

He rubbed his bloody palm off on his breeches, saying "I think we need a little more research into those chains. I've never heard of them traveling outside Sedara. I know they use them in interrogation. I don't know much about them, to be honest. I don't know how much is written. But logically … I mean, the chains wouldn't be incredibly useful if *anyone* could control them, would they? Your enemy could just grab them and turn around and use them on you. I'm pretty sure they've got some kind of magical code to activate them."

"Sard!" I clenched my fist.

"Whoever controls these chains controls the wearer completely?" Connor asked Declan.

"I … I'm not sure."

"Mind *and* body?"

Declan shrugged.

"Why don't you and I go back to Wyle's chamber and raid his library?" Connor suggested.

"What are you thinking?" I asked.

Connor pressed his lips into a thin line. "Abbas has been very good at blocking both Quinn and I from infiltrating his mind. But if he thinks he has control, complete control over someone, then he might let his guard drop—"

"That's too dangerous!" I protested. "What if we can't get control back?"

Quinn slid his hand around my waist. *Would you deny one of my men the opportunity to protect their country? Save it from an invader?*

"Not fair."

We have to protect Evaness, Dove.

Quinn, Connor, and Declan tromped back toward Wyle's tower, leaving the chain (and me) with Ryan. They wouldn't let me go with them.

"You need to bathe. You haven't eaten today. And it's going to take them three hours to get you into that golden coronation monstrosity with the giant collar," Connor twisted his hand out of my grip.

Ryan guided my unwilling feet the rest of the way to my chamber. He rang for maidservants and helped me out of my mourning dress himself so that no one else would see the bloodstains.

As I slipped into the steaming water I asked the question that was making my stomach churn. "What secret do you think Wyle gave up?"

Ryan stared into my eyes. "Honestly? I think he told them about you."

"How'd he get around the geas?"

"Djinn magic is different than ours. I don't know. You just asked what I thought."

Sard. I felt the truth of what he said in my bones. Someone out there knew my weakness. Knew I wasn't really a threat. Knew how easy it would be to defeat me. I sank below the surface and stayed under as long as I could. The hot water surrounded me like a cocoon. It made me feel separate and safe. It was an illusion. But I clung to it.

Eventually, Ryan's hand dipped below the surface and pulled me up. "You were starting to scare me."

"Sorry. I just … they just passed this morning. And already, Lady Agatha and her son and—"

"Deep breath, Bloss. Soldiers perform better under pressure. You've been training with that insane mother of yours all your life. You've had drill after drill for this. Look at me," Ryan grabbed my chin and gently turned my face to his. "Tell me what you'd tell her. What do you want us to do?"

My mind raced. Images flew through my head, but they were so quick and fleeting I couldn't pull any of them down. I couldn't see them. This wasn't just a drill. And my mind knew it. My body knew it. I pulled back from Ryan and looked down, disappointed in myself. Ashamed. "I don't know."

Ryan grabbed my waist and hauled me out of the tub, ignoring the fact that I dripped water all over him. He turned me around and put my hands on the tub, bending me forward over the water. The dark strands of my hair danced along the top of the water, floating, as I stared at my reflection.

"You have one minute to come up with a plan before I spank you, Little Dearling," Ryan said.

I gasped. My core clenched. The physical response of my body to Ryan's dominance was immediate. His hand caressed my backside and the fear and swirling images in my mind disappeared. My brain cleared. My body and mind were focused on only one thing. His touch. The soft trails left by his fingertips that slowly disappeared as he backed away.

Smack!

The impact of Ryan's hit sent my chest into the side of the tub. It hurt. But at the same time, my core fluttered. My breathing quickened. My breasts, hanging down, bobbed with need, with the desire to be touched, grabbed, man-handled until sensation rocketed up from my core to my spine.

But Ryan didn't caress me again. Didn't move to rub the spot he'd hit. Didn't sneak his hand around my thigh to feel how achingly wet I was. He simply growled. "One minute, Bloss."

I scrambled to think. To focus. To pretend this was all just a training session. But, just as I had gathered my thoughts—

Smack!

He hit me again. The second time, the reality of the situation sunk in. I had to think. Quickly. I opened my mouth and spouted out the first things that came to mind. "Willard needs to be scared. We need to limit his capacity for damage, quickly. He and his mother know about the dragons. I'd give Lady Agatha a hallucinogen, so she starts spouting off nonsense for a few days. With her age, people would think it was an episode. That she's deluded. Willard —maybe he needs a fall from his horse. A good kick to the head. To scare him. And incapacitate him long enough to give me some time to think. Abbas ... I'm not sure yet." I cringed, waiting for a smack for my indecision.

But Ryan whirled me around, pulled me flush against him and kissed me. Hard. So hard he stole my breath. "That was sarding amazing, Princess. God, I love your mind almost as much as this body," he teased.

His kisses grew more frantic. Desperate. His hands roamed up my sides, pushing me back slightly so he could tweak my nipples.

I moaned into his mouth. This was what I wanted. This was the kind of release I needed after everything that had happened.

One of Ryan's hands abandoned my breasts, swirled down over my stomach, and started sliding over my opening. Up and down. Up and down. He spread my lips slightly and slid his finger just below them, still caressing my center. Up and down. He added a back and forth motion as he went, tracing a literal lightning bolt over my pussy. I shuddered against him.

"Yes," I breathed, when our kiss broke and he lifted me off the ground so he could suckle a breast, one hand holding my back, the other maintaining friction on my core. Having a half giant hold me suspended, vulnerable in midair, while he fully controlled my body—the very thought of it made me wild. That I could buck and kick and scream and no matter what, he was completely in control. And I was completely safe with him.

Ryan twisted his fingers. Sensation shot out to my thighs in warm ribbons. And then in shocking bolts. I started to buck against him, to ride his hand.

"Yes, Ryan!" I whispered his name.

He kept up the movement against my clit with his thumb as he slid a finger into me. That send me over the edge and I screamed, bucking hard against his hand, drawing out the moment, the mindless haze of sensation. Until it faded and I collapsed, my head falling to Ryan's shoulder.

"That was quite a show," Declan's dry voice made my eyes pop open.

My other husbands stood, watching, as Ryan slowly let me slide to the floor. Ryan grinned at them. Then he stuck his wet fingers in his mouth.

Connor moaned.

Ryan smacked his lips as he pulled his fingers out. "I was just rewarding our wife. She came up with a plan for Willard and Lady Agatha."

"Good." Declan nodded curtly. "Because we have one for Abbas."

CHAPTER THIRTY-ONE

*S*hite. Shite this is heavy, I thought.

I made my way to the Great Balcony at the front of the palace, where my coronation would be held, so that the crowds gathered below could see.

The stupid golden collar of my dress was as high as my head and served as a blinder, so I couldn't see behind me unless I turned my entire body. The dress I wore was a daringly low-cut gold brocade, sewn with so many pearls that I felt I might as well be wearing armor. Armor that was so heavy it was about to fall forward and expose my nipples to the entire kingdom. I cursed my mother and the dressmaker, who had conspired together to create this awful 'statement piece.' And even as I cursed them, tears filled my eyes. This was the last thing my mother had done that I could curse. I fingered the sleeve of my dress, as if touching it would somehow connect me to her.

The sun was setting in the distance, painting the sky a blushing pink. Burnt orange clouds hovered above the horizon. The sky was too beautiful for the day. But the wind, the wind was just right. The wind bit at my eyes. It turned my nose red and chapped my lips. I stepped to the rail of the balcony and waved as I was supposed to. I gazed down at my people. They smiled and laughed and joked with one another. Nobles and commoners from the capital Marscha mingled together. They carried lanterns, wore fur-lined hats, and held steaming mugs of hot cider passed out by vendors. The sweet scent of warm apples drifted up to me where I stood. I inhaled, wishing I could share in their joy.

Instead, I waved, with a painted-on smile as I watched those who had gathered to swear allegiance to the new queen. Sometime in the past, someone had decided that continuity was more important than heartbreak. Stability was more important than mourning. Evaness couldn't go a single full day without a new queen.

I would be crowned before the sun dipped below the horizon.

I saw Ryan's contingent below. I spotted Lady Agatha, who looked rather tipsy. My lips curved at that, assuming Quinn's people had helped her along, so she could start spouting nonsense. Willard was nowhere to be seen. She kept trying to speak with Lord Aiden and his wife, and the pair kept edging away from her.

The other nobles from the other provinces all had at least one member representing them.

The ambassadors from the seven kingdoms all stood together. I gave a polite nod to Meeker, determined not to show the anger I felt. I quickly moved on to smile to Mateo and his father and the delegation from Macedon.

Then I made a game of smiling at Ryan's contingent of palace guards and random commoners. Until I spotted Kylee in the crowd and couldn't resist a happy wave. Not that the tavern owner remembered me as myself. But he seemed delighted to have gotten a smile from the queen. And so at least there was that.

I also gave a discreet wave to one woman in the crowd who wore a hood. The woman I'd asked Ryan to fly out and fetch this afternoon. The woman I'd decided would be my new castle mage.

Cerena nodded back at me, signaling that everything was ready.

I bit down on my grin and focused once more on my people.

Seeing the crowd below me only increased my sense of responsibility. Only increased the weight of the crown. It made me more certain that I needed to quash the threats I faced in order to keep them safe. The innocents below knew nothing of the perils that plagued Evaness. Nothing about how we teetered on the precipice of war. They knew nothing of my fear or the twisting misery that crawled through my stomach, pinching and showing no mercy. My sweet people only saw their Beast Tamer Queen, about to take her crown. That's what Connor told me the locals had started calling me. My stomach roiled.

This plan better work, I worried internally, though I smiled brightly.

I didn't look at my knights or Avia, knowing they were standing off to my side, tense and hopeful. They all stood in full armor, except Quinn, who wore his traditional black, along with a clean and gleaming elven chain around his neck.

Knowing it was there made my fingers twitch, eager to rip the evil thing right off him. But I couldn't. Not yet.

Abbas appeared at my side. I hadn't even seen him approach.

"Your Majesty, your personal butler, Jorad, has asked me to have the honor of escorting you up to the platform as you are crowned," he leaned closer than was necessary to speak softly into my ear.

I didn't flinch, though I wanted to.

Jorad had asked Abbas to assist on my orders. The game had begun. My heart hitched.

"I would be honored if you'd escort me, Prince Abbas," I replied, making eye contact.

He looked handsome. He was in a deep blue jacket that offset his tan skin. The sunset gleamed against his black hair, which curled slightly at his shoulders. He held out a hand with a glowing blue ring on it.

I smiled and took his hand.

I fought my nerves. I had to play this just right, like a musician. This was a performance. Or like a gambler. This was poker. For a minute I wished I'd taken Kylee up on his offer to work in the gambling hall. I'd only seen bits and pieces of the bluffs that players pulled. I'd seen courtiers and grown up with them. But this was the biggest wager I'd ever made.

Quinn's life—and the future of the kingdom—depended on it.

"Your Majesty," Abbas purred. "How are you feeling this evening?"

"Rather disappointed. My mage died this afternoon."

"What a somber day," Abbas' mask of polite indifference didn't crack.

"Yes. It was particularly disappointing to discover he'd betrayed me."

"Betrayed you?"

"He was spelled to explode upon betrayal."

Abbas' raised a thick black brow. "Well, that's one way to ensure loyalty."

I waved at the crowd. "An unfortunate way, don't you agree?"

"Very."

"What I found even more interesting than his betrayal was the elven chain that he'd been wearing."

Abbas' eyes glittered. "I've heard such chains are powerful."

"They'd have to be, to overcome the geas my mother placed on anyone who knew about my power."

Abbas hid his smirk almost immediately, but I saw the minuscule quirk of his lips. He was growing smug. Good.

"I found it interesting that you left the chain behind. It was rather a mess, true. But I wondered all afternoon why you'd leave such a valuable weapon. I concluded that you wanted me to know it was you."

"Sedara has plenty of those elven chains," Abbas said.

"I have a Sedarian husband who could just as easily have told that country what they wanted to know."

"Your husband would betray you?" Abbas put a hand to his chest in mock horror. "May I suggest an upgrade?"

"I believe you have, several times."

"Well, perhaps, you've now come to your senses and will take me up on my offer."

"You are now aware," I paused and gave a special wave to two jumping children in the crowd, "that the alliance you seek with me, may not be entirely beneficial for you."

"I disagree."

I turned to face him and study his expression for a moment in the torchlight. He seemed earnest. But that was the problem with nobles. They always seemed earnest.

"This evening …" I began slowly, dragging the words out through my teeth as if they were painful for me, "there was a mistake. A servant mistook your chain for ornamental coronation chain. They placed this chain on one of my husbands."

Abbas held still. I knew he was already aware of this 'mistake.' Quinn had been dull and lifeless since the chain had been placed over his head, against my vehement protests.

"Darling princess, I find it as hard to believe that was a mistake as you found my leaving the chain behind to be."

I wasn't certain if Abbas realized his admission. I did. He'd admitted to killing my mage. And it made my stomach twist as we moved into the next steps of the game. He'd already taken a life. And Quinn had bet his life the moment my hair-brained husbands had agreed on this scheme. I swallowed my emotions and kept my face passive as I asked, "What do you really want, Abbas?"

Abbas grabbed my hand and brought it to his lips. "I've already told you."

"You want Evaness? Is that it? You want our fertile crops? Our land? Our ports? Access to the treaty with Sedara? What?"

"My family may be interested in all those things. But ... as I've said. I'd like *you*."

"What do you need peace power for?"

"Ah ... now darling, why do you think it's only your power I want?"

"You might be slightly interested in my body. But you're half-djinni. Power means more to you than anything." I met his eyes head on.

He raised his eyebrows. "You're such a smart little thing. So, I have to ask myself, why would such a smart girl allow her knight to do something as stupid as put my chain around his neck?"

I ground my teeth together. This was the part of the negotiation I didn't want to go through. The part where I put everything on the line. My nerves turned my insides into a bubbling tar pit. I smiled wider to hide what I felt. "I asked you here tonight to offer you a choice. Clearly, my power needs to remain secret. You may have my mind-talker, as a gift, given your written guarantee you'll never breathe a word about what Wyle told you. Or ... you can have the engagement you seem to desire so much."

"Beautiful girl, why would I want your husband when I could have you?"

"I highly doubt your sincere interest. And I like to hedge my bets," I gave Abbas a cold look.

"And is this how you treat your husbands?"

"Their duty is to Evaness first," I spit out the words Declan had coached me through, trying to sound as cold and calculating as I could, instead of like the quivering little girl I felt like inside.

Abbas reached for my hand. "I want to work with you for our mutual benefit," Abbas raised his lips to my hand and gave it a gentle kiss. "And I will give you your mind-talker back in exchange for our official engagement."

My insides collapsed in fear and relief. Fear for what I might be taking on with Abbas and relief for Quinn. A brief flash of gratitude toward Declan also passed through my head. Everything had worked out exactly as he'd said it would. And so I stuck to the script, continuing to act reticent and cautious. "I don't like going into this blindly. Without knowing your end game."

Abbas leaned forward and brushed my forehead with a kiss. "My end game is the same as anyone else's."

"I highly doubt that."

"Well, what do you think I want?"

"To escape your father's control?" I guessed. "To be the only one of your brothers to have a claim on Evaness. To--"

"To fall in love?" Abbas asked.

"No," I scoffed. "World domination is more likely."

He bit his lip and grinned. "You see right through me. I like that."

I sighed. "You can stop with the compliments. Release Quinn and you'll get your way."

"You gave me Quinn. You want this alliance as much as I do. You're desperate for it, even."

I grabbed Abbas' hand and raised our entwined fingers. That was the signal. The herald trumpeted beside us, blasting my ears. And then he took up his bullhorn and announced our engagement as a sign of peace and treaty between the kingdoms of Cheryn and Evaness.

Below, Meeker looked furious. He cut a path through the crowd, no doubt to send a pigeon carrying an angry message to Sedara.

Everyone else cheered.

Abbas waved at the thronging masses below and turned to me with a bright smile.

"So eager, love," he grinned at me. "You must feel backed into quite a corner."

I gave a false look of worry after Meeker, who was just a speck in the distance at this point.

Abbas followed my glance, calm resolution settling over his features as he saw what he thought I perceived as my biggest threat.

"The chains," I reminded him. "I don't even know how you got an enchanted object through the gates."

Abbas shook his head. "A man can't reveal all his secrets. Where's the magic in that?" He raised his hand and mouthed a few words.

The blue glow around Quinn's neck ceased, and Connor pulled the evil thing off of Quinn, tossing it onto the ground. It skittered across the stone, landing near my feet.

I stared at Quinn long and hard as he rubbed his chest and then shook the feeling back into his hands, as though they'd been asleep.

Are you okay? I asked.

Yes. And I think I got what you wanted when you went into the world domination bit. Abbas has memories of the dragon. He's the one who met with the rebels.

I turned to Abbas and smiled, taking in the how the torches lining the balcony offset the rich golden embroidery of his undershirt. I met his deep brown eyes dead on. "Would you please place my crown on my head, darling?" I asked in an annoyingly saccharine voice as a servant brought up the crown of Evaness on a pillow. The crown was tall, studded with seashells and diamonds and turquoise.

"Of course," Abbas grinned darkly.

I tried not to smirk at his superiority. I dipped into my curtsy and allowed him to fit the crown to my head.

I waited while the herald said the words that made me queen. I didn't listen to a single one, all of my attention focused on what came next.

"And now," the herald cried out, "your Queen and the Prince of Cheryn will sign their engagement documents."

A quill and a scroll were brought forward. The same document each of my other suitors had signed. With one special addition from Cerena.

I signed on the line indicated and handed the quill to Abbas, letting nervous worry cross my features for a single second before I smothered it.

Abbas caught the look and grinned. "You should be nervous." He signed his name with flourish. "For all the things I plan to do."

I put a hand to my chest in mock worry.

"Oh no, Prince Abbas. You don't plan to mislead or desert me, do you? You are aware you just signed a *magically binding* document?"

"What?"

"Oh yes. This particular engagement document ensures you'll never find release with another woman again."

Abbas' face turned puce. "I'm nearly immortal."

"Yes. Oh dear. That could be problematic. Unless of course, you're into corpses?" I held up my hands and gave a suggestive shrug. "It also does one other thing."

"What?" Abbas snapped.

I leaned forward, my voice a hoarse, angry growl. "If you ever betray me, you'll end up just like Wyle."

I let Abbas stew in his anger for a minute before I added to it.

I turned to wave happily to the crowd. Through my fake smile, I said, "You wondered why I made this so easy for you. Your brother flying around my lands, eating cattle and poisoning the crops with his breath, being led toward my little sister, is rather a nuisance. And since I'm going to kill him, I don't want your father declaring war on me."

Abbas jaw dropped. Just minutely. But enough for me to read the shock in his gaze.

I turned pressed a kiss against his furious face.

The crowd went wild.

CHAPTER THIRTY-TWO

To my shock, Abbas transformed the kiss. He slid his hand around the back of my neck and pulled my face closer. His tongue snaked in between my lips and tangled with mine. He sucked my tongue into his mouth and tugged on it. Then he released it and bit down on my lower lip. He feathered his lips over mine as he pulled back and met my eyes.

He left me panting.

"Like I said before, Bloss, it's adorable when you bring out your little claws." He let go of me then, took a step backward, and held up the blue ring he wore. He stroked it once with his finger.

A terrible roar filled the sky.

And there, in the distance, backed by the setting sun, appeared a black-winged nightmare. A dragon.

"Shite."

I whirled to see my knights, their jaws gaping, their expressions shocked.

"Get Avia below! NOW!" I screeched at the servants. They all scrambled to get inside, dragging my sister with them.

I grabbed up the bullhorn the herald had dropped. The crowd below could not see the monster yet. I had to get them out of the courtyard but avoid mass panic. "Everyone please form orderly lines and proceed into the palace, immediately. My first action as Queen of Evaness is to invite you all to share a feast with me. Noble and common alike. Tonight, we celebrate Evaness."

A cheer went up through the crowd.

Ryan stepped to the edge of the balcony and gave a hand signal to his soldiers, who immediately helped everyone into orderly lines. At a second hand signal, his troops even started diverting people to side entrances and servant entrances.

I turned to find Jorad facing me.

I stared sternly at him. "Fire War protocol, Jorad. Get everyone to ballroom, get the food. Then make the announcement that they need to relocate to the fireproof dungeons. Only make that announcement once Ryan's men have the ballroom secured."

Jorad gave a brisk nod and left.

I turned back to spy the beast flapping its wings, coming closer. The last of the sun's rays glinted off its iridescent blue scales. The beast released a jet of black flame.

It was as though I had tunnel vision. The dragon was the only thing I could see as my heart thrummed like a war drum in my chest. Nothing else existed.

This was why I'd come back. To save my sister from this beast. To save Evaness.

I took a deep, bracing breath. I ignored the tremors that shot through my limbs.

"I need a gargoyle," I whispered.

"No," my husbands' chorused. Even Connor.

"I can't fight it here."

"Darling," a deadly purr sounded in my ear. "Why ever not?"

In my shock, I'd completely forgotten Abbas. Everyone had. Seeing the dragon had made him cease to exist. He was a lesser threat. What was one man compared to a monster?

He had capitalized on that. Used the moment to scoop up the elven chain. A chain he now slid over my head.

"I think you should fight the dragon. Right here." At his words, the metal started to melt and meld with my skin and the chain gave off a blue glow.

My knights surged forward.

"I suppose I could have her throw herself off the castle," Abbas said.

They froze.

"Climb up on the railing, Bloss," Abbas ordered.

I tried to fight it. But my limbs moved separately from my mind. They moved as though they were tugged by invisible strings. They were slightly jerky, like puppet limbs. I was tugged up onto the railing by those strings. I struggled with my massive ball gown. I nearly slipped and tumbled twice.

Hands wrapped around my waist and lifted me into place. Large hands. Ryan's hands.

"Take your hands off her," Abbas commanded.

Ryan slowly removed his hands, once he was sure I had my balance.

"Don't!" Connor whispered. I don't know if he was begging me not to jump or begging Abbas not to make me.

I tried to lift my hand. I couldn't. I tried again, swallowing down bile. I tried a finger. I couldn't move anything. My body felt separate from me. As if there was a thick barrier of bandages between my brain and my limbs. I was still inside. But I couldn't break out. I was trapped.

If Abbas bid me to jump I'd have no choice. I knew it. I felt the surety of it. I had no control. Even though I tried to fight it, I had no control.

I kept my gaze firmly ahead, though my stomach churned. I cared less about my death than the death of the men behind me, the knights who'd saved my kingdom when I'd run away as a melodramatic teenager. Their faces flashed through my mind as the dragon grew close enough for me to see the orange-red color of his eyes. Connor. Ryan. Declan. Quinn.

Can you hear me? Quinn's voice cut through the gauze surrounding my body and penetrated my mind.

Yes! I shouted internally in my relief. I could still reach someone. Someone knew I was still there, buried inside a spell.

Abbas leaned forward at that moment, stroking my ankle as the dragon approached the capital city, Marscha. "Your Majesty, I am so eager to see how you defend your kingdom. Raise your hands."

My hands flew up of their own accord, making me lose my balance. I tilted forward. The cobblestones of the courtyard leered at me. I felt myself tilt through the air.

Ryan's arm snaked out and grabbed my waist; he was the only reason I didn't fall to my death. He didn't let me go this time.

Abbas didn't seem at all disturbed by the near-loss of his puppet. His next command was smooth and even. "Blast that dragon with peace power until you've ended it or it has ended you."

He let go of my ankle as my hands started to emit a green burst of peace power. My wrists ripped open, blood trickled down my arms.

Fear bubbled up from my stomach and filled my mouth; I was drowning in it.

Ryan let go of me and I tilted forward again; I was as frozen as a porcelain doll, still blasting peace power from my hands as I fell—two sets of arms pulled me out of the air. Declan and Connor tried to pull me down from the railing, but my body wouldn't allow it. Abbas had ordered it. And so they helped me balance on it.

I heard a thump behind me. I hoped that Ryan had smashed Abbas into the stones so hard the other man's brain littered the floor.

Quinn's voice sounded inside my head. *Ryan says you have one minute to come up with a plan, or he's going to spank you.*

Was that Abbas? Did he knock him out? I need a gargoyle. I need to leave—

Smack! The hit didn't do much to penetrate my ball gown. But it shocked me as my body rocked forward in Connor and Declan's arms.

I was planning dammit! I was planning.

Leaving isn't an option, Dove. You need a plan for all of us.

Declan's the planner. Sard! Can't he just... I dunno, transform the dragon into a rabbit?

Quinn went silent for a minute. The hands around my waist shifted. Declan's left.

"I've never used my power on sentient things," Declan said.

"Test it on Abbas," Ryan ordered.

396

"Well, he's knocked out, so he's not really sentient," Declan pondered.

"Just do it," Connor yelled. "That thing's almost here!"

The screams had started in the capital, as people on the streets spotted the monster. As it grew closer, its colossal size became more and more apparent. The dragon's black wings stretched as wide as two houses. Smoke curled out of its nostrils. It opened its mouth and I could see the red-hot glow—

"NO!" I blasted more peace power, ignoring the fact that a jagged cut ripped open in my right thigh. Blood shot out with each beat of my heart. It gushed down my legs. It soaked my skirt. The pain made it impossible for me to hold weight on it; I shifted and Connor struggled to keep me balanced.

In the distance, the dragon shook his head as though startled. But he didn't flame the house beneath him.

I didn't revel in that tiny victory. I was past emotions. I was fading. I felt lightheaded. My eyelids flickered.

I think I'm going to faint, I told Quinn.

Ryan! Quinn's mindspeak blasted all of us. *Heal her now. And don't stop healing her! Forget us! Heal her.*

Wait. Were they hurt? Did I hurt them? I asked myself.

I fought to stay awake. I thought the arms around my waist might feel wet. Sticky.

Sard.

Ryan and Quinn held a silent argument behind me.

Until Quinn's shout accidentally reverberated through our heads. —*We won't drop her!*

"I'll siphon off whatever rage I can," Connor said. "Just do it, Ry. She's getting pale."

I started to wobble. My vision blinked in and out.

Warm pink light surrounded me. The magic buzzed over my skin, knitting it together. But the magic wasn't just healing. It was tenderness itself. It felt like a summer night full of lightning bugs. It filled me. Until I felt like a shimmering pink light myself. Like a stained-glass window. Like the dawning sun.

The magic faded and my eyes opened. I could see clearly again. And there was no summer night or pink dawn. There was the wind, growling at me. And the howl of a dragon making the hairs on my arm stand up.

Ryan's voice sounded near my ear, "Bloss, he made you use your power. But tone it down. Wait. Until the beast gets closer." He stroked my hair once; his hand trembled as he struggled for control.

Awe filled me.

He's right. He's a genius. What was I thinking? I'm an idiot! I shouted at myself.

I toned down the green glow until it was hardly visible. And though my wounds reopened, they bled more slowly.

They were the slashes of a thin knife, instead of the jagged hacks of an ax.

Footsteps sounded and then I heard a *thunk, thunk, thunk* as Ryan pounded the wall behind us. He roared. The sound made the hairs on my arms stand up. Pebbles clattered to the ground. The wall wouldn't last long.

Is everyone inside? I asked Quinn because I was too scared to look below. Too scared to take stock of how many people I might shred to pieces.

Quinn didn't answer me.

Is everyone—

Shut it. I'm helping Dec.

I focused back on my foe, determined not to distract Quinn and Declan. The dragon was halfway through Marscha. Five more beats of his wings and he'd be in the dead space in front of the castle.

Declan! Can he—

"Sard!" Declan's curse answered my question. Whatever he'd done, whatever he'd tried, wasn't working. "Sentient creatures are a no-go!"

Bloss, you have another minute. We need a new plan.

I, what? No! It's almost here! Run. You all need to run. Or I'll drain you. Save Avia. Save the people in the castle.

Smack! Somehow, my ass stung. Even through the skirt.

Another minute. Go, Bloss.

Near the dragon I saw a flock of birds appear. They swarmed the beast. He paused momentarily, and then flamed them. But instead of dropping, they just disappeared. Quinn was distracting the beast with hallucinations.

What's the plan, Bloss? I heard the fatigue in Quinn's inner voice. That had taken a lot out of him. I doubted he could do it again.

Ryan needs to get Meeker. We need the spell to unlock this sarding chain and get it off me.

Ryan has to heal you. Quinn's voice bellowed through all our heads. *Connor. Take the edge of his rage. Drink it in. NOW!*

Make Connor hold my hand as he does it. Have them both get their hands into my peace blast.

Two sets of hands reached out along my arms. Ryan's pink power glowed around me. Connor's power was absorption, and he siphoned off some of my pain and some of Ryan's rage. I heard him grind his teeth together. I could only hope he didn't try to take on too much. I was about to tell Quinn to stop him when—

Smack!

I screamed internally at Quinn. *Asswipe! I came up with a plan!*

I sent my men after Meeker. We need more!

Sard! I—my brain felt empty. Tapped out. I didn't know what to do.

If Dec can't just minimize the dragon, what can he do? He can't maximize my power. That will kill us all. It would take too much blood. The words slammed into my mind like a battering ram.

I yelled at Quinn. *What's the opposite of blood?*

What?

Dec reduces the opposite. What can he reduce to make blood?

Lips pressed against my arm.

What's the opposite of blood? Quinn yelled at us all.

The dragon was almost to the moat. Sarding hell. It was too late. I might have thought of a solution. But it was too late. My brain started shorting out in panic. My heart started pulsing so hard I felt it in my throat.

He's crossing the moat! Quinn, you have to go—

The moat! Quinn yelled. *Water!*

Suddenly, the water in the moat surged overhead. It rose in a ring around the castle, floating above the towers, rippling in the wind.

I heard Declan's voice muttering next to me. Yellow light shot toward the water droplets, which suddenly turned black. An iron stench filled the air. My breath caught. My heart skipped when I realized the droplets weren't black. They were red. Red as blood.

Blood started to rain down on all of us as the dragon flew over the first tower and spewed flame.

I could feel my power swell with the presence of so much blood.

And for the first time, the rush of adrenaline in my veins carried the edge of excitement with it.

This beast wanted to attack my castle? Let it try.

My arms automatically swung to follow the dragon. I pushed out every last ounce of power I had. Green light exploded through the sky. The ring of blood shriveled, evaporating as my power consumed it.

I met the dragon's orange eyes head on.

Its eyes flickered, turned brown. And then it fell, smashing into the cobblestone courtyard.

CHAPTER THIRTY-THREE

Meeker was brought up by two of Quinn's spies. He'd been caught trying to leave Marscha when the dragon was spotted.

At first, the Sedarian ambassador refused to disclose how to work the elven chain. He said it was a betrayal of Sedarian state secrets.

But Quinn was not my spy master for nothing. He was eventually able to persuade the ambassador that disclosing that information was in Meeker's best interests.

Though I had defeated the dragon and was able to stop using my powers, I wasn't able to climb off the balcony until Meeker provided the counter spell. So when I came down, it was on shaky limbs.

I collapsed into Connor's arms.

Ryan personally drug Abbas into our deepest dungeon and chained him there.

Declan went to find our beast master, to see what might be done about a dragon who'd collapsed in the courtyard and was snoring peacefully.

Jorad and Avia made an appearance to check on me.

Neither were very impressed by the state of my clothes, the state of the balcony, or the state of the courtyard. I didn't get a single clap for defeating the dragon.

Instead, Jorad's lips thinned as he surveyed all the damage he'd need to get repaired, the blood stains he'd need to get out of the stone, and the awful state of his queen and her knights. The ledger-keeper in him was tallying up the expenses of my first day as monarch. Watching that almost made me laugh.

He stiffly reported that the citizens had been calmed but would expect a speech from their ruler. I nodded and waved him off.

"In a moment."

He gave a curt bow before going back to do … whatever he needed to do.

That's when Avia launched into me.

"You idiotic strumpet! You got engaged to that lunatic? And then, sent me below like some, like some—" she collapsed into dramatic teenage tears.

"I needed Abbas to feel in control."

"He had a sarding dragon! He was in control!"

"Well, yeah. We didn't know it was that close."

Avia smacked me. Hard. "Don't you ever do that again!"

"I'm your queen. I'm allowed to do that."

"You're my sister and you're never allowed to do that! And that's final!"

I bit my lip to hide my smile. "Well if you say so—"

"I do say so. You big stupid shite!"

"Oh, stop squawking," I pulled her into a hug.

When I released her, I turned to Connor. "Do you mind doing most of the talking? You're better at not being offensive than I am."

Connor gave me a tired half-smile and nodded. He grabbed my hand and intertwined our fingers. "Of course, Bloss Boss."

We made the announcements to a stunned crowd and then put Jorad in charge of answering questions and politely kicking everyone out of the castle.

The dragon woke before Jace and Declan could figure out how to wrangle him. The beast took off and was followed by Ryan's guards as he headed north.

I doubted we'd seen the last of him. But, at least now, we knew we stood a chance. We knew we could fight him, so long as we fought together.

"What do you think of a moat permanently filled with blood? It could be kind of neat." I joked.

"I nearly puked from the smell alone," Declan responded.

"Alright. But the Blood Queen has a ring to it, doesn't it?"

"No," Connor responded.

"Bloss, the dragon killer?"

"How about Bloss, the spanked?" Ryan retorted with a yawn.

I pretended to pout. "You all are no fun at all."

We are exhausted from saving your beautiful butt, Quinn said.

I turned in outrage, ready to lecture him.

Just joking, Dove. Let's save the nicknames for a time when we're not utterly spent.

We went to the royal wing together, bathed, and everyone piled into my bed. In under two minutes, we were all asleep.

🐚

The next morning, I woke to four naked men, standing at the foot of my bed, stroking themselves.

I yawned and stretched. "Well, if that isn't a sight for sore eyes."

"Your eyes aren't going to be the only thing sore today, Wife," Ryan said.

He walked forward and pulled me out of the bed. He hugged me to him for a moment before he set me down. Then Ryan tore at my clothes. He ripped my chemise in half with his bare hands and shoved it off my shoulders. It fell to the floor in a heap and I was left shivering in the brisk morning air.

Four pairs of eyes raked over every inch of me.

"Dearling," Ryan murmured.

Declan came up and hugged me from behind as Ryan ran his hands over the newly healed scars on my thighs. Connor and Quinn came to stand on each side of me.

Ryan stroked the scars. "Never again, Dearling. You will never do that again." His voice grew rough. "Say it."

"Which part?"

"You'll never come up with a stupid plan. Or get engaged to another man. Or fight a dragon. Or try to send us off—"

"That's quite a list. What if I don't have a choice?"

Ryan growled, his fingers curling around my thigh. His hands were so large he covered nearly half of it. His eyes burned down into mine. "Bad girls talk back. Say: I won't put myself in danger again."

"I won't put myself in danger again … sir."

Ryan groaned, and his fingertips dug into my thighs.

Declan pushed aside my hair and whispered in my ear. "Blossie, I think you need to be punished."

Ryan roared and spun me around so that I was facing Declan. Declan held my hands and bent me forward so my breasts dangled. I had a clear view of his erect cock, pointed up at my mouth. But he wouldn't lower me enough to let me touch it.

"Not yet," Declan breathed. "You're in trouble."

Quinn stepped forward and cupped my right breast, squeezing softly. He released it so I felt the weight as it fell back toward the floor.

Bloss, he moaned in my head.

Having the three of them touch me all at once set off something wild inside me, something untamed. I hummed with need. My eyes sought out Connor, who was standing back, taking in the scene as Declan cuffed my wrists in his hands and Quinn bent and sucked my right nipple into his mouth.

Connor's tousled curls fell over his eyes but he didn't bother to move them. His hands were busy on his shaft. One of his thumbs slid over the sensitive head of his dick as he pleasured himself. I could only imagine the sensual picture the four of us made.

But I ached to feel all of them at once.

"Connor, come here and touch me too, please," I begged. "I need all of you."

Connor stepped forward slowly and sank to his knees under my belly. He kissed from my belly button downward, leaving a feather light trail that made my nerve endings light up.

Ryan's finger traced a trail down my spine and over the curve of my ass, under each cheek.

Then Ryan's finger left my body. He gave me a smack, pushing me into Declan's chest just as Quinn grabbed my left nipple and pulled, just as Connor's tongue touched my slit.

I bucked like a wild colt and only Declan's arms kept me in place.

Having all of them stimulate me at once was amazing and overwhelming.

But then they all stopped. They waited. I looked up at Declan but his eyes were on Ryan, awaiting orders. I turned my head to look at Ryan out of the corner of my eye.

Ryan held his hand up, poised to smack my ass again. But he stayed there, frozen. "I can't," he said. "I'm actually mad. I can't spank you again." His eyes softened as he dropped his hand. "You scared me so bad, Bloss."

Declan released me. I stood and turned to reach for Ryan, but Declan grabbed me.

"You might not be able to spank her. But I can punish her." Declan spun me around, smashed me into foot of the bed, pushed me over so my back hit the mattress, then yanked my body so my legs were off the sides.

He wrapped my legs around himself. And then slid slowly down until his face aligned with my core, which was perched on the edge of the bed, gaping open from the position he'd put me in.

Declan started to kiss my skin softly, gently. Then he began to kiss up and down my seam. He was careful not to build up friction. He made sure he kissed just hard enough to tease. My body warmed. I pulsed with need.

I whimpered. My breath started to come faster.

But Declan continued to kiss me at a snail's pace, content to watch moisture gather at my opening.

Connor joined us on the bed, so he could watch Declan from a better angle. He'd always been a voyeur. He perched on his knees near my shoulder. I watched his ball sack stretch as he stroked himself again and again, eyes roaming my naked body and heaving breasts as Declan teased me.

"Dec, please," I begged.

"No!" He stopped.

"But—"

Declan loomed over me. "You pissed us all off. You still tried to send us away yesterday."

My eyes filled with tears. I looked at each of them, and their faces shimmered. "I'm sorry. I just love you so much. I can't bear the thought of anything—"

"Say that again," Ryan growled, stepping up to the foot of the bed and standing beside Declan.

"I love you." I said it to each of them, holding Ryan's brown eyes for a moment, then Quinn's grey gaze. Declan's baby blues stared at me, and he stroked my slit with his fingers as I said it to him. And then I looked up at Connor, who had paused his stroking to watch me as I said it to him.

Declan slammed into me while I was still looking at Connor, surprising me.

"You're ours! Say it." Declan slammed again, making my body slip back along the sheets.

"I'm yours," I groaned as Declan's dick touched my cervix. There was a spike of pain, but not enough pleasure yet to set me off.

"Please," I moaned, hoping any of the others would take pity on me.

Connor's legs suddenly loomed over my face. He strad-dled me as he lowered his dick toward my mouth. He laid the shaft over my lips and waited for me to open. "Suck me," Connor commanded.

I took Connor's thick red shaft between my lips as Declan smashed me again, this time grinding slightly to rub against my clit. The flicker of pleasure at my clit, along with the bone deep soreness of him slamming into my pelvis, started to build up pressure. My legs started to tremble.

I rode that line of pleasure and pain as Declan slammed and ground against me again. I moaned against Connor's shaft. I began to arch my back, searching for that perfect angle. I was close. So close. There. I found it as Declan slammed again.

My eyes fluttered, when out of the corner of my eye, I saw a bluebird. It flew across the room to hover over me. And then it shite right on my face.

"Ah!" I screamed. I pushed Connor's dick aside as I swiped at my nose and mouth. But my face was bare.

I turned to my right, to glare at Quinn, who was steadily watching Declan and Connor, who shoved his dick back into my mouth and started pumping, holding my hair.

What the sarding hell, Quinn?

Dec may get you first, Dove. But you're still being punished. Besides, your first orgasm is mine. Only mine. His grey eyes flashed.

Oh God, my mind shuddered at that. His possessiveness sent sparks down my spine. My brain began to unfurl like a flower in the sun.

Until I saw a racoon scramble across the bed and bend to nibble at my nipple. I nearly bucked Declan off. I couldn't help it. My mind was operating on an instinctual level at this point.

"Dammit Quinn!" Connor cursed and climbed off me. "She nearly bit my dick!"

"What's going on?" Ryan asked.

Quinn leaned toward him.

An evil grin spread over Ryan's face. Ryan turned to me. "Seems only fair you have to wait, Dearling. After what you put us through."

"No. No," I moaned, shaking my head back and forth against the mattress.

Connor spoke on my other side. "I think Quinn's generous to say he'll let you cum at all."

I turned to face him, and saw he was back to steadily pumping his own shaft, watching my tits bounce as Declan thrust into me again and again.

Heat built up within me once more. But before I could get more than a tingle built up, Declan groaned. I felt his dick pulse.

And then he slid out.

Ryan grabbed me and flipped me over. "Up on your knees," he barked.

I complied, pulling my knees up on the satin sheets and resting my weight on my elbows.

"Oh no, Dearling, get up," Ryan gently pulled my hair until I was up on my hands. And then he pulled a little more on my hair until my back arched and my head was tilted back slightly. My throat was exposed. Ryan pushed on my back to arch it and expose my ass at the same time. I'd never felt so controlled. My nipples throbbed. I wanted to beg Ryan to touch them, but I knew I couldn't.

"You're ours. Say it."

"I'm yours."

Ryan thrust into me. He was so thick, his girth spread my lips and rubbed against them, shooting sensation over my entire lower half. And then his balls hit. Ecstasy and pain at once. His balls were thick, heavy. They slammed into my clit again and again.

Ryan's hand smacked my ass. The spark traveled through me, up my spine toward my head. So close.

He smacked me again.

"Sir!" I cried. "I'm yours, sir!" The words alone sent me spiraling. One more thrust and I'd detonate.

But Ryan stilled. "Let me know when she's calmed down."

"Quinn!" I screamed. "That's not fair."

A silent chuckle tickled the skin on my chest as Quinn positioned himself under me and began to slowly lick a nipple. *It will be amazing when you do cum for me, love. It will take you into another plane. Now ... suck Connor's cock like a good wife.*

I looked up to see Connor propped up on his knees in front of me. His large red shaft was already slick with precum. His eyes were heavy lidded with desire. "I need you, Bloss."

My heart cracked, hearing that. "I need you, too."

"Damn straight you need us," Ryan shoved into me, driving my face toward Connor's cock. I opened my mouth and his cock slid in. It was salty against my tongue. I lapped at it, able to control little beyond my tongue since Ryan still rode me.

The sensation was overwhelming: Ryan's huge dick splitting me open, rubbing against my sensitive pussy lips with each thrust; Quinn sucking my nipple and sending sensation shooting down to my womb; Connor murmuring he loved me as his dick touched the back of my throat.

Ryan roared when he came, bucking against me hard and fast.

Connor came in my mouth seconds later, gushing warm hot fluid down my throat. I swallowed all of it that I could.

I collapsed on top of Quinn, feeling wound up and exhausted at the same time.

Oh, no. Dove. The best is yet to cum. Get it?

He wrapped his arms around me and pulled me off the bed.

"No," I groaned in protest. My legs could hardly hold me up. But Quinn had me stand and hold onto the bedpost as he yanked pillows off the bed and tossed them on the ground. Then he led me over and had me lay on the rug in front of the fire.

"Mmmm." The heat felt good, so good I was drowsy.

But then—sarding ass—Quinn opened a window. And the ice-cold breeze made my nipples pucker and goosebumps rise on my belly.

What are you doing?

Sensory stimulation, Dove. Your nerves are alive right now. Quinn grabbed my pelvis and lifted it. He waited until my eyes met his and then he deliberately stuck out his tongue and took a long slow lick up my opening.

I gasped. The cold and the heat and his mouth on my core. It was a rainbow of sensation. All the feelings at once. It was bliss.

My hands fisted in the rug. I struggled not to thrust against him wildly.

He licked again. And I couldn't help the tiny jerk of my pelvis. My eyes grew heavy.

One more lick. I was there, teetering on the brink.

Quinn shoved two pillows under my ass and thrust home, the giant mushroom tip of his dick splitting me open and rubbing inside me. He thrust just enough to hit my g-spot and then hovered there, twisting his hips. His hand came down to touch my clit.

I exploded. The room went dark, then light, then dark. Tingles ran all the way to my skull. I was abuzz with energy, light, floating bliss. I thrashed and screamed and cried out. The orgasm seemed to go on and on, like a wave in the ocean. An endless current of pleasure.

Hell yes, Dove. Give that to me. Give me your rapture.

I started to come down, and I met his eyes. *Can you ... feel that?*

I can see your thoughts. Experience it that way. Connor over there was cumming again himself, lucky bastard.

We both turned to watch Connor, who was mopping cum off his stomach.

Declan and Ryan watched Quinn and me hungrily. They'd both recovered and were touching themselves.

I turned back to Quinn. I want you to cum. And I want you to share it with me.

He grinned. *As my Queen commands.*

And he thrust until we both saw stars.

All of us lay in my bed together after. Each of them stroked some part of me. My hand, my hair, my foot. And I knew without a doubt that I would rather face death with them than alone. I'd rather face anything with my knights at my side than without them. Because if we could conquer a dragon together, we could do anything.

EPILOGUE

The next morning was cloudy. A chill in the air threatened snow. I pulled my fur cloak tighter around me as Connor helped me ascend the stairs to the temporary dais set up beyond the moat, in the open stretch of land between the castle and the capital.

I took my seat in the middle throne as my husbands and Avia sat beside me. I watched the executioner as he sharpened his blade.

The crowd gathered slowly. First the nobles came riding their horses and tittering with gossip. And then the villagers walked up the cobblestone road. Everyone gathered to watch a man die.

Vendors began hawking their wares: turkey legs and mince pies. I'd never been a fan of their determination to turn executions into 'events' rather than warnings or lessons. But there was little I could do about it now.

I tried not to tap my foot impatiently as I waited. Ceremony required pomp and circumstance in order to demand respect, and that required time. So Mother had always said anyway.

Avia leaned toward me muttered, "Something feels wrong. He didn't argue with you. Didn't fight. It felt too easy."

"He's given up," Declan shrugged.

"What's there to fight? He summoned a dragon to attack our monarch while on a diplomatic mission. There were witnesses. He's done for," Connor spoke up.

Avia shook her head. "Aren't djinn supposed to be clever?"

"He's only half-djinn and the least powerful of all his brothers," Declan said. "Though, I do agree, I'd have expected an escape attempt from him last night."

"Do you think his brothers sacrificed him, then?" Avia asked.

Ryan shrugged as he joined the conversation. "If they did, he went along with it all."

We all sat for a moment, stewing in our own thoughts before Avia spoke again.

"Oh, look, there's Mateo. I'll be back in one minute," Avia sprang up from her seat and darted away.

She had just reached the gap between the dais for our thrones and the dais for the nobles when a scream issued from the crowd.

I stood, scanning the throngs. The crowd began to break, like a wave, going in every direction, frothing, frantic, crazy. They tripped and tumbled over each other, running away from the dais. People were trampled underfoot. A cart was overturned.

I shot peace over the crowd before I could figure out what was causing the riot. They mellowed slightly as I searched for the reason for their fear.

One small child stood frozen, his finger pointed skyward.

I turned and looked at the sky behind me.

A black creature swooped down out of the clouds.

The dragon snatched Avia up before I could blink.

My heart exploded in fiery rage.

Avia's scream lashed the air, cracking like a whip. The dragon was back in the clouds before our archers could react. Avia was gone.

"Nooo!" I screamed.

Just then, the guards dragged Abbas out. The prince was chained and grimey, his hair full of dirt as it tumbled to his shoulders. His golden outfit from the night before was caked in dried blood from the night of the battle and the filth of the dungeon. But the eyes that met mine were triumphant. Gleaming.

The guard brought him to the edge of the royal dais.

"Good morning, dearest," Abbas grinned at me. "You look a bit pale. Would you like me to warm you up?"

A jet of black flame shot down through the clouds, stopped only by the magical barrier in the sky my mother had erected after the last Fire War.

Avia screamed again. The crowd rushed away through the field.

My stomach dropped until I heard the string of curse words that followed Avia's scream. She wasn't hurt. Yet.

That dirty, liver-eating shitehole. If he thought he'd won, he had another think coming.

I blasted Abbas with peace power until he stood complacent. Then I grabbed the chain holding him from his guard. I'd need him for leverage.

I turned to my knights. "Suit up. We have a princess to save."

MIDKNIGHT: TANGLED CROWNS
BOOK 2

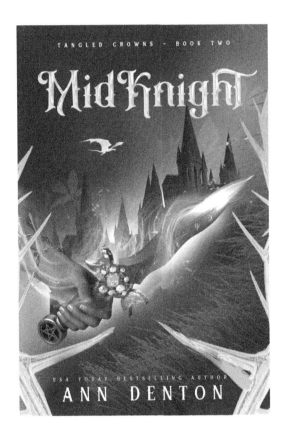

MidKnight - Tangled Crowns Book 2

Now Available at Amazon.com

AFTERWORD

Thank you so much for reading! You are amazing, and you are the reason I can keep dreaming up beautiful worlds. If you liked this book, please leave an Amazon review. It's how indie authors like myself make it into the algorithms at Amazon so other readers can find us.

Book 2 of this series is Available Here.

There will be six books in this series, five of which are out now!

ACKNOWLEDGMENTS

A huge thanks to Rob, Raven, Ivy and Makayla. Thanks to my cover designer, Nichole Witholder, at Rainy Day Artwork, and my amazing ARC readers.

ALSO BY ANN DENTON

Choose from books on the following pages based on your current reading mood.

The standalone or the first book in each series are listed by mood. The darkest reads appear first and grow progressively more light-hearted so it makes it easy to find just what you're looking for next. I also tried to add some basic mood info at the bottom of each series page for you.

FERAL PRINCESS SERIES
(Completed Trilogy)

A hot, dark shifter omegaverse with dub con, a steamy alpha, a loving beta, and a sassy omega who thought she was going to be an alpha female. She was sooo wrong, but when she's claimed by the pack alpha, make no mistake, she has something to say about it.

Defiant - Book 1

Mood - #DARK #DIRTY #ALPHA

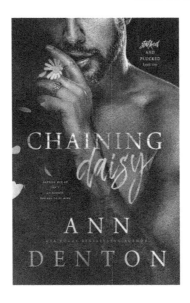

STALKED AND PLUCKED SERIES
(Series of Standalones)

A fast-burn, contemporary MF romance series with very morally gray men who stalk their ladies before claiming them. The series follows a group of college girls who are best friends.

Chaining Daisy - Book 1

Mood - #HOT #HOLYHELL #NEWKINKUNLOCKED

PINNACLE SERIES
(Completed Duet)

A medium-burn paranormal romance about a girl who gets herself sent to a reform academy on purpose, so she can recruit criminally-minded guys to pull off the magical heist of the century. (Reverse Harem)

Magical Academy for Delinquents #MAD - Book 1

Mood - #BADASS #FUN #SEXY GAMES

LOTTO LOVE SERIES
(Completed Duet)

A medium-burn, contemporary romantic comedy reverse harem about winning the lotto and doing whatever the hell you want with it, even if that means holding a Bachelorette-style competition for an entire harem of hotties.

Lotto Men - Book 1

Mood- #LOL #BLUSHING #NO WAY

RUBY - JEWELS CAFE SERIES
(Standalone)

A medium-burn, fated mates reverse harem with an angel on her last strike, some nerds and a tech demon determined to help her, and Christmas miracles.

Ruby

Mood - #SWEET #AWWW #GIGGLES

DARK TEMPTATIONS SERIES
(Incomplete)

A fast-burn monster reverse harem in an alternate reality where monsters rule the earth. A human woman is captured and auctioned off to the Four Terrors who will haunt her nightmares and her dreams alike.
Cowrite with Katie May.

Ravaged by Monsters - Book 1

Mood - #DARK #FATED LOVE
#WILD SEXY TIMES

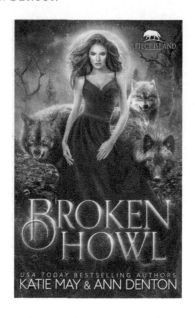

BROKEN HOWL
(Standalone)

A female omega rejects her mates so she can escape her abuser. She's sent to an island for rejects but her mates refuse to let her go…
Cowrite with Katie May.

Broken Howl

Mood - #CRYING #HEALING #FIGHTING

DARKEST QUEEN SERIES
(Incomplete)

The devil is a woman. And this is the story about she fell from Heaven only to rise as God's greatest enemy... (A reverse harem spinoff of the Darkest Flames series) Cowrite with Katie May.

For Whom the Bell Tolls - Book 1

Mood - #FURY #SOUL-DEEP CONNECTIONS #BATTLE OF WILLS

DARKEST FLAMES SERIES
(Completed Trilogy with a novella)

A medium-burn paranormal romance about a girl who tries a love spell on the hot guy at school and accidentally summons demons instead. It contains psychotic, alpha males, and student/teacher relationships. (Reverse Harem)
Cowrite with Katie May.

Demon Kissed - Book 1

Mood - #OOPS #NAUGHTY LAUGHTER #FORBIDDEN HEAT

Demon's Joy
(Standalone)

Santa's daughter has to save Christmas from demons! And all she's got to help her are five funny reindeer. (A reverse harem spinoff of the Darkest Flames series) Cowrite with Katie May.

Demon's Joy

Mood - #SILLY #HOLIDAY CHEER #YUM

MAGE SHIFTER WAR SERIES
(Completed Duet)

A medium-burn paranormal mafia romance. A fae princess is taken captive by three shifter criminals.
(Reverse Harem)
Cowritten with Elle Middaugh.

Fae Captive - Book 1

Mood - #BONNIE&CLYDE #BADASS #HOT

HAMMER TIME
(Standalone)

A medium-burn paranormal comedy featuring Thor's
daughter and a quest to save demigods from prison.
Expect lots of ancient deities and potty humor. (Reverse
Harem)
Cowritten with M.J. Marstens.

Hammer Time

Mood- #PUNTASTIC #NOYOUDIDN'T #SNORT

CONNECT AND GET SNEAK PEEKS

Do you want to read exclusive point of views from different characters, make predictions and claim your book boyfriends with other readers, see my inspiration for these books, and hang with fellow romance lovers? Then join my Facebook Reader Group! I promise you'll love it!

Join Ann Denton's Reader Group

Facebook.com/groups/AnnDentonReaderGroup

ABOUT ME

I have two of the world's cutest children, a crazy dog, and an amazing husband that I drive somewhat insane as I stop in the middle of the hallway, halfway through putting laundry away, picturing a scene.